RENFIELD

RENFIELD

Slave of Dracula

Barbara Hambly

BERKLEY BOOKS, NEW YORK

THE BERKLEY PUBLISHING GROUP
Published by the Penguin Group
Penguin Group (USA) Inc.
375 Hudson Street, New York, New York 10014, USA
Penguin Group (Canada), 90 Eglinton Avenue East, Suite 700, Toronto, Ontario M4P 2Y3, Canada
(a division of Pearson Penguin Canada Inc.)
Penguin Books Ltd., 80 Strand, London WC2R 0RL, England
Penguin Group Ireland, 25 St. Stephen's Green, Dublin 2, Ireland (a division of Penguin Books Ltd.)
Penguin Group (Australia), 250 Camberwell Road, Camberwell, Victoria 3124, Australia (a division of
Pearson Australia Group Pty. Ltd.)
Penguin Books India Pvt. Ltd., 11 Community Centre, Panchsheel Park, New Delhi—110 017, India
Penguin Group (NZ), Cnr. Airborne and Rosedale Roads, Albany, Auckland 1310, New Zealand (a
division of Pearson New Zealand Ltd.)
Penguin Books (South Africa) (Pty.) Ltd., 24 Sturdee Avenue, Rosebank, Johannesburg 2196, South
Africa

Penguin Books Ltd., Registered Offices: 80 Strand, London WC2R 0RL, England

This is an original publication of The Berkley Publishing Group.

Copyright © 2006 by Moon Horse, Inc.
Cover photo by axbgroup.
Cover design by Rita Frangie.
Text design by Tiffany Estreicher.

First edition: September 2006

Library of Congress Cataloging-in-Publication Data

Hambly, Barbara.
    Renfield / Barbara Hambly.—1st ed.
       p. cm.
    ISBN 0-425-21168-1
    1. Dracula, Count (Fictitious character)—Fiction.   2. Vampires—Fiction.   3. Transylvania
(Romania)—Fiction.   4. Whitby (England)—Fiction.   I. Title.

    PS3558.A4215R46   2006
    813'.54—dc22

                                                                                        2006007627

PRINTED IN THE UNITED STATES OF AMERICA

10   9   8   7   6   5   4   3   2   1

For George

With special thanks to Neil Gaiman

All passages indicated with an asterisk are taken
verbatim from Bram Stoker's *Dracula*

CHAPTER ONE

R.M.R.'s notes
20 May
7 flies, 3 spiders

I've filled many notebok pages and scraps of paper with these daily reckonings. Sometimes I look at them and they make no sense to me, nothing at all but scratchmarks. In more sensible moments, I think the counting is just a sad form of mental mischief. It's a way to avoid thinking about the truly essential question, which is, of course, what does a single housefly *mean*?

Letter, Miss Mina Murray to Miss Lucy Westenra
20 May

My dearest Lucy,

I am writing this to you in the happiest of moods. Can you guess why? Yes, I've heard from Jonathan today! He writes from Bistritz, the post-town nearest Castle Dracula—to receive a letter a mere two weeks after it was posted is a miracle, for

Transylvania. What a great thing it is, to be living so close to the threshold of the twentieth century! He still has heard little concerning his client the Count, save that he is rumored to keep not one but *three* beautiful wives. This may be proper form beyond the woods and east of the Danube, but I know you will agree that it is two wives too many. I've always felt that I am too trusting or too unimaginative to know the pangs of envy. Still, I must admit to a moment of jealousy, and in my idle dreams these women cannot help but notice how fine a man my Jonathan is.

I know that it would be unreasonable of me to expect Jonathan's business with the Count—the purchase of property here in England somewhere—to be finished in more than a few days, yet already I begin to fret that he has not outdistanced his own letter and arrived on my doorstep before it. I will write Mr. Hawkins, Jonathan's employer, that after Jonathan and I are married, when my husband must travel so on company business, I must go with him. Naturally I will tell Mr. Hawkins that I can be of great benefit to his firm with my record-keeping and skill at the typewriter, and further, that the company need not pay me a shilling. I don't know if I could bear another such separation, and I know that Jonathan surely feels the same—when he can turn his thoughts from the Count's captivating wives.

Well, dear Lucy, you mentioned that you will be having dinner soon at Rushbrook House. I have not met your Dr. John Seward, but you have written that he is handsome and quite out of the ordinary. I should suppose so. No ordinary man would invite a young lady to dine at a madhouse.

Your loving,
Mina

* * *

"Cook says, must she obey every order from that Mr. Blaine? Because if she does, she says she won't be able to get the chicken on the table in time."

Dr. John Seward briefly closed his eyes and didn't even try to imagine what contradictory order given by the elegant butler Blaine—borrowed for the occasion from the local baronet, Sir Ambrose Poole—would preclude Mrs. Davies having the chicken ready for dinner with Mrs. Westenra and her daughter. Ordinarily the maid's question would have intrigued him. (Did he command her to polish the borrowed silver tureen that Sir Ambrose sent along with him? To fetch newer and fresher lettuce-leaves wherewith to line the platter?) Now it represented yet one more minor monster tussling with his trouser-leg as he prepared for the major encounter of the evening.

In the quiet, steady voice he'd perfected in a decade of dealings with the insane, he replied, "Please tell Mrs. Davies to use her best judgement, and to refer Mr. Blaine to me if there seems to be a conflict. Tell them both that getting the food on the table for dinner is my first priority."

The housemaid Mary nodded, the expression in her eyes clearly proclaiming that there was some major portion of Seward's instructions which she hadn't understood, and she darted back through the door of the little pantry and clattered down the corridor to the kitchen. Seward wondered if he should go after her and ascertain what part of his instructions were going to be garbled in transmission this time, but the chiming of the pantry clock claimed his attention like the salvo of a battle's opening guns.

Eight.

Dear God, they would be here any minute.

You've confronted cannibal savages in the South Seas on that round-the-world voyage with Lord Godalming's daffy brother, Seward reminded himself. *You've faced off against Comancheros in Texas out to murder you and your friends for your boots. Can one respectable English matron out to secure A Good Match for her daughter be worse?*

Of course she can.

As he passed through the dining-room—its faded silk wall-papers and graceful proportions a reminder of the house's patrician origins—he encountered Dr. Hennessey, his night surgeon, pouring himself what was clearly his third or fourth cognac of the evening.

"Cheer up, Johnny," encouraged the older man with a rather hazy grin. "This girl—she has money, eh? And she's pretty? How about this mother of hers, then . . . She has money, too?"

Seward blenched at the thought of the fat-bellied and sweaty Irishman—the best that Rushbrook Asylum could get for its rather limited funds—sidling up to Mrs. Westenra with propositions of a double wedding, and said, "I believe the money is all secured in an unbreakable trust," a patent fabrication that he hoped would hold for the evening. "As for Miss Westenra . . ."

The bell pealed and the attendant Langmore, bedight in livery borrowed like everything else for the evening from Sir Ambrose, strode through from pantry to hall, shouting, "I'm comin', then, keep your . . ."

Seward strode ahead of him, cutting him off at the hall door and preceding him into the small and rather gloomy entryway that had been carved out of what had once been the house's library. All the grand rooms in the main block of Rushbrook House had years ago been converted for the use of the doctors and the patients: the original dining-room into a clinic with a dispensary in the pantry, the drawing-room into a day-room for the quieter patients, the morning-room for hydrotherapy, and the billiard-room—rather grimly—equipped with several patent "tranquilizing chairs" and a Swing. Many of the rooms of the wing alotted to the Staff had a tinkered-with look, where a side door had been given the trappings of a main entrance and rooms originally spacious had been divided to approximate a normal household.

Mrs. Westenra was taking in all these alterations with a cold blue eye that missed not a halved window nor a single square inch where brick had been substituted for marble. "How very cozy," she said as Seward escorted her and her daughter across the threshhold, and through the hall into the rest of the original library, now doing duty as drawing-room for the Superintendant, i.e. himself. "What a very clever use of space."

"I think it's charming." Lucy shrugged her wrap into Langmore's waiting hands, giving the attendant-cum-footman one of those sweetly dazzling smiles that, even glancing, had won Seward's heart the night he'd first encountered her at a party at Lord Godalming's. Then she turned the full brightness of her eyes on him. "Are those hyacinths from the garden here at Rushbrook, Dr. Seward? I thought we saw a garden, didn't we, Mama, as we drove up?"

"You did indeed, Miss Westenra. Several of our patients enjoy working with plants and flowers. Not only enjoy it, but seem to find it calming to their minds and nerves." He took her gloved hand, and guided her to a chair: a delicate girl, too thin for her medium height, her flaxen hair dressed in a feathery chignon that further emphasized this ethereal quality.

Mrs. Westenra gave an exaggerated shudder. "I hope you don't have them coming into this part of the house and arranging the flowers, too, Dr. Seward." Like her daughter, she was a thin woman, her pallor an exaggeration of Lucy's alabaster delicacy, her eyes the chill antithesis of her daughter's hopeful trust.

She glanced pointedly at Langmore. "Or do you use them in your household? I daresay it would take more courage than I possess, to live never knowing when I'd come through the door and find myself face-to-face with a lunatic." She turned as she said it, and drew back a little as Dr. Hennessey entered, red-faced and swaying slightly, a now-full-again glass of cognac in his hand.

"Dr. Hennessey," Seward introduced through slightly clenched teeth, "who is in charge here at night." *And sleeps it off during the day.* Hennessey was a relative of Lady Poole—upon whose husband's patronage Rushbrook House depended—and his employment here owed as much to this fact as to his willingness to work for what Seward was able to pay. Seward was familiar with such links. His own stint of shepherding Lord Godalming's brother, the erratic Harry Holmwood, through South America, Russia, and the South Seas had resulted in his acquaintance and friendship with his patient's nephew, the Honorable Arthur Holmwood: the true prize, Seward knew, in the widowed Mrs. Westenra's matrimonial quest.

And why not? he reflected, as Blaine entered to announce dinner. The Honorable Arthur was as handsome as a Burne-Jones engraving of Sir Galahad, curly-haired, square-chinned, unfailingly polite (even to the pavement-nymphs they'd patronized in Tampico, San Antonio, Vladivostok, and Singapore), and stood to inherit a very large fortune and the title of Viscount Godalming. Seward had watched his young friend's eyes at that party at the Godalming town-house and knew he adored Miss Westenra.

The only problem was that Seward adored her, too. Even at

nineteen, she had the tact, taste, and vivacity to make a perfect London hostess. But she also, Seward guessed, watching her as he seated her at his left at the cramped dining-room table, had the instinctive empathy to be a doctor's wife.

Even a mad-doctor's.

As Blaine brought forth the fish course—a sorry turbot adorned with a half-lemon carved into a crown—and Hennessey launched into a rambling Nietzschean toast, Seward reflected that it was going to be a long evening.

"Sor?"

It was Langmore, tiptoeing out of the pantry to whisper in his ear. The attendant's livery was mussed, his old-fashioned stock pulled askew.

"It's the big new 'un, sor. He's scarpered."

Mrs. Westenra was questioning Hennessey—since Seward's answers had proven unsatisfactory—about the number and variation of patients represented at Rushbrook, turning every now and then to Lucy with little cries of, "How horrible!" when the Dubliner doctor obliged her with a particularly bizarre example of behavior. Unlike many private asylums, Seward had insisted, when he'd been hired, on treating all prospective patients, not merely those who were easiest or least troublesome. Hennessey was regaling the ladies with accounts of Mrs. Strathmore's assault on Mrs. Jaimeson with the scissors, and Seward only hoped he wouldn't go on to detail the more revolting aspects of the notorious "Lord Spotty," as the attendants called him.

"Please excuse me," said Seward, rising. "There's a small matter that needs my attention. I'll be back in a moment."

Dr. Hennessey, refilling his glass, didn't even think to ask if help was needed. Probably, reflected Seward, just as well.

As he was leaving, Mrs. Westenra said, "Those cries! Do the poor souls always howl so?"

Seward paused in his tracks, and reflected that he must be well-fitted to his business. It had been some time since he'd even been aware of the howling.

Letter, R. M. Renfield to his wife
(Undated)

My beloved Catherine,

I hope this letter finds you in excellent health and the most congenial of spirits. I'm aware that it's been some time since I've written to you, and I beg both your understanding and your forgiveness. It's been a busy time for me, as I slowly grasp the changed nature of my life. I must accept new ways, puzzling ways, sometimes inhuman ways—but toward what final design? I do not know.

I have barely a moment to myself each morning and again each night. That's certainly not enough quiet time for me to order my thoughts and compose such letters as deserve your attention. In fact, I was hoping against reason that you would visit me this last week-end. We might have enjoyed some tranquil time together, you and I, to speak or share the silent moments as we always did.

It's spring and the air here is scented with honeysuckle, the sweetness of England for which I so longed among the heavy perfumes of foreign lands. But these are not the flowers you tended so carefully, nor the blossoms that cheered me nightly when I returned home from the City. Without you all things have lost their savor.

Please consider visiting next week-end, or the one thereafter. I will believe that you are arriving soon, bringing with you everything that gives color and freshness to the dawn, and rest and comfort to the twilight. And—I need not say this, I'm certain—please tell our precious Vixie that she will always be the joy in my life wherever I go, howsoever we are separated, and that she (and you, my dear Catherine) will go with me everywhere, always.

> Please believe me,
> Forever your most loving husband,
> R. M. Renfield

Chapter Two

A slanted coign of roof sheltered the rear door of the Staff wing of Rushbrook House. Beyond it, rain that had started during the soup course pattered sadly in the darkness. Rushbrook House stood a few miles from the last houses of Purfleet, and beyond the wall of the extensive grounds, the Thames marshes lay as they had lain since time immemorial. Even the grounds, though planted with trees and crossed by two or three drainage canals discreetly disguised as ornamental brooks, tended to squishy muckiness and standing pools in the slightest rain.

"How long ago did he escape?" Seward shrank in spite of himself from the idea of a chase through the morass in his single presentable evening-suit.

"Just now, sir, when Hardy was takin' him his supper." Langmore had acquired a lantern in one hand, a strait-jacket rolled up under the other arm. The patient Renfield, though gray-haired, stood over six feet tall and was built like an oak-tree.

"Bashed me up against the wall like I was a kid, sir," added Hardy, stepping out the door behind Seward. He was easily Renfield's size, towering over Seward's five-feet-ten-inch slightness. The side of his face was purpling where he'd been struck. "And him so quiet and gentlemanly-like." He shrugged into an oil-skin mac.

"Like I's tellin' you, Hardy." Langmore shook his grizzled head. "It's the quiet ones you gotta watch. Sly, they is." He glanced at Seward, like a soldier waiting for his captain to lead him to battle.

Seward took a deep breath. "Check along the wall by the road first," he said. "Then check the east wall. That's the lowest, and in the worst repair. If he goes over there, he'll just find himself in the grounds of Carfax. Thank God the place is deserted, and the house well-locked. Blow your whistles if you need assistance."

The two burly night attendants looked momentarily nonplussed as it sank in that Seward wasn't going to go with them, then took a second look at their employer's dinner-jacket and polished shoes, and nodded, belatedly putting two and two together. Seward supposed, as they faded into the utter darkness beyond the thin pools of gaslight from Rushbrook's windows, that if they had even average intelligence, they would have been able to find employment as something other than hired strong-men at a madhouse.

Yet having dispatched them to an adventure he considered himself too well-dressed to participate in, Seward found himself unable to simply return to the house. It was his duty to make sure Renfield got back to his room in safety. He had branded himself already in his own eyes as a shirker by staying here on the relatively dry rear step. He could not further betray his trust by settling down to a comfortable dinner with the girl he loved while one of his patients was loose—the more so because he was fairly certain that if Renfield *wasn't* found, neither Langmore nor Hardy would interrupt him at his dinner a second time.

Damn it. Seward fumbled in his pocket for his cigarette case. *Curious, how the mad always had such fiendish timing in their outbursts. As if they could tell which were the most important events in the lives of those around them, and waited for the most utterly disruptive moment to make their move.*

Could they? he wondered. *Did they have an extra sensitivity, an extra faculty of observation?* He shivered, for the night was raw and bitterly cold. *Everyone speaks of the connection between madness and artistic talent—do both states share roots in a greater capacity for perception of detail?* He would, he reflected, have to write to his old teacher in Amsterdam about the matter. Van Helsing was always fascinated by such connections.

His heart warmed a little at the thought of the sturdy old Dutchman, a pleasant recollection washed away entirely by a gust of wind that blew rain over him, soaking the shoulders of his jacket.

So he might as well have gone out running through the mire after all.

Good God, what horrors was Hennessey telling Miss Westenra and her mother in his absence?

Lanterns flashed dimly through the trees, jogging up and down as if the men were running. They vanished then, but Seward's jaw tightened. Along the eastern wall, then, which being built of large stones rather than bricks made it far easier to climb. He strained his ears for the sound of the whistles. If Renfield got over the dilapidated barrier that divided Rushbrook's park from that of Carfax, the long-neglected estate immediately to the east, it could easily take them the rest of the night to locate him. Like Rushbrook, Carfax was an enormous house, but it was infinitely older and falling into ruin. When first he'd come to Rushbrook, Seward had gone over the wall himself and ascertained that the old house and its attendant chapel were at least tightly locked. An escapee would have had a hard time going to earth inside. But its park was a jungle, nearly twenty acres of overgrown groves and woods, mired with standing pools around a small lake.

Damn, thought Seward again. *Damn, damn, damn . . .*

A fine future I have to offer poor Miss Westenra. What made me ever think she'd consider my offer? He recalled his own inner smile when, a few days ago, his friend Quincey Morris had spoken to him of his own adoration for the delicate blonde girl. Quincey was a stringy, awkward-handed Texan whom Seward and the Honorable Arthur had met during their adventurous year of travel in the company of the Honorable Uncle Harry. Arthur had invited Quincey to spend a season in London with him, and though the Texan's speech still bore the twang of the American plains, his manners were meticulously good and his self-made fortune—in land, cattle, and Colorado gold—had made him marginally acceptable to a certain segment of the more impoverished Society mamas.

Though Seward liked Quincey enormously, he had never for a moment considered him genuine competition for Lucy Westenra's hand. He couldn't imagine that lively, sociable girl agreeing to go live in a ranch-house in San Antonio, be it never so spacious and comfortable. The memory of his own patronizing attitude sliced him now like a flaming whip: *And you think she would be any more likely to revel in "cozy" quarters in Rushbrook House, listening to the screaming of the mad on still nights?*

But the flare of hope was like a little white flame somewhere behind his sternum. *She might . . .*

And the memory of the scent of her hair, and the thoughtful pucker between those delicate brows, warmed him again. She was an exceptional girl. He would assure her that this situation was only temporary—

Darkness thickened in the darkness, first a bumbling outline, then a Laocoön that resolved itself into three inter-tangled shapes, Renfield's bowed gray head and enormous shoulders seeming to dominate the attendants who walked on either side. All three were covered with mud. The lanterns had gone out. Renfield was strait-jacketed and there was blood on Langmore's lined face, but there was no suggestion of violence now, only a kind of sly petulance in Renfield's eyes as he was pushed into the reflected light near the house.

"I'm not trouble," he muttered, twisting his head to look down at Langmore. "I'm not trouble to anyone."

"If you're not trouble, mate, I'd like to see what is," retorted the little attendant. "But you come along quiet, and we'll go easy with you this time. Won't even put you on the Swing, will we, Hardy?"

Renfield flinched at the mention of the Swing, something Seward noticed with annoyance. Hennessey swore by the Swing, claiming that the motion of being swooped up and down blindfolded for hours calmed the patients' minds. In the six months he'd been Superintendant, it had not escaped Seward that for all Hennessey's claims of theraputic value, his colleague had only to threaten its use for most patients to calm down immediately, in terror at the nausea and disorientation the "calming" device produced.

"We'll be kind to you, oh, yes," agreed Hardy, with a bad-tempered look. "First one's free, innit?"

"*I'm* not the one you should be looking for," added Renfield, turning his head over his shoulder to speak to the bigger attendant. "I'm not the one."

"He did come along quiet, once we'd both laid hold on him, sor." Langmore wiped the raindrops from his eyes to look at Seward. "Gave us a nasty run, though. You want him in a crib for the rest of the night?"

Seward, watching Renfield's face, again saw the twitch of dread at mention of being locked into what was to all intents and purposes a latticework metal coffin, barely the depth of a man's breast or the width of his shoulders. Unable to move, unable to turn over, unable even to reach one arm across to scratch an itch . . .

More humane than chaining, of course, but in Seward's opinion, not much more. *All very well to go on about moral treatment, lad,* Hennessey had said patronizingly, when Seward had begun making changes in the House's patient routines. *You just see how your "moral treatment" answers when you've got some foaming mooncalf coming at you swinging his bed round his head like a club. You'll be putting those wall-rings back into the cells quick enough.*

He pushed the soaked hair out of his eyes. "No, take him to his room and strap him to his cot. I'll be along in a moment and give him some chloral hydrate. He should sleep through 'til morning. Once you've done that, please go on back to the dining-room. I'm sure Simmons and Mr. Blaine need your help."

Langmore's grin was wry. "Like nuthin' never happened, sor."

"Exactly." Seward shivered with the cold, and crushed out his cigarette on the wet stone of the doorstep as he turned back to his recaptured patient. Standing on the step, he was at eye level with the bigger man. Dark blue eyes, Seward noted again, under an almost anthropoid shelf of brow. Though Renfield's hair was graying, his heavy eyebrows were still nearly black. "Mr. Renfield, your family—and you yourself—have been as-sured that there's nothing to fear from me or from anyone else at Rushbrook House. Why did you flee?"

Under the dripping brows, the muck-plastered hair, the dark blue gaze was calm and altogether sane. "My question," Ren-field replied, "is, *Why do you not?*"

* * *

Lucy got quickly to her feet as Seward came back into the dining-room, and would have crossed to him in the pantry doorway had not her mother halted her with a glare. The girl hesitated, napkin still in hand, then asked, "Is everything all right? Did they find the poor man?"

"'Course they did, *acushla*." Dr. Hennessey jovially lifted his glass to Seward in a mock toast. "Told you they would. That Langmore has a nose on him like a bloodhound. *And* he's a good tracker besides!" And he relapsed into gales of iniebriated chortles of appreciation at his own jest.

Across the curdled remains of the fish course, which had not been removed in the nearly seventy-five minutes that had elapsed since Langmore's hesitant summons, Mrs. Westenra regarded Seward with a gaze like frozen slag.

"My dear Mrs. Westenra!" Seward cried, identifying the immediate priority in the situation, "I am most terribly sorry! I instructed Simmons to carry on in my absence. I cannot imagine what happened . . ." He held Lucy's chair for her as she reseated herself. "Yes, Miss Westenra, to answer your question, the patient was brought back safely and unhurt. I've just come now from giving him a sedative injection . . ."

And changing into gray tweeds that looked hopelessly out of place next to Hennessey's rumpled and straining dinner clothes, and the expensive silks of the two ladies.

"You don't actually let your patients roam loose about the house, as Dr. Hennessey said?" Lucy looked timidly up over her shoulder at Seward. "Do you?" To her left, Hennessey grinned drunkenly and winked.

When Langmore and Simmons brought in the *Hindle Wakes*— a German specialty slightly beyond Cook's skills—the chicken was stone cold and the lemon-cream sauce had separated.

The rest of the dinner proceeded in silence.

"I told you how it would be, Lucy," Seward heard Mrs. Westenra's voice as their carriage pulled away. "I doubt that even that absurd American would have subjected you to . . ."

Rain, darkness, and the sloppy squish of hooves and wheels obliterated the rest. Seward quietly closed the door, made his night rounds of the thirty-six lost souls under his charge—most of them sleeping heavily under the calming magic of laudanum, chloral hydrate, or tincture of *Cannabis indica*—then returned to his room, to dictate the account of Renfield's escape and recapture into the phonographic daybook. That chore accomplished, the entire fiasco of the dinner-party began to unfurl itself, like infinitely repeating performances of a bad play, across his mind. Of course there had been no question of asking Lucy's mother for her daughter's hand after deserting her to Hennessey's company.

I'll be in London Tuesday, he told himself. *I shall send a note to their house on Chatham Street, call on them. They aren't leaving for Whitby until next week. There is still time to speak to her, still time to ask her—*

Plans for the future produced more anxiety, if anything, than a review of the immediate past. At last, Seward went downstairs to the dark dispensary, made up an injection of chloral hydrate for himself, and returning to his room, joined Renfield and the others in the relief of oblivion and dreams.

* * *

Renfield felt the cold, heard the howling of the wolves long before the rest of the dream came into focus.

He shivered. He had always hated cold, always hated the bleak chill of London, the gray dreary wintertides in Nottingham after the thick heat and riotous color of India. Since his return from half a lifetime in the East, the sounds of England had seemed harsh to him, like dropped money clanking on stone. Clattering carriages, rattling shoe-heels, nattering nasal voices, after the slower rhythms, the multifarious voices of bird-calls, the eternal hum of insects.

His dream was a dream of silence.

The silence of the dead.

It was raining there, too, a bitter whisper against stone walls. Renfield saw firelight, like handfuls of jewels, nearly lost in an immense hearth whose overmantle was supported by carved grotesques, wolf-faces whose shadow-cloaked grins mocked the young man imprisoned in that unknown room. Renfield knew he was a prisoner because he saw him try the door, not once but many times—saw him pace like a caged animal, as he himself, Renfield reflected, had paced for days now in his cell. When the young man came near the hearth, he saw his face, hollow and haunted under a tumbled shock of dark hair.

Saw his breath, a whisper of flame-dyed smoke when he walked more than a stride or two from the fire.

Saw him cross to the window and jerk aside the velvet curtains, revealing an ill-fitting casement of tiny panes, and beyond it—when he pulled it impatiently open—bars.

The young man struck the wall with the hammer of his fist, once, twice, the tired motion of a man who has pounded that wall, who has confronted those bars, for weeks.

Renfield watched dispassionately, knowing what it was, to pound a wall.

Firelight leaking through the window sparkled on shimmering rain, like an infinity of gold and blood. The rain fell through fog, and in the darkness the fog coalesced, until it seemed to Renfield that the forms of three women hung in the air outside the window, their pale dresses and their long hair drifting about them like seaweed beneath the sea. The young man at the window saw them—Renfield heard the intake of his breath—but said nothing. Only gazed, like a man hypnotized or under a spell.

It seemed to Renfield that the eyes of all three gleamed red in the darkness, catching the firelight like the eyes of rats.

Two were dark, the third, luminously fair. They stretched out their arms to the prisoner, and it was the fair one who spoke, in a voice like crystal tapped with a silver spoon. "Jonathan," she said, "Jonathan, let me come to you," and Renfield noted with interest that the language she spoke was the sweetly musical German of the south.

He thought wonderingly, *They are the Valkyries, just as in the opera.* And in his heart the music of Wagner, god-genius of Bayreuth, stirred like the breathing of the Earth.

They are the Choosers of the Slain. The ones who lay their hands upon the men who will die.

"I am called Nomie, Jonathan. You have only to wish it, and I will come."

The man Jonathan stood now so close to the bars that his face pressed against them, his hands clutched the wet iron. He was trembling with terror and desire. "I wish it," he murmured. "Come."

A noise, like the crashing of a cannon, boomed and echoed through Renfield's dream. Jonathan fell back a pace from the window but did not—maybe could not—turn around to see what might have been behind him, and Renfield, too, saw only the three women—Valkyrie, Graces, goddesses, or the fate-weaving Norns—hanging in the whispering dark. One of the dark-haired women screamed a curse in German, and slowly, flesh and hair and garments dislimned once more into lightless mist. Only for a time their red eyes remained, glittering in the night like unholy stars.

Jonathan staggered, as if waking from some terrible dream, and whirled. Renfield saw then what he saw, that the sound had been the chamber's door, slammed open with stunning violence against the wall.

The doorway was empty. Only darkness lay beyond it.

But the prisoner did not flee. Instead he shrank from the open, empty doorway, his breathing fast with terror. Though the night was icy, sweat jeweled his face. For a long time he stood, only staring at the open door, and the thin mist that curled across the flagstones. Then slowly he edged forward, like a man approaching a coiled snake, extended a hand visibly trembling, and with a quick move, slammed his prison door shut again.

Then he stumbled to the fire and collapsed on his knees on the hearth, his face buried in his hands.

CHAPTER THREE

R.M.R.'s notes
21 May
8 flies, 1 spider

22 May
9 flies, 2 spiders
I find my facility of patience and focus increases with practice. There is a knack to trapping a fly, as much mental and perceptual as physical. I find myself hampered in my efforts by the abject stupidity of the attendants here. Like all men of petty intellect, they cling to regulations as to spars in the storm which the world appears, to them, to be. I have explained repeatedly the nature of my mission here, yet the man Langmore persists in removing the baits I put down, and even in freeing my quarry. Incapable of perceiving underlying patterns, his system, like those of his fellows, seems capable only of animal fear, like buffalo fleeing a thunderclap because they imagine that the release

of atmospheric electrical tensions has something to do with them.

Prune madecoine and beef obtain best results

23 May
10 flies, 4 spiders

24 May
10 flies, 3 spiders

25 May
16 flies, 4 spiders
A long talk with Dr. Seward today. Though I explained my business to him carefully, I came away with the impression that he understands nothing. He seems to me a man of good heart but decidedly mediocre mind. Still, though nearly as rigid-mindedly fearful of change as all the others, he did agree with my request that the cook include quantities of honey, sugar, and various confitures in my rations here.

Letter, R. M. Renfield to his wife
25 May
My beloved Catherine,

Simply the writing of your name raises my spirits, setting before me as it does your lovely face. I must be brief, for I cannot make the fools here understand my need for paper not only to communicate with you and our lovely Vixie, but also to proceed with my work. It is a matter I dare not yet take up with Dr. Seward, the Superintendant, though he and I have begun to come to an understanding regarding the work itself. I thought, in my conversation with him today, that he appeared downcast.

Rumor among the attendants is that he has suffered a reverse in love. If that is so, my heart goes out to him in pity. What it would have cost me, my dearest one, had your family prevailed in their opposition to me, and prevented our union, I cannot bring myself to think.

The dreary rains of spring have ceased at last, and the garden here riots with hyacinth, iris, and the first sweet roses of summer. From my elevated window I look down on the marshlands beside the river, and see them gay with wildflowers, spangled with reflected light, and alive with the birds of the air.

I understand the difficulties you are having in getting letters to me here. Better that I should suffer a pang or two for want of your dear comfort, than that those who seek to keep us apart should learn of your whereabouts, and so undo all our plans and strivings. Kiss my dearest Vixie for me, and tell her that her papa shall be with her by and by.

> I remain forever,
> Your most devoted husband,
> R. M. Renfield

* * *

"Lady Clayburne." Dr. Seward set down the card that had been sent in, got to his feet as Mary showed his visitors into the office. "Lady Brough."

The younger of the two, a stylish matron of Mrs. Westenra's type, extended two kid-gloved fingers with the air of one who hoped Seward would not actually touch them. The elder, erect and disapproving in extremely stylish mourning weeds, simply folded her thin hands more tightly around the ebony head of her cane and regarded Seward with a reflexive and ingrained contempt.

"Please sit down." Seward fetched them both chairs. Lady Brough scrutinized the seat of hers as if to make sure no one had inadvertently left fresh pig entrails on it, then perched on the edge. Her daughter, Lady Clayburne, settled a little more firmly, but Seward had the impression that she, like her mother, had been carefully schooled that no lady ever let her spine touch the back of any chair she sat on, under pain of death. His aunts and his sister subscribed to that belief as well. "Mary, please bring tea."

As the housemaid departed, Seward resumed his own seat behind his desk and switched off the phonograph into which he'd been dictating his notes. "You are here to see Mr. Renfield?" He had not had the impression, when Ryland Renfield's family brought him to Rushbrook House, that they were the sort of people who would remain in London past the fashionable season for their afflicted relative's sake. "I'm sure he will be most gratified to have visitors."

"We are here to see *you*, Dr. Seward, not my brother-in-law." Georgina, Lady Clayburne, folded her elegantly gloved hands and the permanent grooves of disapproval which bracketed the knife-slit of her mouth deepened slightly. "I am certain there is little to be gained by an interview with Ryland himself. How does he here?"

"Much the same as when he was brought in," answered Seward. "On one occasion only he attempted to escape, but offered no resistance when apprehended." He cringed inwardly at the memory of that disastrous dinner-party. At the recollection of how Lucy's eyes had filled with tears, when he'd knelt to propose marriage yesterday—had it been only yesterday?—at her mother's villa of Hillingham. How she had blushed when he'd asked her, *Is there someone else?*

Knowing full-well that there was.

"Beyond that, he has been the most cooperative of patients. He occupies his time with trapping flies—spiders and flies, I should say. Did your sister ever mention his keeping such odd pets?"

"My sister does not hold with pets, Dr. Seward, and never would have them in the house. As for flies, I am shocked that you permit such a filthy pastime." She looked around the office as if expecting to see assorted tumblers and fruit-jars on every windowsill and in every corner, roaring and buzzing with captives.

Lady Brough added, in a thin harsh voice, "I thought my son-in-law was brought here to restore the balance of his mind, not to have his crochets indulged."

"Of course that is so, Lady Brough," agreed Seward. "But sometimes one cannot discover the key to madness without observing the tendency of its delusions."

"Nonsense. My second daughter—Lady Norrington, she is now, and we never thought to make so respectable a match for her—conceived the notion when she was a girl that she was in danger of contagious infection whenever she went out of her bedroom, and insisted on remaining there and having her meals sent up. A few sound whippings broke her of that caprice." The old lady's gaze flicked back to Seward, a bleached and colorless hazel, and cold as stone. "Has my daughter been here to see her husband?"

"As a physician," said Seward carefully, "that matter is between my patient and myself."

"Don't mouth platitudes, young man," snapped Her Ladyship, "as if you were a priest under seal of the confessional. Neither my daughter Catherine nor my granddaughter Vivienne has been seen by any member of the family since Ryland's incarceration, nearly four weeks ago. Catherine, of course, may do as she chooses. She always has." There was both contempt and loathing in the old woman's voice. "But Georgina and I have a responsibility to Vivienne and we will not be turned aside."

"It is very like Catherine," added Lady Clayburne, "to go into hiding in this melodramatic fashion and leave my mother and myself to deal with this most unpleasant and awkward situation." Where Lady Brough's voice was soft and cold, like the silk of a garrot, her daughter's had the clang of a headsman's ax. "Completely aside from the *outrageous* fees demanded in this place"—she gestured impatiently around her—"there is the matter of the funds settled upon Catherine by my late father, money which it was understood was to be used in educating Vivienne and establishing her creditably in the world. This Catherine—encouraged by her husband—has *not* done. I blame Ryland entirely. What can one expect of a money-grubbing merchant who's spent all his life in heathan parts among tradesmen?"

"Catherine was always as bad," put in Lady Brough. "With her séances and her Theosophical Society lectures and her Ancient Music."

"Of course she is, Mama," agreed Lady Clayburne quickly. "You are quite right. But at least one had *some* control over Catherine. But Vivienne—Vixie, she is called in the family—is due for her come-out next year. The poor child has been raised on a rubbish of philosophers and economists, with the result that when she does come out, unless something is done to take her education in hand, she will be entirely too *outré* to make anything resembling a respectable *parti*. Catherine should have known better, but of course neither Mother nor I could ever tell her a thing. Now that Ryland is, thank goodness, out of the way,

Mother and I agreed that it is the perfect opportunity to take that poor child under our wings and make something of her before it is too late."

"I see." Seward reflected that if Lady Brough were *his* grandmother, he'd go into hiding, too.

Mary entered with the tea-tray, and dipped a little curtsey to the two ladies as she set it down on the corner of Seward's desk. What there was about the tea things that didn't meet Lady Clayburne's standards, Seward had no idea. Neither the cups nor the saucers were visibly chipped, the bread-and-butter was fresh, no sugar had been spilled, and the milk was wholesome. But Lady Clayburne's thin mouth compressed still further, as Mrs. Westenra's had when Seward had re-entered the dining-room the other night in his gray tweeds, and Lady Brough regarded the tea-cup Seward offered her through her lorgnette for a long moment before, reluctantly, accepting it.

Lady Clayburne demanded, "*Has* my sister come to see Ryland?"

"It remains a matter between herself and me, as Mr. Renfield's physician, but no, she has not." Quite possibly, guessed Seward, because Mrs. Renfield suspected that her family would attempt to trace her in precisely this fashion. But it was curious, he thought, that Renfield had mentioned to him neither wife nor child. "The girl Vivienne is Mr. Renfield's only child?"

Lady Clayburne sniffed derisively. "The dear Lord only knows what he got up to in India, all the years he was there, but Vivienne is my *sister's* only child."

"Ryland was married in India." Lady Brough set her tea aside untasted. "My solicitor, Joseph Wormidge, has instituted inquiries among the business and Army communities of Calcutta and has found little against him save his passion for Wagner. Horrible, dreary racket!" Her pale eyes narrowed. "Nevertheless, the inquiry is not yet concluded."

"When his first wife died—I understand she was an invalid for many years—Ryland returned to England to manage his business from here," went on Lady Clayburne. "He met Catherine at one of those dreadful theosophical lectures she was patronizing that year. We did everything in our power, Mother and I, to keep her from throwing herself away on a tradesman and a man twenty years older than herself into the bargain. Well!" She took the tiniest sip of her tea, with the air of one making a heroic sacrifice to prevent her host from killing himself with well-deserved chagrin, and set the cup and saucer firmly aside. *So much for* THAT. The bread-and-butter she simply ignored.

"Understand me, Dr. Seward. Mother and I have only Vixie's good at heart. Goodness knows how we're to keep it quiet that there is insanity in the family long enough to find her a husband, even *with* a year or two at a good Swiss boarding-school to straighten her out . . . the cost of which Mother and I are quite prepared to shoulder. Once we locate them, of course, we have instructed Wormidge to begin proceedings to re-claim Father's trust funds, which Catherine has quite clearly misused."

Seward said nothing. A parson's son who had been raised on the edges of Society, he knew with deadly exactness what options lay open to a woman once control of her own money was taken out of her hands.

"Neither Catherine nor Vivienne, as I have said, have communicated with any member of the family since Ryland was found wandering the streets of London in what can only be described as confusion." Anger glinted in Lady Brough's soft voice. "Their house in Nottingham was closed up, and when Wormidge effected an entrance, he found their clothing missing, as if for a long stay elsewhere. Ryland's house in London has clearly not been re-opened, but he was a wealthy man even *before* he married Catherine and helped himself to her inheritance. Because *his* solicitor, Mr. Lucius Bolton, dropped out of sight at the same time, we suspect that Catherine and Vivienne are in hiding somewhere, and using Bolton as a go-between. We intend to find them."

The cold determination in her voice, and the self-righteous expression on Lady Clayburne's face, reminded Seward of the reminiscences Lucy had shared with him of her one nightmarish year in a French finishing-school. She had begged her mother to at least let her return to England, to go to school with her friends.

Lady Clayburne opened her tiny reticule of jet beads, withdrew a card-case. "A young lady's future is at stake, Dr. Seward," she said, and laid a card on the desk. "Please do not make her life more difficult than it will already be with an impossible tradesman—let alone a lunatic—for a father. When she comes here—*if* she comes—please do what you can to urge Catherine to return to Mother and myself. In any case, I expect to be notified of her visit."

She slid a second card across the desk at him. "This is Mr. Wormidge's card—our solicitor, in Bedford Row. If Ryland should make any reference to Catherine, or say anything that might indicate where Catherine or Vivienne might be found, please contact either myself or Mr. Wormidge."

Seward murmured, "Of course," and slipped both her card and the solicitor Wormidge's into his desk drawer. It was his duty, as Superintendant, to keep Rushbrook House a paying proposition, entirely apart from the fact that his usefulness to its patients depended on his remaining on good terms with their families. At least Lady Brough and Lady Clayburne were not obviously insane themselves, as were the relatives who had had Lord Alyn locked up.

He wondered if Vixie Renfield had begged her parents not to send her to "a good Swiss boarding-school" to "straighten her out." Had pleaded to be allowed to remain in England, with her friends.

Letter, Miss Mina Murray to Miss Lucy Westenra
2 June

Dearest Lucy,

No time for more than a note, as this is the busiest time of year at the school. The weather has turned hot here, and damp. *How* I envy you, walking along the cliffs and downs of Whitby! It seems like a year, instead of only a month, until I join you. Tell your mother again how much I look forward to it, and how grateful I am for the invitation.

One of the dearest aspects of true friendship is that, in all the years we've played together and worked together over those *dreadful* samplers at Mrs. Druggett's school, whenever one of us has been sorrowful or afraid, the other has been able to cheer her up. Lucy, I am both sorrowful and afraid now. I have had no letter from Jonathan since the middle of May—nearly two weeks now—and though I know perfectly well that they do not have the penny post in far parts of the world, and that I cannot expect him to take time from his work to write to me often, still I cannot rid myself of the fear that he is in some terrible trouble.

There! Now tell me I'm being a goose—as I know perfectly well that I am.

So good that your dear Arthur *is* in civilized parts (or as civilized as Ireland ever gets!) and you can get those daily notes you write of. They do, indeed, bring the sound of the voice, the sight of the face, before our eyes—as your notes to me have done all this week.

Thank you, my dearest friend, for being my dearest friend. You know and I know that wherever he is, Jonathan is just fine.

All my love,
Mina

Chapter Four

R.M.R.'s notes
5 June
14 flies, 1 spider
I knew this would happen. Seward ordered me to "get rid of" my "pets" as he calls them, though I have explained to him—or thought I explained—the critical importance of what I do. I obtained three days' grace. What can one expect, when surrounded by the pettiness of ordinary minds?

Dr. Seward's Journal (kept on phonograph)*
18 June
[Renfield] has turned his mind now to spiders, and has got several very big fellows in a box. He keeps feeding them with his flies, and the number of the latter has become sensibly diminished, although he has used half his food in attracting more flies from outside to his room.

1 July

His spiders are now becoming as great a nuisance as his flies, and today I told him that he must get rid of them. He looked very sad at this, so I said that he must clear out some of them, at all events. He cheerfully acquiesced in this, and I gave him the same time as before for the reduction. He disgusted me much while with him, for when a horrid blow-fly, bloated with some carrion food, buzzed into the room, he caught it, held it exultantly for a few moments between his finger and thumb, and, before I knew what he was going to do, put it in his mouth and ate it. I scolded him for it, but he argued quietly that it was very good and very wholesome; that it was life, strong life, and gave life to him . . .

Letter, R. M. Renfield to his wife
(undated—early July)

My dearest Catherine,

I trust that this letter finds you in the best of good health, and that you and Vixie are enjoying the mellow beauty of this English summer. It gives me daily comfort to picture your sweet faces. Though I now realize how difficult it would be for you to visit, still I hope and pray that one day you and she may find a way to do so without drawing undue attention to yourselves, for I miss you sorely.

My work proceeds apace, though unbelievably hampered by the stupidity of my colleagues here. Seward is well-meaning, but beyond imbecilic. His mania for regulations has forced me to begin on the next stage of my efforts prematurely. I pray that no ill will come of it, knowing how much depends upon its successful progress. His colleague, Hennessey, is not only venal, but dangerous. Only yesterday, in Dr. Seward's absence, he entered my room with three young gentlemen from one of the London colleges—not medical students, but simply young rakes who paid him half-a-crown apiece "to see the loonies," as they put it. When I was moved to protest, he threatened me with the Swing, a most appalling "treatment" that "calms" through nausea and dizziness. Valuable in dealing with the truly mad, of course, but as horrifying to a normal man as the rigors of the Spanish In-quisition.

So I am reduced to accomplishing what I can, with what I have. You know that I would do, quite literally, anything, in or-der to assure your safety; that there are no lengths to which I would not go to protect our beautiful daughter from harm.

Your loving husband, forever,
R.M.R.

R.M.R.'s notes
3 July
10 flies, 2 spiders, 1 sparrow
-7 flies → spiders
-5 spiders → sparrow

6 July
9 flies, 2 spiders, 1 sparrow
-6 flies → spiders
-4 spiders → sparrows
Seward in Town again today. Hennessey admitted a pair of young gentlemen who wanted to "observe" the lunatics, in particular, they said, the women, and did any of them rip off their clothing in their fits? I thought Langmore would object, but he said noth-ing. I have noted that Langmore frequently seems the worse for

opium, whose symptoms became tediously familiar to me in my years of dealing, not only with the native Indians and coolie Chinese, but with the colonial clerks and wives as well. I have also frequently overheard Hardy and Simmons speak of Langmore's abstractions of chloral hydrate from the dispensary. If they know of this, Hennessey certainly must.

Oh, to be attempting such a work as mine, and to be surrounded by such human detritus!

9 July
8 flies, 3 spiders, 1 sparrow
-9 flies → spiders
-12 spiders → sparrows

10 July
10 flies, 6 spiders, 2 sparrows
-9 flies → spiders
-6 spiders → sparrows

Letter, R. M. Renfield to his wife
11 July
My dearest Catherine,

A line in haste. This afternoon from my window I observed the execrable Hennessey walking along the tree-lined avenue that leads to the high road, a most unaccustomed exercise for a man who raises sloth to an art form. Following him with my gaze, I saw him stand talking by the high-road gate to a short, stout gentleman in a green coat, who even at that distance was clearly recognizable as Lady Brough's solicitor Wormidge. Though the trees on the avenue prevented my seeing clearly, I thought they talked for some little time, and that something—papers? money? letters?—was passed from hand to hand.

The sight filled me with rage and despair. Not so much that I fear your discovery—indeed, the fact that your mother seeks to trace you through me here reassures me that she has no clue concerning the false identities and alternate bank accounts we established for your concealment—but because I understand that it will be that much more difficult for you to contact me, much less see me.

Still I remain, as Shakespeare says, "rich in hope." Watch and wait, my darling—my darlings—and all things will be made well.

Forever your loving husband,
R.M.R.

Dr. Seward's diary (phonograph)*
19 July

We are progressing. My friend has now a whole colony of sparrows, and his flies and spiders are almost obliterated. When I came in, he ran to me and said he wanted to ask me a great favor . . . "A kitten, a nice little, sleek playful kitten, that I can play with and teach, and feed—and feed—and feed!" I was not unprepared for this request, for I had noticed how his pets went on increasing in size and vivacity, but I did not care that his pretty family of tame sparrows should be wiped out in the same manner as the flies and the spiders . . .

10 p.m.—I have visited him again today and found him sitting in a corner brooding. When I came in, he threw himself on his knees before me and implored me to let him have a cat; that his salvation depended upon it. I was firm, however, and told him he could not have it.

20 July

Visited Renfield very early, before the attendant went his rounds. Found him up and humming a tune. He was spreading out his sugar, which he had saved, in the window, and was manifestly beginning his fly-catching again . . . I looked around for his birds, and not seeing them, asked him where they were. He replied, without turning round, that they had all flown away. There were a few feathers about the room and on his pillow a drop of blood.

11 a.m.—The attendant has just been to me to say that Renfield has been very sick and has disgorged a whole lot of feathers. "My belief is, Doctor," he said, "that he has eaten his birds, and that he just took and ate them raw!"

11 p.m.—I gave Renfield a strong opiate tonight, enough to make even him sleep . . .

R.M.R.'s notes
21 July

HE IS COMING!!!

Letter, R. M. Renfield to his wife
21 July

My darling Catherine,

Something has happened which alters everything! How well I remember when you used to chide me for my attitude of materialism—so strange in one who espouses the romantic ideals of Wagner, you said. And I, in my blind superiority, would reply that romanticism, while all very well to inspire the heart and the spirit, cannot put bread and butter on the table. Blind, blind, foolish and blind, to say those very words!

Yet the gods hear even the maunderings of fools. And sometimes, their eternal hearts are moved to compassion by the very blind stubbornness of those who deny them.

Oh, my beloved, forgive me for the blindness that continued my work, my mission, in the selfsame narrow crevice of scientific methodology for which I so scorned my poor benighted colleagues here! That I continued it stubbornly, seeing nothing beyond what I thought was "truth," while all the while a greater truth was approaching, like the inexorable descent of thunderclouds from the Simla hills to the plain!

He is coming, and we all of us—you, me, Vixie—will be saved!

*   *   *

Dreams of blood. Dreams of life, like specks of flame, coursing and sparkling through his veins. Deep in opiated sleep, it seemed to Renfield that he was yet awake, aware of each separate life in the world, like individuated atoms of searing light.

When he had taken opium in India, he had had such a vision. He had felt himself separately conscious of every beetle, every monstrous roach, every solitary white ant in the swarms that dwelt beneath his bungalow, every bird in the trees and every snake in the weeds, all of them: a seething mass of life soulshaking and wonderful in its hugeness.

Even in this thin chilly climate, he was aware. Flies, spiders, sparrows . . . the brilliant dots of their individual lives glittered and danced in his veins. The kitchen cat he'd seen through the window the other day, who had fired him with such wild hopes, so cruelly and unnecessarily dashed. Fools, all of them . . . ! From the window he'd seen her looking at him, gazing across the space between them with round golden eyes.

In his dream those eyes returned to him, drawing him to them through darkness. But he saw now that they were a man's eyes.

Cold gripped him, the damp cold to which even eighteen years back in his native country had not accustomed him. Cold, and the smell of the ocean. In his dream he was standing, and underfoot the rough boards of a ship's hold rocked. He heard the slosh of waves against the hull, smelled the familiar stinks of a cargo-hold, rats and bilge-water and dirty leather and rope, and above all else the thick, mouldy smell of earth. The ship was transporting boxes of dirt—Renfield mentally calculated the cost per pound of shipping, and concluded that someone must be both rich and mad. In Rome he had visited a monastery whose chapels had been floored with earth brought from Jerusalem, that the monks who died might be buried in the holiest ground in Christendom without the inconvenience of making an actual pilgrimage. Was there, he wondered sardonically, some equally pious coward still at large in England?

How did he know the ship was bound for England?

Then he saw the eyes. Not gold now, but red, gleaming from a dark shape which rose up from among the earth-boxes. A cloaked form, hiding power in the folds of its garments, like the Pilgrim God in Wagner's *Siegfried*: the Wanderer stepping from the shadows, concealing yet unable to conceal all of what he is.

Renfield sank to his knees. "Who are you?" he whispered, and to his lips came the words in German of Mime the Dwarf from that opera. "*'Who has tracked me to this retreat?'*"

A voice which seemed to emanate less from the column of darkness before him, as from the dark at the back of his mind, whispered, echoing the words of Wagner, "*'Wanderer' the world calls me: wide are my wanderings; I roam at my will all the earth around.*"

A vast shudder shook Renfield's bones. He managed to breathe the name, "Wotan . . ." but could make no other sound.

The dark shape continued: *I've mastered much and treasured much; I've told wondrous tales to men. Men have believed their wisdom great, but it is not brains that they should treasure.*

"*I have wit enough,*" Renfield gasped—Mime gasped. "*I want no more . . .*" Yet in his mind, in his heart, he saw the dozens of glass tumblers begged singly from Langmore and Hardy, with his painstakingly collected flies buzzing beneath them. Saw the crumpled sorry boxes of spiders, the hard-won fragments of his great work kicked aside by fools and Fate, as in the opera the sword Nothung had been shattered, beyond his poor power to re-forge.

"*What was good, straightway I gave them,*" murmured that deep, harsh voice from out of the shadows. "*Spoke, and strengthened their minds.*"

Renfield whimpered, "Lord . . ."

His head bowed into his hands, he only heard the sough of the great cloak as that column of darkness stepped forward—as Wotan the Wanderer, lord of the gods, stepped forward—and smelled the rank, intoxicating stench of graveyard earth and decaying blood. The hand that rested on his head was heavy, cold as the hand of a corpse.

"*Behold, the bridegroom cometh,*" said Wotan's voice, in the dark at the back of Renfield's mind. All around them the waters surged against the boat's wooden hold, but though the lightless space stank of rats, not a single whisper of their skittering did Renfield hear. "*And ye know not the day or the hour.*' But I come. Then those who are known to me shall have their reward."

It seemed to Renfield then that he was back in his bed in

Rushbrook House, back in his opiated sleep. But his mind was awake and aware, aware of everything: of the voices of Langmore and Simmons as they played their endless, stupid games of cribbage at the little deal table at the far end of the hall; of the kitchen-cat hunting in the long grass and poor old Lord Alyn in the next room crying and mumbling over and over to himself how he did not deserve to live, how great his sins were and how powerless he was to stop himself . . . Of the soft deadly clinking in the study directly below him, as Dr. Seward made up for himself his now-nightly injection of chloral hydrate, so that he could enjoy the sleep he so blithely handed out to his patients. He was aware of the fog that lay on the marshes, of the boats moving down the broad estuary to the sea.

He was aware of the sea. Of a small ship with tattered sails, driven on by storm-winds that moaned in its rigging, of the pounding of waves on distant rocks. It seemed to him that he could rise from his bed and fly on the wings of that storm—on the crest of that darkness.

Fly to the ship, where Wotan waited . . . where the Wanderer God sat in darkness, with all his power and wisdom gathered into his strong hands, to help those who did as he willed.

Fly to Catherine . . .

He saw her, auburn hair half-untangled from its nightly braid, face peaceful in sleep. Like the Prince in a fairy-tale, he thought he stood over her, her beauty breaking his heart as it always did, always had, since first she'd stood up at that theosophical lecture and questioned the lecturer about the astral plane. So many nights when she would turn over and sleep, after their final good-night kiss, he had simply sat awake, looking at her slumbering face by the glow of his little reading-lamp, relaxed and so young with all its small daily worries sponged away. Joy beyond joy.

I will save her, he thought. *Wotan will help me. I will make him help me.*

The thought of that terrible ally filled Renfield with dread, for he knew to the marrow of his bones that the thing in the hold of the ship was not to be trusted. *I will make him help me, but I cannot, must not, ever, ever let him know where Catherine and Vixie are hidden.*

He didn't know quite why this was so, or what the nature of the danger was. But the column of shadow within shadow, darkness within dark, had glowed with a nimbus of peril.

I will be clever, he vowed. *Clever and strong. I can get his help without his knowing. I can keep that secret, buried in my heart. Then no one will put my Catherine or our beautiful Vixie in danger, ever again.*

Chapter Five

Mrs. Violet Westenra
Requests the honour of your presence
At the marriage of her daughter
Lucy Marie
To
The Honorable Arthur Holmwood
Saturday, the 8th of October
At twelve o'clock noon
St. George's Church, Hanover Square

Breakfast and reception immediately follow
At
Godalming House
Grosvenor Square

Dr. Seward turned the invitation over in his fingers. Even the paper was rich as creamy velvet in the patch of strong August sunlight that lay upon his desk.

It interested him that he felt no pain. Only a kind of dull shock, as if he had taken a mortal hurt but wasn't yet aware that it would kill him.

A ridiculous conceit, he thought numbly. *Of course I'm not going to die of love. I shall recover from this, as I recovered from a rattlesnake bite on the Texas plains and from nearly having my head cut off on the Marquesa Islands.*

Oh, Lucy. Was this your idea, or Art's? Two people he loved equally—of course they'd both want him to be there, when they gave themselves over wholly into one another's keeping. He recalled how Lucy had wept when he'd asked for her hand, how she'd blushed when he'd asked, *Is there someone else?* Of course there was. He'd seen how Art watched the fair-haired girl at that ball at Godalming House, how his young friend had maneuvered always to be close at hand when she wanted a cup of punch or a sliver of cake. He'd seen, too, the melting approval in Mrs. Westenra's chilly eyes, that had turned to daggers whenever Seward had claimed Lucy's attention.

Get away from my daughter, you . . . you mad-doctor. Can't you see she's fascinating the heir to a Viscount who has twenty thousand a year?

Not for one instant did Seward doubt that young Arthur Holmwood loved Lucy Westenra to distraction. He would make her a fine husband, and knowing the man as he did, Seward would take oath that—pavement-nymphs in Tampico notwithstanding—his friend would never give her the slightest cause for suspicion or tears.

And at nineteen, Lucy was old enough to know her own mind, Seward recognized.

And yet what returned to his thoughts again and again was Mrs. Westenra's satisfied voice as the carriage pulled away into the rain: *I told you how it would be, Lucy.*

And the deprecating contempt in her tone as she looked around the tiny drawing-room: *What a clever use of space.*

What else had she said to her daughter, to steer her thoughts away from a man who had no fortune, to one who had a great one? All for Lucy's own good, as that harridan Lady Clayburne had spoken of taking Vivienne Renfield from her mother and sending her to a finishing-school in Switzerland, so that she could later make "an eligible *parti.*"

Growing up as he had, with the standards and position of an old family to maintain though the money to do so was long since gone, Seward had had a front-row seat on how the ladies of Society could damn with faint praise, could manipulate the hearts and thoughts of their daughters with that agonizing amalgam of duty, love, and guilt.

Was that why, after he'd received the small legacy which had raised him from Out of the Question to modest eligibility, he had never trusted those hopeful lures tossed out by the daughters of the lesser social ranks?

Seward sighed, and raised his head, to gaze out the window of his study into the green of the walled park. Through the trees he could see the black roof-slates of Carfax Hall. Last week the FOR SALE sign had been taken down from its rusted gates, and hired men had gone in yesterday to scythe clear the drive. So the place had found a buyer. Wealthy, one hoped, for it would cost a fortune to put that dilapidated pile back into anything resembling livable condition.

Through the endless months of June and July, while he had buried himself in work to forget the ache of hopes raised only to be dashed, he had written to Lucy in Whitby, where she was staying for the summer with her mother. She had written back once or twice, polite notes about country walks with her school-friend Mina, or descriptions of the old churchyard on the East Cliff, where the headstones would occasionally tumble down to the sea beneath: copybook exercises in friendly correspondence that could have been addressed to anyone.

Yet what did he expect? Declarations of love? He didn't know whether these cordial letters were worse, or better, than nothing at all.

He turned the invitation over again in his fingers. October eighth. Sixty days away. Time enough to determine whether he could not endure to be there, or could not endure to stay away.

With a sigh he leaned across to the cabinet and wound up his phonograph, set the needle on the wax cylinder, and picked up the small mouthpiece. If nothing else, there was still work. Though everything seemed to taste of ashes these days, at least he could do some good for someone, no matter what he was feeling inside.

"August seventh. With the prohibition against sparrows in effect, Renfield's mania for flies and spiders has returned full-force, and his room is now filled again with his boxes and jars. In addition to feeding the flies to the spiders, both Langmore and Hardy have seen Renfield eating both species, confirming my hypothesis of a new type of mania, zoöphagy. For two weeks it has seemed to me that the man has grown more secretive, and I have come upon him repeatedly with his face pressed to the window bars, in an attitude of listening . . ."

Letter, R. M. Renfield to his wife
9 August

My dearest one, in haste—

If I have hitherto hoped that you would somehow find a way to visit me here, now I must—and you must—put that thought from our minds.

Well did the ancients depict their gods bearing saving fire in one hand, and in the other the bow of death! Salvation walks side by side with destruction, and wise indeed is the man who can steer the course between them.

HE IS HERE. His feet tread English soil, and nightly he whispers in my dreams. I saw as in a vision the ship that bears his sleeping body driven ashore by the storm-winds that are in his keeping. Where he made landfall, I do not know. Amid rain and fog I was aware of picturesque small houses, of cliffs looming over the harbor, crowned with a tiny church and its tombstones. But through the very ground beneath this house it seemed to me that I felt the press of his foot, somewhere in this island realm.

And he is coming here! I know this as I know my name.

And I fear for my very soul.

Guard yourself, my beloved! Compared to him, such creatures as your mother and Wormidge are nothing! Take every precaution against discovery. Only the knowledge that you are safe—that Vixie is safe—gives me the strength to carry on.

I am taking what steps I can, to strengthen my soul against his power, that I may not be utterly swallowed up.

The light of his majesty floods my mind, yet I tremble. As I tremble, your name is on my lips. It is all, *all*, for you.

Forever your beloved husband,
R.M.R.

R.M.R.'s notes
9 August
15 flies, 4 spiders

10 August
12 flies, 2 spiders

Attempt to obtain a sparrow interfered with by attendant—fool! I must be more careful. So much depends upon my strength.

* * *

Dreams of moonlight, and of the long stair that led from the little coastal town up to the churchyard on the cliffs above. Renfield felt himself again aware of every living thing in that town, sleeping now, sleeping deep: each child dreaming of pony-rides or magic palaces, each man of stammering unprepared through classroom-lessons unlearned. He saw the dark houses with their windows shuttered, the pretty gardens robed in darkness. Saw the white slip of movement, as a blond girl in a nightdress strolled unconcerned through the town with a sleep-walker's unseeing stare.

She was beautiful, and Renfield's heart was touched by her. Where the night-breeze flattened the thin batiste against her body, it showed a shallow breast, the sharp point of a too-slender hip, a delicate form childlike and vulnerable without the womanly defenses of corsetry and draped silk. She was not many years older than his daughter. Loosed for sleep, her flaxen hair shivered to her hips.

The girl climbed the stairs—hundreds of stairs. Slabs of stone, or carved into the living rock of the cliff, and Renfield knew what waited for her at the top. He wanted to cry out to her, to wake her, to warn her, but he knew what Wotan would do to him if he did this—Wotan would not be pleased.

Wotan would withhold from him the gift of life that he so desperately needed. Worse, Wotan would whisper into the dreams of others, of Georgina Clayburne and that stone-faced harridan mother of hers of where Catherine and Vixie lay sleeping tonight.

Then all would be in vain!

Heart pounding, body quaking with pity and with cold, Renfield watched as the blonde girl walked past him—for he seemed to be standing on the long stair from the town—and on up to the churchyard on the cliff.

A tomb lay close to the cliff's grass-grown edge. For a moment Renfield thought that the thing that lay on it was a dog or a wolf, but the next moment the dark form rose, elongating into the unmistakable shadow of a cloaked man, and red eyes gleamed where they caught the moon's sickly light. From the top of the steps Renfield watched, as the sleep-walker passed among the graves with the confidence of a child. The figure beside the tomb held out its hand. Renfield's ears seemed to be filled with the buzz of swarming flies.

Don't do it! he wanted to shout to her. *Don't go to him!* He was aware of her face, relaxed in sleep as Catherine's was all those nights beside him, like Vixie's when she was little, when he'd go into her room to check on her and see her asleep in the night-light's tiny glow. *Please don't hurt her . . .*

Wotan gathered the girl into his arm, the white of her nightdress disappearing in the velvet folds of the cloak. His hand, huge and coarse, with pointed nails like claws, cupped the side of her face, turning her head aside to expose the big blood-vessels of the throat. The roar of flies swamped Renfield's mind and for a time his dream was only that he was sitting in his room at Rushbrook, with the window wide open and flies buzzing in, landing happily on his hands, on his knees, on the pillow of his bed, and letting him eat them like candy while spiders lined up in an expectant file, waiting their turn.

The glow of life washed over him, filled him, burning, warming, intoxicating. For a few moments every cell in his body was conscious, and cried aloud with relief from a lifelong hunger he had never even known had weighed upon him so heavily, until that instant of release.

His mouth sang with the metallic flavor of fresh blood.

His brain, with the scent of the girl.

He thought she cried out.

Distant and dim, as if seeing with someone else's eyes, he became aware of the girl again, lying on the cliffside tombstone as if upon a bed. Beyond her, the moon shone with a cold pewter gleam on the shingle-beds of the harbor where the tide had gone out. It made the feathery coils of her hair pale as ivory, where they lay over the edge of the granite slab, and trailed on the ground. Renfield heard a girl's voice call softly, "Lucy!" and saw a second girl striding among the graves. She was a little taller and of sturdier build, hurriedly dressed in shirtwaist and walking-skirt. Her dark hair was already coming out of a hasty braid that slapped between her shoulders as she ran.

"Mina?" the blonde girl whispered, as her dark-haired friend sat beside her on the tomb, raised her up in her arms. The blonde head fell back, turned aside, curtained by that cascade of moon-colored silk. Her breath dragged in thick frantic gasps. The dark girl, with brisk decisiveness, wrapped Lucy in the heavy figured shawl from around her own shoulders, pinning it at the throat. Then she took the shoes from her own feet and put them on

Lucy's before turning to the task of fully waking her. Renfield heard her voice, a gentle, lovely alto, speaking soft nothings as his consciousness drew back from them. Their image grew smaller and smaller, tiny in the light of that enormous moon, but just before it winked out, Renfield saw Mina get Lucy to her feet, and help her back toward the stairway that would lead them down to the town.

He awoke ravenous, starving, the yellow moonlight a glowing shawl dropped on the floor of his room. Hand trembling, he emptied confused flies and sleepy spiders from their boxes and tumblers and jars, devoured them without even stopping to chew. Spiky legs, brittle wings.

Their tiny lives sparkled like electricity in his veins.

But his hunger was not even touched.

Chapter Six

R.M.R.'s notes
12 August
14 flies, 5 spiders, 2 slugs (sugar-water dripped on sill)
Must have more. Asked for extra sugar, received it. Know not to
try for sparrow. Always they watch me. *He* watches me, too.

*   *   *

"Dr. Seward?" Renfield spoke for the first time during Seward's
visit that evening, rousing himself from his desperate preoccu-
pation of mind. He had to be careful, he knew, yet even as he
hoped to wrest from Wotan the additional life that he needed,
it might be possible to use Seward, unsuspecting, to obtain
the knowledge that—as Wotan had so accurately said—men
treasure.

Renfield reflected that the young doctor was stupid enough
to be manipulated into telling him anything.

"What is it, old chap?" Seward turned back from the door,

which Renfield noticed Langmore was quick to lock again. They feared him, did they?

Anger flashed through him. He'd give them cause to fear.

The anger must have shone in his face, because Seward hesitated. Renfield forced his rage down. "As a doctor of the mind, have you—or anyone in your field—come to any theory of what dreams are, and why we have them? Are they truly—or can they be—agents of communication, as even the ancient Stoics argued? Or do you believe, like Freud, that they are merely the mind's way of ordering the events of the past, of sorting them into larger mental categories determined by past experience?"

A spider tiptoed in through the open window, past the bars; Renfield caught it with the adeptness of long practice and popped it at once into his mouth, dug his notebook from his shirt-pocket and added it to the tally, then turned back for Seward's reply.

"I believe they can serve the mind as a means of assimilating experience," agreed Seward, his dark eyes watchful on Renfield's face, as if—which Seward so often did—he sought to guess what lay behind the question. He went on, "I have heard—both here and in America, and in the islands of the South Seas—stories of how dreams do communicate events of the past or present, though as a scientist I'm inclined to wonder how such a thing could be proven empirically. My old teacher—a Dutchman from Amsterdam—is of the opinion that the ability to dream developed as human intelligence grew to the point that men were in danger of harming themselves and others through too exclusive a reliance on that intelligence. That God gave man the ability to dream as a channel to deliver warnings from sources that cannot be quantified. But he may have been joking." And Seward smiled.

"And if one dreams of things that are taking place far away—

evil things, events that bring danger to the innocent—is there a way to warn those one sees in danger? A way to know where these events are taking place, or whom to warn?"

Seward's eyes narrowed sharply. "What do you mean?" he asked. "Did you dream about your wife, for instance? Catherine, I believe her name is? Or your daughter?"

Georgina Clayburne has been to see him. Rage seared through Renfield, as if a match had been dropped on a trail of kerosene. He felt his face heat, forced himself to look at the wall beyond Seward's shoulder. Forced from his mind the delicious joy it would bring him to pick the slightly built doctor up and smash his brains out against the wall, to twist his head from his shoulders.

They would strait-jacket him. Put him in the Swing. Give him castor-oil and ipecac to weaken him with vomiting.

When Wotan came, he would not be ready.

Breathing hard, Renfield said, "I didn't dream about nobody, sir." He knew he should make up a convincing tale but he couldn't think. His mind was filled with the roaring buzz of flies. "I was just asking."

*   *   *

When Seward left, Renfield returned to the window, pressed his face to the bars to drink in the evening's cool. Rushbrook House was set at an angle to the road, so that through his window he could see the gates to the high-road, as well as a portion of the crumbling wall and overgrown trees of the estate next door.

Yesterday he'd seen a handsome new carriage come through the gates, its team of matched blacks familiar to him. He had thought the woman inside looked like Georgina Clayburne.

And he didn't think it was the first time she'd come to call on Seward.

Asking what? What did she know already? What had she guessed, and what information had she bought from Hennessey? She had almost certainly had the house in Nottingham searched. That didn't trouble Renfield particularly, for he had made sure, when he, Catherine, and Vixie had left it, that no trace of paper remained to tell where they'd gone. The other houses in London, like the bank accounts he and Catherine had set up, were under other names.

Was that why Seward watched him so closely, took down notes of what he said? Was he sending every word, every speculation, on to Georgina and that ghastly mother, even as Hennessey was doing?

He watched the shadow of Rushbrook House stretch out over the garden, reaching toward the dark wall, the dark trees, of Carfax. The voices of the attendants rose like incongruous bird-calls in the air, as they began to close up the windows, put up the shutters for the night. From a room near-by, the woman the attendants referred to as Queen Anne began her nightly howling. Many of the patients, Renfield had observed, grew worse at this hour, pounding on the walls and babbling, or sinking into uncontrollable tears. Footsteps hurried in the halls, to give Her Majesty the drugs that would silence her, would push her over the edge into her own dreams.

What if those dreams, like some of his own, were infinitely more dreadful than the waking that she could not struggle back to no matter how much she tried?

Renfield closed his eyes, and told himself that he must be strong.

That night he dreamed of the girls again, as he had dreamed the night before. Dreamed—as he had last night—that he was in their bedroom, looking down on them as they slept, and their faces were relaxed in sleep, as sweet and young as Catherine's looked in the mysterious blue radiance of the waxing moon. Mina, the dark-haired girl, wore a little pucker between her brows. Though she was probably no older than her friend, she had the air of a young woman who has had to make her own way in the world. The nightgown-sleeve that lay on the tufted counterpane was plain muslin, and much worn, in contrast to the fantasia of batiste and lace that swaddled the delicate Lucy.

When fear came into the room, and the chilly breath of the grave, Renfield tried to reach out to Mina, tried to shake her shoulder—or he thought he tried . . . or he wanted to try. *He is coming,* he thought as the air in the room grew colder and colder and a small black shadow began to circle erratically outside the moon-drenched window. *Wotan is coming.*

His heart pounded in terror. He had to wake them up, so they could flee.

He had to wake up himself, so that he wouldn't see what would happen.

But he could neither move, nor waken.

Mina whispered, "Jonathan," in her sleep, and sank deeper, almost into the sleep of death, Renfield thought. But Lucy turned on her pillow, her shut eyes seeming to seek the window, and in the moonlight Renfield could see now that the thing outside was a bat, fluttering and beating its wings at the casement.

He pressed back into the shadows, his hands covering his mouth.

Wotan would see him. And seeing him, would take his vengeance, not only on him, but on Catherine and Vixie as well.

Oh, Catherine, Catherine, he thought wildly, *if I can see this, if I can be here, why can't I be at your side instead?*

But he shut the thought from his mind like the slamming of a door, lest Wotan hear him and know then that someone named Catherine even existed.

Lucy rose from her bed, her head lolling, and with the pre-ternatural clarity of dreams Renfield saw the wound on her neck, the two tiny punctures above the vein, unhealed, white-edged and mangled-looking. All the moonlight seemed to be failing in the room, and the shadow of the bat grew still, seeming to swell in size, so that it covered the whole of the window in its wings. Out of that shadow its red eyes gleamed, like the far-off lamps of Hell. When Lucy stumbled to the casement and fumbled open the latch, the dark form of Wotan stepped through as if he had strode there upon the air of night.

Lucy sagged forward into his arms. In the moonlight Wotan smiled—or the thing in the ship's hold that had spoken to Renfield with Wotan's words. *He could not be Wotan,* thought Renfield muzzily, *for he has two eyes, not one like the Wanderer God: eyes as red and reflective as the eyes of a rat.* But then, when Wotan had spoken those words to Mime the Dwarf, he had not yet traded his eye for wisdom. His mustaches were long and iron-gray, his face was not the face of a god, but of a man who has gone beyond what other men are, into some unknown zone of experience.

A face of power. A face like iron, that no longer recalls what it was to be a man. A face maybe that never knew in the first place.

He cupped the side of Lucy's face in his short-fingered pow-erful hand, drew back his lips from long canine teeth, like an animal's fangs. Renfield closed his eyes as the blood began to flow down, hid his mind in thoughts of flies. Big fat horse-flies the size of lichis, each bursting with the electrical fires of life. He did not even dare think, *Let her alone . . .*

Wotan—or whatever that thing was truly called—would not like that.

Already Renfield understood that what that shadowy deity wanted, maybe more than life, was power. For him, there could be no disloyalty.

R.M.R.'s notes
19 August
The bride-maidens rejoice the eyes that wait the coming of the bride; but when the bride draweth nigh, then the maidens shine not in the eyes that are filled.

* * *

"It's Renfield, sir." Grizzled little Langmore blinked in the dimmed gas-light of the hall. He'd clearly expected to find Seward in bed. "He's escaped."

Seward had been expecting it. All day Renfield had been restless, prowling his room by turns wild with excitement and darkly sullen. When Seward had turned in after his final round among the patients, though depressed himself, he had elected not to inject the chloral hydrate which had, he realized, become something of a habit over the past three months. Instead he'd prepared for bed, but sat up re-reading Lucy's latest note, short and polite though underlain with sadness, for she suspected her mother was far more ill than she was letting on . . . all the while listening, as if he knew there would be trouble with Renfield as the night grew deeper.

"I seen him not ten minutes ago, when I looked through the judas, sir." Hardy pushed open the door of Renfield's room as Seward and Langmore came striding down the hall. "Sly, he is. Layin' on his bed lookin' like butter wouldn't melt in his mouth."

The muggy cool of the night-breeze met them as they entered the room, where the window-sash had been literally wrenched from its moorings in the wall, bars and all. Seward shivered, thinking of the strength that would have taken.

A sudden paroxysm of rage or terror? He hoped so. The thought of the madman being actually that strong at all times was not a pleasant one. He glanced around the little room, to make sure there wasn't some clue, but it looked much the same in the light of the attendants' lanterns: the narrow cot-like bed had not been displaced from its position along the right-hand wall, the assortment of tumblers, cups, and boxes that contained Renfield's living larder were still neatly ranked on the floor opposite.

Stepping to the window, he caught the pale flash of what might have been a nightshirt, dodging among the trees by the intermittent whisper of the waning moon. The yellow gleam of a lantern told Seward that Simmons was already on the trail. Heading for Carfax, it looked like.

"Bring a ladder and follow us to the east wall," he instructed Hardy, took his lantern, and hung it on his belt. With more than a slight qualm, he slithered through the torn-out ruin of the window, hung by his hands from the sill for a moment, then dropped to the ground. Langmore at his heels, he set out through the darkness on Renfield's trail.

CHAPTER SEVEN

"There he goes, sir," Langmore whispered, and Seward held up his hand. Renfield's hearing was sharp—he'd demonstrated more than once his ability to track a fly by its buzzing above the sound of conversation—and he'd be listening for the smallest noise of pursuit. *Or would he?* Seward had encountered madmen and madwomen who seemed to think that mere escape was enough; that they could elude pursuers as if they were birds.

> *With a heart of furious fancies,*
> *Whereof I am commander;* sang the old ballad—
> *With a burning spear*
> *And a horse of air*
> *To the wilderness I wander . . .*

Not for the first time he wished his old friend Quincey Morris were with him, Quincey who'd learned tracking from a couple of Commanche who'd worked on his father's Texas ranch.

Quincey could be relied upon to keep quiet and obey orders without question, something Seward wasn't sure he could count on from most of the attendants.

The white blur of Renfield's nightshirt shone against the dark of the Carfax wall long before the pursuers were anywhere near him, then vanished as he dropped down the other side.

Seward cursed. In addition to exploring the Carfax park itself, he'd walked around the perimeter wall, both outside and in, and knew it to be badly dilapidated, low enough in several places for a man to easily climb. It might take Renfield a little time to find such spots, but the thought of chasing him through open countryside in the dead of a pitch-black night made him shudder.

Thank God at least Hardy had the wits to move quietly, or as quietly as a big man carrying an eight-foot ladder without a lantern might be expected to—

"Stay here," Seward breathed, as Hardy set up the ladder against the wall. "He may think he's safe for the moment; if he thinks we're on his heels, he'll be away like a hare." When he put his head over the fern-grown capstones, he could glimpse Renfield again, making his way toward the dark bulk of the house. "Slip over as quietly as you can and spread out," he whispered, retreating down the ladder a few steps and looking down at the upturned faces of the three attendants. "Hardy, circle around to the right, Simmons and Langmore to the left—whatever you do, try to keep him from getting out the gate onto the high road."

Had the new tenants—or at any rate the carters who'd lugged in the dozen huge crates of their goods that afternoon— remembered to lock those rusted gates of oak and iron? Had they been able to make the crazy old locks work, either on the gates or on the house?

Seward tried to push the thought away. "And for God's sake,

keep quiet," he added. "Keep your lanterns as dark as you can manage. If you hear me shout, come running." At any rate, thank goodness, he reflected as he slipped over the wall in what he hoped was an inconspicuous fashion, Carfax wasn't inhabited yet. He might have to go chasing a semi-naked madman down the highroad and into the marshes, but at least he wouldn't have to deal with neighbors enraged or terrified by a midnight incursion. Since the FOR SALE sign had disappeared from the gates, he'd watched for signs of habitation—or even of preparation for habitation, so as to get the address of someone to write to—but so far there had been nothing. It was as if, having purchased the place, the buyers had been content to let Carfax sit in its crumbling Gothic glory, as it had sat since at least the Napoleonic Wars.

Tangled ivy crunched underfoot. Something—fox or rabbit—darted wildly away through the undergrowth that choked most of the park. Carfax had clearly begun life as a small castle, of which part of the keep and a chapel remained, a ruinous appendix clinging to the side of a four-square, mostly Tudor dwelling now largely swallowed up in ivy. The gardens were in as poor a state as the house; twice Seward's path was blocked by tangles of overgrown hedge, and once he found a fragment of cotton nightshirt snagged up on a half-dead rosebush. He could hear Renfield's footsteps, a dry harsh rustle in decades of dead leaves, making still for the house.

I shall have to find the new owners somehow, thought Seward, *and speak to them about having that wall repaired. The house agent must have warned them, in any case, that they were buying property next door to a lunatic asylum.* The thought of Renfield breaking out again after the new owners were in residence flitted nightmarishly through his mind. *Probably no*

danger to them, but God help Fido or Puss if he happens to en-
counter them in the park.

". . . Master . . ."

The word breathed in the darkness, and Seward froze. A
mutter of speech. *Speaking to whom?*

Seward could have sworn the house was empty.

He crept nearer, not breathing, straining to listen as he
rounded the corner of the black leaf-shrouded bulk.

The clouds had parted, letting through a thread of moonlight
that showed him the half-circle of the chapel, the stained but-
tresses ragged with ivy and the arched clerstory windows sunken
eyeless sockets in the wall. There was a door set in the wall,
flanked by columnar attenuated saints leperous with moss. Renfield's white nightshirt made a blur in the embrasure.

"I am here to do your bidding, Master. I am your slave, and
you will reward me, for I shall be faithful." He brought his
hands up, filthy and stained with moss, as if to caress the iron
handle, the padlocked bars. "I have worshipped you long and
afar off. Now that you are near, I await your commands, and
you will not pass me by, will you, dear Master, in your distribu-
tion of good things?"

Selfish old beggar, thought Seward, suddenly amused. *He believes he's in the Real Presence of God and his first thought is for
the loaves and fishes—particularly the fishes.*

Still, there was something in the intensity of Renfield's hissing
voice that set alarm-bells ringing in his mind. Religious mania
took a number of truly unpleasant forms. He wouldn't want to
deal with the complications it would add to the existing obses-
sion with zoöphagy . . .

"*Who is there?*" Renfield swung around, his square, lined
face convulsed like a demon's.

Lantern-light flashed in the darkness. Langmore, Simmons, and Hardy threw themselves out of the shrubbery, catching Renfield as he tried to bolt. Seward, who'd sprung forward and seized Renfield's arm, was thrown back against the chapel wall as if he had no weight at all. For a moment it seemed to him, watching the struggling men, that the madman would hurl them all aside and disappear into the night. Renfield bellowed and cursed, then screamed like an animal as Langmore twisted his arm, but Seward thought the madman would have gone on struggling, letting the attendant break his bones, had not Hardy struck Renfield a stunning blow on the head. The big man sank to his knees; Langmore whipped forward the arm he held, and Simmons jammed it, and the other, into the sleeves of the strait-jacket they'd brought.

Whatever momentary fears Seward felt about that blow dissolved on the way back to Rushbrook House. Renfield kicked, thrashed, howled like an animal until he was gagged; twisted like a man in the throes of convulsions. At one point Seward feared that the lunatic would manage to tear himself free of the strait-jacket, and when they got him into the house—with all the other patients setting up a cacaphony in sympathy like the howling of the damned in Hell—ordered extra bindings strapped around him before he was chained to the wall of the padded room.

When Seward returned to his own bedroom, he was shaken to the bones: *Dear God, and I once harbored the delusion that I could bring Lucy to live with me in this place?*

He sank down onto the bed, trembling. The transformation of a man whom he'd thought of as basically harmless, to other human beings if not to himself or to any fly or bird that came within his reach, brought home to him what his old teacher Van Helsing had said to him once: "We are the guardians of the frontier of darkness, my friend. And that means that for the most part, we must stand our watches alone."

Ah, Lucy, he thought despairingly, *you deserve better than this—better than the danger you would be in, living here with me, no matter what I could do to protect you. I underestimated the dangers of that dark frontier. I will not do so again.*

In the east-facing windows of his room, past the irregular darkness of Carfax's broken roof-line, the summer sky was already staining with first light. Through the walls of his room Seward could hear his patients howling. And above their cries, a powerful voice bellowed like that of a Titan in chains:

"I shall be patient, Master! It is coming—coming—coming!"

Seward injected himself with chloral hydrate and passed out without even removing his clothes.

Letter, R. M. Renfield to his wife
Undated (late August?)

My beloved,

I beg your forgiveness for not having written. I was unavoidably prevented, by the stupidity and, I fear, downright malice of the men with whom I am forced to work in this place. Nothing but the most urgent consideration would have kept my pen from paper, would have silenced the words of love that every day dwell in my heart.

Tell our Vixie that her papa loves her, and will be with her again by-and-by.

Your own,
R.M.R.

CHAPTER EIGHT

Hanging in chains on the wall of the padded cell, Renfield dreamed.

For three days he hung there, raving and sobbing at what he saw, at what he knew was happening, would happen. They gave him laudanum to quiet him, forcing it down his throat when he twisted his head aside in a vain effort to refuse further dreams.

Don't send me back there! he wanted to scream at them. *He is hunting her, stalking her as a hunter stalks a doe! Waiting for her to come.*

But these words he dared not say aloud, for Catherine's sake, for Vixie's and his own.

Wotan was near. Wotan was present, was there, not just in England but less than half a mile distant, lying open-eyed in his coffin in the crumbling chapel of Carfax, blood-stained hands folded on his breast.

Waiting.

Peace came with nightfall and moonrise, for in those hours

Wotan's mind was elsewhere, occupied with the business that men occupied themselves with during the day. The sense of release, of relief, was nearly unbearable. Renfield would lie on the floor of the padded cell each night when at Seward's orders he was released from his bonds, listening only to the dim howling of the other patients, to the murmur of Langmore and Simmons as they played their unceasing games of cribbage in the hall, to the steady soft ticking of the hallway clock. Yet he was at all times aware of the Traveler, aware of his nearness. Aware of his power.

Wotan was there, Wotan who held the gift of life in his hand.

Wotan whose anger infected his brain and drove him to screaming rages in the daytime, so that he was chained again on the wall.

Watch yourself, traitor, if you betray me now, Wotan had said to Loki, in the shivering music of *Das Rheingold. I, of all the gods your only friend . . .*

Wotan, too, dreamed. In his dreams the Traveler God could hear and see, through those others whom his mind had touched. His thoughts spread like poisoned mist through the air, making nothing of distance. Wotan would know what Renfield said, if he shrieked to the guards what he knew, what he saw during his daytime visions. Wotan would hear, and would not forgive.

I do not want to see the kill!

*   *   *

That first day in the straps he saw the girls in the train-station. Pretty Lucy looked much better, with a trace of rosiness returning to her delicate cheeks, and she hugged her dark-haired friend like a sister. "You have your tickets?"

"Exactly where they were when you asked five minutes ago." Mina patted her handbag, and Lucy laughed. "You're in danger of forgetting that *I'm* the schoolmistress, *you're* the giddy young thing who goes to parties and is going to be the daughter-in-law of Lord Godalming by the time I get back."

"Darling!" Lucy giggled, her rosiness deepening, and the older woman who accompanied the girls—she had Lucy's blue eyes, Renfield thought, and Lucy's flawless complexion—folded her gloved hands and smiled.

But her smile was wan. There was a haunted shadow in the back of those blue eyes, transforming what had been the cold face of a lady of Society—a lady who reminded Renfield alarmingly of his sister-in-law Georgina, Lady Clayburne—into a mask of exhaustion and deepest tragedy. She watched the girls as if it were she, not the dark-haired Mina, who was about to depart, with a hungry longing and a terrible regret. Her face was both puffy and sunken, with a waxy cast to it that Renfield knew well from long acquaintance with his countrymen in India's unhealthy clime.

She has had her death-warrant, he thought, his heart aching suddenly for her as he never thought it could have, not for that species of woman. *She knows it, and her daughter does not.*

"And this Sister Agatha didn't say what had happened to Jonathan?" Lucy was asking. "Other than that he had brain-fever?"

"It was all she said." Mina reached into the pocket of her jacket—sensible brown linen and, like all her other clothing, a little worn, a few years out of fashion—and drew out a much-folded square of yellow paper. "Only that he rushed into the train-station at Klausenberg shouting for a ticket for home. Klausenberg seems to be the central market-town of the Carpathian plateau, if the atlas is correct and if Klausenberg is the same as Cluj. There seems to be only one train per day there from Vienna, at nine-fifteen in the morning. Since the night-train from Munich arrives at just before seven, that should give me plenty of time—"

"You and your railway timetables!" laughed Lucy's mother, her weariness dissolving into genuine pleasure at the dark girl's company, and Lucy hugged her friend again impulsively.

"Oh, darling, you're so brave! Going out like this to the ends of the world! Not even knowing the language!"

He is watching her, thought Renfield, aware of Wotan's mind, Wotan's shadow—aware of those red eyes gleaming, like a rat's eyes, in the shadows of that cheerful provincial train-station. *Watching her and waiting for her . . . and smiling. Smiling like a damned leering devil in the dark of his coffin.*

NO!!!

Renfield tried to twist his mind away as he became aware of that grinning, ironic, ancient thought watching him, too. Enjoying his pity for the sad-faced mother in her stylish walking-dress, deriving wicked amusement from his fears for that too-fragile, too-pale fair-haired girl. Renfield tried to dream something else, tried to think of something else: great pools and smears of treacle, spread all over the floor of his cell, and huge black horseflies roaring through the window to become mired in them, waiting smilingly for his hand.

Not the sparse and aenemic insects of England at all, but the meaty gargantuan fauna of India. White ants swarming forth from wood like trails of animate milk, rice-beetles that would blunder and blunder at the same wall without the wits to go around. Those were insects indeed!

He tried to force himself to see them, to force himself to see the yellow buildings of Calcutta, the market-places aswarm with brown half-naked farmers, with Brahmins in their golden robes and shy-eyed farm-girls and great white cows making their way through the dung and the dirt and the crowds. Tried to will himself back to that place, where life dripped with the scents of clarified butter and spices and the painted idols stared out from every street-corner and door.

But it was as if he moved his eyes and the vision dissolved and he was back in that cool neat train-platform in England, with the smell of the green fields in his nostrils and the taste of the salt sea near-by, and Mina clasping the older woman's hands saying, "There's no way I can ever repay your kindness in buying me my tickets, Mrs. Westenra, and giving me money for the journey. But believe me, I *shall* pay you back."

A smile twitched the wrinkled gray lips and Mrs. Westenra laid a loving hand on Mina's cheek. "My dear child, do you imagine it's money out of *my* pocket? By the time you come back, Lucy will be the daughter-in-law of Lord Godalming, and I shall have gotten the money out of her lord."

They all laughed merrily at that, as the conductor began to drone his call for travelers to board; in the shadows at the back of the platform, Renfield could see the cloaked shadow of the Traveler, red eyes glinting, white teeth glinting as he smiled.

No!

"We'll take your trunk down to London the day after to-morrow. You must bring Jonathan to Hillingham the very moment he's well enough to travel. Darling . . ."

"Darling!"

The girls embraced on the steps of the train, the bright silks and laces of the one like the most fragile of flowers against the earthy brown linen of the other. Somewhere in his mind Renfield felt the gloating greed, the amused pleasure, of the watching Traveler and he began to thrash in his dreaming, to scream, *Let her alone! Let her alone, you devil!*

He knew the girls would never meet again.

The roaring of flies filled his mind, the taste of them in his mouth. A thousand flies, a million, all mired in those sweet pools of treacle and all smiling up at him with Lucy Westenra's face.

* * *

He is hunting her. He is waiting for her to come.

In those cool hours of release while the moon flooded Rushbrook's lawns with wan silver, Renfield tried to tell himself that he knew nothing of the girl Lucy. She might be stuck-up and cruel, as calculating as her mother. She was, after all, about to marry a lord, and that sort of thing surely didn't happen by accident. But this he could not believe. During the course of his second day of laudanum-induced visions, of the gloating, grinning presence of the Traveler in his mind, he glimpsed Lucy and her mother in the rock-walled garden of what seemed to be a small summer cottage, having tea with a golden young Apollo in Bond Street tailoring. Saw with what exquisite care and tact the girl dealt with her mother, fetching and carrying for her and laughingly denying that she did so out of worry.

"Nonsense, darling. Arthur told me he liked helpful women and I'm trying *very* hard to impress him!" When she passed his chair, young Arthur's gray-gloved hand sought hers. The look that passed between his blue eyes and hers tore Renfield's heart.

* * *

Such prey is the source of his strength, he thought, lying the next night on the thick canvas flooring of his cell, the reek of ancient filth and decades of carbolic rising dimly through it from the matted coir beneath. *Without her death, there would be no life in his hands, to give out to those who serve him.*

Renfield pressed his face to the padded floor and wept. He wanted Catherine desperately, wanted only to see her smile again, to hear her voice. *Where Life flows,* Loki had sung—Wagner's music had sung—*in Water, Earth, and Air . . . What could a man find, mightier than the wonder of a woman's worth? . . . In Water, Earth, and Air, the only Will is for love.*

How long had it been since her laughter had bubbled in his ears, sweet as spring rainfall? He could not even recall. Now it was only with terror that he thought of her at all, fearing that even in these dark hours, while Wotan's mind was elsewhere, Wotan would somehow learn of her, somehow know where she and Vixie were hidden.

Fearing that he would find them, as he would find Lucy no matter where she went.

Renfield hugged himself, as if he could crush his bulky sixteen-stone-plus into a ball the size of an apple, the size of an apple-seed . . . too small to be found by those all-seeing crimson eyes. Hurting for comfort, he called to mind—just once, like a quick glance at a photograph hastily stowed in hiding again—Catherine's face as last he had seen it, asleep and so peaceful, with her long dark lashes veiling those pansy-blue eyes and her red hair unraveled over the pillow.

Beautiful Catherine. Beautiful Vixie, as delicate as Lucy but with Miss Mina's exquisite darkness, laughing over some passage in her Latin lesson or holding out her finger in breathless wonder as a yellow butterfly floated in from the garden, landed on it with tiny pricking feet.

Just let me be with them again, Renfield whispered to the

God whom he knew Wotan would never allow him to petition. *I know my sins are many, my offenses rank in your sight, but please, please, let me finish my task here, and return to their side.*

Day was coming. They would strap him up again, pour laudanum down his throat. He felt the Traveler's mind, as the thing he knew as Wotan drew near to his lair in the rotting chapel at Carfax again, seeking the bed of earth upon which he must sleep. *Why earth?* he wondered. *Why that particular earth, which he'd brought in such quantity upon the haunted ship?* He wanted to ask, but dared not. He was there only to serve, only to do the bidding of the Master who, for all his terror, was his best and only hope.

* * *

Seward had left the door of the padded room unlocked through most of the night—Renfield heard them whisper about it in the corridor. But beyond a flicker of contempt for such an obvious attempt at trapping him, he felt no interest in the matter. The Traveler was abroad in the night; of what use was it to knock upon the door of his empty house? And Renfield was weary, weary unto death, and hungry with a hunger that he knew could never be filled. No fly, no spider, not the smallest ant crept into the dreary canvas confines of the padded cell. Only, if he listened, deep beneath the matting he could hear the rustle of tiny creeping beetles, of crawling fleas.

And they did him no good at all.

Catherine, my darling, he thought as he felt the Traveler's mind begin sinking into its day-sleep, begin to burn like creeping fire at the edges of his own, *dream of me now, between your sleep and your waking. Remember that I love you.*

He heard the key turn in the lock.

Not many minutes after that he began to scream.

Letter, Dr. Patrick Hennessey, M.D., M.R.C.S.,
L.K.Q.C., P.I., etc., Rushbrook House, to Georgina,
Lady Clayburne
22 August

Received your check. Many thanks.

I searched through Seward's correspondence again this week and found no attempt on the part of Catherine Renfield to get in touch with either her husband or Seward. Nor was there any letter in a hand that matched the sample you sent to me. I will continue to observe.

R.M.R. has been under heavy restraint for two days, after an escape attempt on the 19th, and violent much of that time. So far as any of the attendants has heard, he has not uttered your sister's name, nor given any clue as to her whereabouts or those of your niece.

I will require another 10 s. per week, if I am to continue to collect information from the attendants.

I remain, dear Madame,
Your humble etc.

CHAPTER NINE

Letter, the Honorable Arthur Holmwood to
Lord Godalming
22 August

Dearest Father,

Please forgive my delay in coming up to Ring. I promised to escort Miss Westenra and her mother down to London, and if you could see the uncertain state of Mrs. Westenra's health, I am sure you would agree with my course—nay, command me to it. I hope your own health is improved?

I cannot wait for you to make Miss Westenra's acquaintance. You will pronounce her—in Uncle Harry's words—"sound as a roast." (One inevitably wonders what sort of roast he has in mind?) The two days I have spent in Whitby with her, walking up to the Abbey on its overhanging cliffs, or rowing on the Esk, have been among the happiest of my life, for she seems to carry sunlight about with her. Her mother is a bit of a Tartar—I kept expecting her to tell me, à la Aunt Maude, that *gentlemen* do *not* wear double-breasted waistcoats—but good-hearted underneath. I think she fears to let Lucy go, for with her own failing health she has come to rely on her in a thousand ways.

By the by, the Westenras are *not,* as Aunt Maude would have it, "nobodies." Sir Clive Westenra left Lucy £1100 a year upon her marriage, a quite respectable sum—to anyone but Aunt Maude! Their villa—Hillingham—lies near Primrose Hill, a very quiet, countrified place, surrounded by the sort of old-fashioned garden that makes one think one is deep in the country indeed. I installed the two ladies there this afternoon, and spent a peaceful hour listening to Lucy play the piano. I kept thinking how her fingers would sound on the keys of your harpsicord at Ring, and hoping some day soon to hear the two of you talk about music together. (Her favorite is Brahms.)

Tomorrow I have promised to take both ladies out on the Thames in the *Guenivere*, for it's been far too long since I've had a tiller in my hands. I only wish you could be along as well, to wave at the little sailing-craft as we steam grandly past!

Unless you need me, sir, I shall remain in London until the wedding, which as you know has been moved up to the 28th September. The change of date has made for a great deal of business, and though Lucy handles it all as adeptly as a matron of thirty, still if I can be of service to her and her mother here, I should like to put myself at their disposal.

I look forward very much to seeing you here on the 20th, if that is still your plan.

Until then,
Your loving son,
Arthur

*　*　*

He knows where she is!

Through the heat of the endless summer afternoon Renfield twisted in his chains, emerging again and again from the cloudy delerium of laudanum to the horror of waking knowledge.

He is only waiting for the night, to take her!

He could not say it, could not speak. Wotan in his coffin would hear him, know his betrayal. But he could not keep silent, and like an animal, trapped in rage and in pain, he screamed, and kicked at that filthy gnome Langmore, the whiskey-smelling Hennessey, when they came into the padded room, to dump more laudanum down his throat.

Don't send me back there! If she is to die tonight I don't want to see it!

As if he lay naked, chained like Prometheus to the vulture-haunted rocks, Renfield could feel the passage of the sun across the sky, the inevitable approach of the night.

Someone save her! Someone warn her!

What I do not have yet, Wotan whispered, grinning with his sharp white teeth, *shall I make you a present of, shameful one?*

How many flies will you have to devour, my little Mime, to gain all that one single drink of living blood will bestow?

The blood is the life. You know this.

In India, Renfield remembered, there were sects—whole villages in places—devoted to Kali, the many-handed black-skinned goddess who danced on the corpse of a dead demon, a necklace of human heads about her throat. They said she was the wife of Shiva, Lord of Change, but there was something in her that Renfield sensed was older, deeper, primal as the rotting flesh from which next year's corn sprouted. He'd ridden out one night with a sergeant named Morehouse and a couple of Punjabi policemen to raid the camp of a robber-band along the Grand Trunk: they'd taken two men prisoners, and killed two others in the fighting. The rest had fled. In the camp they'd found the clothes and money of at least twenty-five travelers, some of whose bodies they'd located in ditches near the road the next day.

Are they leftovers from the Mutiny? Renfield had asked, when the screaming, spitting robbers had been bound, gagged, loaded into one of their own bullock-carts for transport back to Calcutta and trial. Even then—thirty years ago almost—the great uprising against the British rulers had been over for a decade, but Renfield remembered it still: the grilling sun beating down on the empty parade-ground at Meerut, the horror of blood and hacked-up bodies he'd seen, when with the relieving troops he'd looked down the Well at Cawnpore.

Narh, said Morehouse, and spit. *They's just robbers.*

And one of the Punjabis, a man named Akbar Singh, had said, *They existed long before the uprising, Renfield Sahib. In those days they were called Thugs, and they were better organized, but it was much the same. Indeed, it was forbidden among them to rob the Gora-log, the English, proof enough that it was only money that interested them, though they claimed to have their Goddess's blessing. It is a poor country, Sahib, and even if a man has a farm, or part of a farm that he shares with many brothers, he often cannot feed his family. Men of this brotherhood speak of harvesting travelers, as if they were wheat, standing in fields that the Goddess had given them. There are many such.*

In his years of living in India after that, Renfield had found that this was so.

Singh's words came back to him, through that endless day, as he felt the yellow fires of the Traveler God's hunger seep into his dreams: harvesting. Harvesting.

And in his dreams he caught glimpses of her, despite all he

could do: running up the stairs with a tray of tea and muffins for her mother, who lay yet in bed; having a chat with the housekeeper—"I worry about her, Mrs. Dennis, she says she feels fine but I know she isn't well . . ." Giving her maid a quick, friendly hug before she snatched up her broad-brimmed straw hat, skipped down the stairs to meet her handsome Arthur, waiting smiling in the hall, or sitting beneath the flapping sun-shade of a small steam-launch that Arthur piloted up the river.

The sun moved across the sky, and the Earth's concealing shadow crawled over the curve of the world. Renfield screamed his despair, and in his mind Wotan only laughed.

If you will turn aside from the harvest, will you then turn aside from the living bounty that it yields?

He felt Wotan's waking like the breaking of a strangler's noose. It was dark in the padded room, and silent, for once, in the hall outside. The smelly air was warm and thick as dirty water. Renfield hung for a time, weeping, in the straps, but twisted his head to one side to dry his eyes on his shoulder when he heard Hardy's footsteps in the corridor. He murmured a pleasant, "Good-evening, Hardy—did you manage to beat Simmons at cribbage today?" and the attendant unlocked the straps, released the metal catches on the back of the strait-jacket, pulled the heavy garment from Renfield's arms.

"There, now, y'old villain, you gonna be good this evenin'?"

"My dear Hardy . . ." Renfield widened his eyes at the big man. "Have I not been good as gold for three days now? *Malicious witnesses rise up; they ask me of things that I know not / They requite me evil for good, and my soul is forlorn.*"

But Hardy, who did not appear to know more of the Bible than a few names and a Commandment or two (if that), only shook his head, and took his leave, to bring, Renfield knew, the usual unpalatable dinner of tepid stew and bread. So he stood in the corner farthest from the room's tiny barred window, head down and hands folded in an attitude of passive dejection. When Hardy returned with the plate in his hand, he was ready for an attack, but Renfield only dodged past him, slammed the door on him, and shoved the bolt shut.

The padded cell was on the ground floor: Hardy's whistle shrilled in Renfield's ears as he ran, but he knew the keepers would go first to the outer doors, not upstairs. He plunged up the small service flight, then along the hall, where the door of his own old room still stood open, awaiting the glaziers who would fix the casement he'd torn out. Let them catch him in time, if only he could reach the dark chapel, if only he could plead with Wotan to find someone else. Surely there were robbers and murderers in England, spiritual brothers of the Thugs, upon whom his hunger could feast?

Darkness outside, the wild smells of summer night and freedom. Shrubs lashed his bare legs, damp grass like a carpet of velvet under his naked feet—it seemed to him almost that he was flying in a dream, flying like the Valkyries, with their wild music in his ears. It would be moonrise soon, moonrise when Wotan would walk out, would make his way to Hillingham House, where, Renfield knew, he had marked the very window of Lucy's bedchamber.

"Master, no!" He threw himself against the iron-strapped oak of the chapel doors. "Master, listen!"

The next instant Seward and his attendants seized him, dragged him back from the door. Renfield screamed in frustration and rage, turned in their grip, and lunged at Seward. *Fool and worse than fool, understanding nothing! You will be the death of that innocent girl, who never did you harm!* But the anger that had all of Renfield's life come and gone from his brain overwhelmed him in red blindness, and the sounds that came from his mouth were inchoate howls of fury. His hands closed around the mad-doctor's skinny throat and he squeezed, twisted, knowing nothing beyond the fact that this man would thwart him, thwart him from doing what he knew to be right.

And as the madness of anger swept over him, he heard laughter, far back down some dark corridor of his burning brain: the laughter of contempt.

Then Wotan was gone.

Renfield stood trembling, shivering, for in the fight his nightshirt had been ripped half off him, and sweat painted his body and soaked his hair. Hardy, Simmons, Hennessey, and Langmore clutched his arms, while Seward leaned against the corner of the chapel wall, gasping and clutching at the collar of his shirt, which had been all but torn away. These things Renfield noted distantly, of less importance than the black wheeling shape of a bat, flittering above their heads in the light of the dropped lanterns and the new-risen crescent moon.

As Renfield looked up, the bat circled overhead, and for one instant Renfield saw the red gleam of its eyes. Then it flew away, not erratically as such creatures fly, but straight, like a homing bird, westward toward London.

Emptiness swept him, and despair.

Langmore had his wrist, clamped under his armpit while he pulled the sleeve of the strait-jacket over Renfield's hand. Renfield looked around him at the men as if waking from a dream. There was so much fear, such deadly grimness in their faces, that it seemed to him almost comical, were it not that he knew what would happen, must happen, tonight.

"It's all right," he said in a normal tone of voice. "You needn't tie me. I shall go quietly."

*Lucy Westenra's Diary**
Hillingham
24 August
. . . Last night I seemed to be dreaming again just as I was at Whitby. Perhaps it is the change of air, or getting home again. It is all dark and horrid to me, for I can remember nothing; but I am full of vague fear, and I feel so weak and worn out. When Arthur came to lunch, he looked quite grieved when he saw me, and I hadn't the heart to try to be cheerful . . .

CHAPTER TEN

R.M.R.'s notes
24 August
4 flies

25 August
6 flies. Sugar and treacle.
Won treacle from Hardy at riddles.

> *A good man proclaimed by God and man,*
> *I sit with my family, two daughters, two wives, two sons.*
> *Each daughter with her only son,*
> *Each daughter's son with his two sisters,*
> *With his father, his uncle, his nephew.*
> *Five chairs there are round the table*
> *And each has a chair, none stands.*
> > *Who am I?*

26 August
5 flies, 1 spider
Spiders harder to catch in padding.

27 August
10 flies. Prune macedoine.

28 August
9 flies.
His voice is silent. Even when I sleep, as I did in today's deep heat, nothing. He is sated.

Every night I see him, standing on the air outside her window, first a small darkness, like a bat, red eyes burning, burning. She comes to the window, sleep-walking in her night-dress, blonde hair streaming down her back and lifted by the breath of the night. Dear God, how thin she looks! Her face is drawn and gaunt, her eyes sunk in shadows. He walks to her across the air and the face she raises to him is like an exhausted child's, uncomprehending. His cloak covers her; he steps down, and into the dark of her room.

Treacle pudding at dinner. Won Langmore's from him at cribbage. Hardy cheats.

29 August
12 flies, 1 spider
Was it Dante who said that the true pain of Hell is exclusion from the beatific vision of God? All the refinements of torment, the rain of fire and the pits of ice, the buffeting winds of the Circle of the Passionate, all are only reflections of that fact: that those souls have forgotten God, and are forgotten by Him.

Wotan the Traveler has forgotten me.

Oh, Catherine, forgive me my failure! I am utterly on my own.

30 August

Will he never make an end to her?

* * *

"John." Lucy rose from the wicker chair among the ferns of the Hillingham conservatory, held out her hand. "It's good to see you."

In the act of surrendering his hat to the maid, Seward froze. His heart seemed to stall in his chest. Art had warned him that Lucy looked bad. But nothing could have prepared him for the ghastly whiteness of her face, the way her stylish pink gown hung now from her attenuated shoulders, the transparent look to her hands, and the faint blueness that lay like a ghost on her lips. *Dear God!*

He forced himself to say, "And it's always good to see you, Miss Westenra," hoping his voice would not betray his shock.

He thanked God—and his long-dead nanny—from the bottom of his heart for the existence of good manners and small talk, that allowed one to go on as if nothing unthinkable were happening.

"We'll be having lunch out here, if you don't mind." Lucy smiled, gesturing through the conservatory's glass doors to the white-clothed table, the cheerful blue-and-yellow china set out among the tubbed feather-palms, the dark-leaved aspidistras. "It's so muggy today." With its long windows open onto the walled garden, even the conservatory was warm, but Lucy kept a shawl draped over her shoulders, as if her own flesh no longer sufficed to protect her bones from chill. From the other white wicker chair, Mrs. Westenra half-rose with a friendly nod—friendly, reflected Seward, now that there was no danger of Lucy giving her hand to one so unworthy as a mad-doctor who had no better social manners than to go off in pursuit of one of his patients between the fish course and the entrée.

"And how are you, Madame?" he asked, holding out his hand to her. Lucy's appearance shocked him, but her mother's sallow skin and puffy hands only filled him with deepest pity. Even had Arthur not warned him about that, too, he would have seen the death-warrant written in her face.

In the awful days following that disastrous dinner, Seward had frequently wished Mrs. Westenra ill. Though he had no superstitious belief that mere sour wishes could bring ill to pass, the recollection of them twisted within him, not out of guilt, but sorrow at how hastily a disappointed lover could hope for fate's vengeance, little realizing that far worse was already in store.

"I'm quite well, thank you, Dr. Seward." Her own nanny's strictly taught good manners allowed her to smile as she lied. "I'm sorry Mr. Holmwood will not be able to join us."

"His father was taken ill, at their ancestral home in Ring." The telegram had reached him that morning, as he'd been writing up instructions for Hennessey to look after various of the more difficult patients. "Have you been there? It's in the Lake District, probably one of the most beautiful old houses I've ever seen." He helped Mrs. Westenra to the little table, just as if she hadn't made sniffy remarks about his quarters in Rushbrook House; held her chair for her and handed her her napkin before seating Lucy, then himself. "I had occasion to spend a few weeks there, when I was first hired to escort Uncle Harry Holmwood round the world and make sure he didn't kill himself or anyone else in the process."

Tales of Uncle Harry kept both women entertained through luncheon—traveling with Uncle Harry had given Seward a stock of stories that would have lasted him through two months in quarantine, and that was only the repeatable ones. His ill-will against Violet Westenra dissolved as though it had never been, petty in the face of mortality's shadow, and he exerted himself to entertain her. For her part, she met his efforts with smiling cheer. Sometimes Seward, glancing at Lucy's face, saw dread and confusion in her eyes as she looked at her mother, but Mrs. Westenra seemed already to be withdrawing from the world of the living. If asked, she would probably agree that Lucy was too thin and did not look well. But she did not seem to see the skull that stared at Seward from beneath Lucy's fragile skin.

"If you young people will excuse me, it's become my custom to lie down for a little after luncheon . . ."

And they were alone.

The last time they had been so was back in May, when Lucy had confessed to him, weeping, that she loved another: that her heart was not free.

He wondered if his would ever be.

The memory of the scene was in her eyes as she looked at him, and Seward said, as if speaking to a new patient, "So tell me what's troubling you . . . Miss Westenra. Or may I yet call you Lucy, as if you were my sister?"

Her fleeting smile showed gums nearly white, and sunken back horribly from her teeth. "I should like to have a brother like you, Doctor . . . Jack. One day . . ."

The maid came in to clear up. Lucy glanced sidelong at her, and said, "Would you much mind coming to my boudoir, if you're going to look in my eyes and at my tongue and all that?" She smiled brightly, but in her eyes Seward saw the same worry that had been there when she'd watched her mother at lunch.

Wondering how much her mother guessed; how much her mother saw.

"Of course." He followed her through the well-remembered front hall, with its Queen Anne chest and the big Chinese porcelain bowl that held visitors' cards, and up to her room, overlooking the back garden on a little balcony and painted white and violet.

The moment the door was closed, she sank onto a chair, her hands pressed to her brow to cover her eyes, as if all her strength had deserted her and she had barely made it to refuge. For a moment she said nothing, but Seward could see the tears flowing from beneath her trembling fingers.

"I can't tell you how I loathe talking about myself." Her voice was barely a whisper.

"I understand," replied Seward softly. "But even were I personally blackguard enough to speak of what another tells me, a doctor's confidence is sacred. Arthur is my friend, and grievously anxious about you, but your trouble is no more his business than the sufferings of any of my patients would be."

"It isn't that." Lucy raised her head then, shook back the tendrils of her hair that had come unpinned around her face. "Tell Arthur everything you choose. It is his business, and no more than I would tell him myself, were he here.

"As for what's wrong . . . I don't *know* what's wrong with me! That's what frightens me so. I feel so weak, and I have trouble breathing, especially in the morning, as if there isn't enough air in the world to fill my lungs. And I have dreams, terrible dreams . . ."

"About what?" Seward asked, though the matter was clearly physical and not in the province of mental fancies. Lucy ducked her head aside, the faintest flare of pink staining the ghastly white of her cheekbones.

"I—I don't recall." Her breath quickened to a sudden, ragged gasp. She got hastily to her feet and went to the window, the pink cashmere shawl sliding from her shoulders in her confusion. Her hands fumbled with the window-catch and the next moment she gave a little cry as the casement jerked up hard. She pulled her hand back, where a corner of the pane cracked at the impact.

Seward sprang to his feet and went to her. She was crying in earnest now, clutching her cut finger, from weakness, he guessed, rather than genuine pain. Or shame perhaps, he thought, as he took her hand and made sure that the cut was indeed superficial. He found it curious, how frequently young ladies were overcome with shame they could not name, when they were exhausted, or hurt.

He said nothing, only took a clean handkerchief from his jacket pocket to tie up the cut. He didn't even think Lucy noticed that he also extracted from the same pocket a small glass pipette, and took in it a few drops of her blood.

"I wish Mina were with me," Lucy whispered, as Seward guided her back to her chair. "Mina Murray, who was in the Fourth Form at Mrs. Druggett's School when I was in the First. Of course I can speak to . . . to Arthur about anything, but . . . but sometimes a girl needs another girl to speak to."

"Of course," said Seward. And in a gently rallying tone, added, "That's a well-known medical fact," and was rewarded by Lucy's hesitant smile. "And I'm sorry," he went on more soberly, "that Arthur could not be here to comfort you. Even were you not affianced, I could name no man better suited to the task."

And she sighed and relaxed, relieved that Arthur's name was not forbidden between them. She turned a little away from him, groping in her pocket for a handkerchief to wipe her eyes.

"Can your Miss Murray not be sent for?" Seward asked. "She was the friend who went to Whitby with you, was she not?"

"She was, but she was called away suddenly, just before Mother and I came home. Her fiancé was taken ill with brain-fever somewhere in Europe, and she had to go to him."

Speaking of her friend's concerns seemed to steady her, and she held out her hand, and opened her mouth, for his examination of nails and gums, with the air of an obedient child. The mucous membranes were nearly white, as he had observed before. *Chlorosis?* he wondered, baffled. It was a form of anaemia that struck girls of her age, but he'd never known it to come on so swiftly. In May she'd been delicate—she was always prone to bronchial complaints—but she'd been pink as a rose and lively as a kitten.

"When did this start?" he asked, expecting her to say—as so many did—that she didn't really know, that it had come on her gradually.

Instead she replied at once, "In Whitby. I used to sleep-walk when I was at school, I think I told you—poor Mina was forever chasing me down the hallways in the middle of the night! In Whitby I started doing so again. One night I went right out of the house where we were staying, and walked clear up to the churchyard that overlooks the town. Mina found me lying on one of the tombstones, like the heroine of a play. We didn't tell Mama."

Again the hesitation, the shadow of fear crossing her eyes—fear of what she half-guessed, fear that she would not even speak of to Seward, and he a doctor. Fear that her fear for her mother was true.

She went on, "I felt ill right after that. I thought I'd just taken a chill, and that it would pass off, and it did, for a day or two. Then it came back, for three, perhaps four days. I felt better for a day or two just before Mina left for Buda-Pesth, and when Arthur was in Whitby, we rode and walked and went boating, and I thought all was well. But now . . ."

She lowered her head to her hands again, and began to cry afresh. "A week ago it began again, the dreams, and the sleep-walking, and this horrible feeling of being in some terrible danger that I cannot see. Last night I woke up lying on the floor between my bed and the window, gasping as if I were drowning and cold . . . so cold! I've tried asking Mother if I may sleep with her and she doesn't want me to. She says she sleeps so lightly she's afraid she will disturb me, or I her. I look at myself in the mirror and I look like Death. I see myself in Arthur's eyes . . ."

She broke off, her hands pressed to her mouth, her thin body trembling as if with bitter chill. "What's wrong with me, Jack?" Her voice thinned to barely a breath. "I know this isn't right. What's happening to me?"

"What's happening is that you're ill." Seward would have given his right arm to cup her thin cheek with his hand; he took her hand instead. Long practice had given him the ability to put into his voice a calm steadiness that he was far from feeling. "All pathologies have an explanation: we simply haven't found the right one here yet. You show some symptoms of anaemia but the onset is all wrong. Are you able to eat?"

She shook her head. It was true she'd only toyed with her lunch.

"The sleep-walking and the dreams may very well have something to do with it, and with your very natural concern over your mother's health. In my work with the human mind, I've observed many cases of some mental stress or upset working its way out in physical symptoms. There's a great deal of new work being done on this subject and it's apparently not at all uncommon. Would it be all right if I came back for lunch the day after tomorrow, and brought a friend with me? He's the doctor I studied with at the University of Leyden, an expert in rare diseases. He may be able to take one look at you and say, 'Ach, it is pollydiddle-itis! She has only to bathe in goat's milk and she vill be vell again!'"

Lucy burst into laughter, her whole emaciated face lightening, and she clasped Seward's hand in both of hers. "Bring whom you will, dear Jack," she said. "Mother will be lunching out; we can be alone. And thank you," she added, as she descended the stairs with him, and walked him to the door. "Thank you more than I can say."

Lucy's laughter, and the brightness that had replaced the frightened lethargy in her eyes, remained with Seward through the long rattling journey back to Purfleet in the two-horse fly he kept—at rather more expense than he liked—for such occasions. Simmons was driving, and came close to tangling axles with half a dozen cabs, drays, and carts on the road.

At Rushbrook House he took a quick glance at Hennessey's

sloppy notes to make sure nothing untoward had happened in his absence—Emily Strathmore had had to be put in the Swing again, and "Lord Spotty" was up to his old tricks—then settled down to write a letter to Arthur Holmwood, and a telegram to Abraham Van Helsing.

CHAPTER ELEVEN

For nearly three weeks Renfield watched, as if from a barred and distant window, as the thing in the chapel at Carfax continued its attacks on Lucy.

When the red-eyed bat had flown from the chapel window, leaving him behind in the hands of his foes, he had feared that he must see the kill. He had had no idea, he thought now, of how long that kill would take, of the drawn-out torment of cat-and-mouse that Wotan played, like a malicious child, with the frightened girl. It was one thing, he told himself, cold with anger, to kill in the delirious uncontrollable rush of rage or lust (*How do I know that?* he wondered: why did the brown face of an Indian girl wink through his consciousness, lying sleeping on the charpoi at his side . . . sleeping with open eyes . . .) It was another to kill by inches, to leave Lucy swooning on the floor of her room, to come again another night and draw her once more to the brink of death.

Yet he could not speak of what he knew. Wotan held the power of life in his hand, life that Renfield desperately needed. Not once in those three weeks did Wotan call upon him or speak his name, but Renfield did not give up the hope—the certainty—that he would.

"All over, all over, he has deserted me," he said one warm September afternoon when Seward came to visit him—to visit him in his old room, whose repaired window looked out over the garden and the tree-lined drive from the gates. He'd spread sugar from his tea over the window-sill, and had caught a dozen flies in the final hour of the day. "No hope for me now unless I do it for myself." Seward, though of too small a mind to comprehend or even guess at Renfield's mission, sympathized and agreed to provide an extra ration of sugar. It was astonishing, thought Renfield, shaking his head, how easily the man could be manipulated.

"He's off to visit that sweetheart of his, that's bound to marry a lord," provided Langmore shortly thereafter, coming in with the extra sugar while Renfield sat at the open window watching Seward's smart black fly rattle off down the drive and through the gates.

"Is she having second thoughts?" inquired Renfield, and the little keeper hooted with laughter and slapped his thigh.

"Lord, let's hope not! That mother of her'n would ass-*assinate* him if she thought it! What a griffin! No—the poor young lady's took ill." Langmore came over to the window, with a glance of wary disgust at the little buzzing cardboard box at Renfield's elbow, and with his eyes followed the black carriage through the gates, and out onto the London road. By his voice, and the pupils of his eyes, Renfield could see the keeper had had a touch of poppy before coming on duty. Not enough to put him to sleep, but enough to make him talkative.

"Funny how a man can be cool and smart as a soldier, when the likes of old Emily Strathmore's tearin' at him like a wildcat, yet since his Miss Lucy's been took ill—and her promised to another man, and that other man the Doc's best friend—it's like he's aged ten years."

"Miss Lucy?" Renfield stared at him.

"Miss Lucy Westenra. Pretty as a daffy-down-dilly, I thought, the night she come here to take dinner with him—with that ma of hers standin' right over her to make sure the pair of 'em didn't have a moment to theirselves for the Doc to pop the question, as I hear he planned to that night. And him borrowin' a butler and silverware and what-all else from Sir Ambrose Poole for the h'occasion. Well, 'tis an ill wind that blows no one good." The grizzled little man cocked an eyebrow at Renfield. "You marry a maid, you marry her ma, and Christ help the man ends up with that old man-trap for a mother-in-law. You know what I mean?"

"Yes," said Renfield softly, thinking of cold-eyed Lady Brough . . . though of course, Catherine was nothing at all like her mother. And that hatchet-faced harridan Georgina Clayburne, who wanted nothing more than to re-claim Catherine's share of their father's money for her precious "family." "Yes, I know what you mean."

Sometimes in sleep he could see Catherine, in that London house they'd bought under the name of Marshmire, dozing by lamplight. Or in his dreams he'd walk up the stairs of their old house in Nottingham, as he'd used to years ago, to see Vixie in her nursery, that bright-eyed nymph face relaxed in sleep, a black curl falling over her forehead. These dreams comforted him deeply, for he missed them both. Even had they been able to get word to him without Georgina and Lady Brough hearing of it and finding a way to trace them—to take Vixie away— communication was now doubly perilous.

And sometimes he would dream of Vixie, waking in her nursery room in that house in Nottingham, not a little girl but the young lady that she was now, sixteen and beautiful, wearing Lucy Westenra's night-dress.

In these dreams she would wake, and sit up in bed, dark eyes wide in the darkness. Outside the window rain fell through fog, and the tiny glow of her night-light sparkled on it as she got out of bed, crossed to the window, threw open the casement. Renfield would struggle to reach her, struggle to cry out to her, *Vixie, don't!*

And He was outside her window. Slowly coalescing from the shadows, as the three Valkyries had coalesced from the darkness, fog, and rain in Renfield's long-ago dream of the hopeless prisoner named Jonathan. The thing in the chapel, the thing Renfield still sometimes called Wotan, though he knew now that it was something else, some other Traveler. Wind lifted and stirred Wotan's black cloak, and in the darkness his eyes were red as flame, staring into Vixie's.

Vixie, no!

Then Renfield would waken himself screaming, and those imbecile attendants would come with their laudanum and chloral hydrate, like rescuers determined to shove a drowning man back down under the waves.

And they wondered that he fought them!

Yet more often, Renfield dreamed of Lucy Westenra: dreamed,

knowing he participated in the dreams of the thing in the chapel, that could touch Lucy's sleeping mind. He dreamed of Lucy waking in the darkness and stumbling to the window, dreamed of the floating shadow, the crimson eyes. Dreamed of the fangs that pierced her throat, of those coarse hands with their claw-like nails, caressing her as if he would mould her flesh into what he sought her to be. Once Renfield saw Wotan push back his sleeve and tear open the vein of his own arm, and press Lucy's white lips to the wound.

"Drink," Renfield heard him breathe. "Drink, or you will die."

Half-swooning, Lucy whispered, "Please . . . I don't want to die . . ." and the dark intruder pulled back her head by a hand-ful of her fair hair, and held the dripping cut up over her mouth, so that his blood dropped down onto her lips.

"Then drink, my beautiful, my beloved one. Drink, and you shall never die. For the blood is the life."

Droplets of the blood splashed on her cheek, mixing with her tears of terror and shame.

Renfield was aware of the old man Seward brought to see Lucy, a short, sturdy septuagenarian with long white hair that hung to his shoulders and a jaw like a pugnacious bulldog's. He guessed it was Dr. Van Helsing, whom Hennessey had spo-ken of as Seward's teacher and master: "Weird old sod, and studies every spook and fairy-tale like they was Freud and Char-cot," the Irishman said, when he came in to check on Renfield a few days after Renfield's conversation with Langmore about mothers-in-law. "Couldn't stick it, myself. Just give me the facts, and keep the metaphysics out of it."

Renfield had read Van Helsing's work since the Dutchman's original studies of Chinese and Indian healing practices in the forties, and had been deeply impressed. But since Hennessey had never demonstrated much interest even in such facts as how many grains of chloral hydrate might be lethal to a screaming patient, or whether there was any way of dealing with recalcitrance other than the truncheon, Renfield didn't attempt to answer. He only continued to stare from his window at the darkening evening sky.

Hennessey went on, "It's his idea old John stay with her tonight—she was took bad last night, seemingly—though the dear Lord knows what he might do if she's took sick again. Wave a bit of incense about the bed, maybe, or chant a wee verse of the Mass?" He shrugged, and scratched his belly, under the gaudy waistcoat dribbled with food-stains. "It's what you'd expect, of a man who says he's a doctor of the mind and then goes and marries a woman who's been locked in a padded room for the past decade. So how's the flies this evenin'?" He hadn't noticed that Renfield had ceased to trap flies three days before, when Wotan's concerted attacks on Lucy had redoubled.

In too many dreams had the flies had Lucy's face.

Or Vixie's.

"In rollicking good health," replied Renfield, which sent Hennessey away in peals of laughter and a strong odor of gin.

Renfield returned to his window, gazing out at the darkening sky.

Seward was gone all night. Renfield saw the smart black carriage turn in at the gates with the coming of dawn. As luck would have it, it was one of the days when Farley, one of the charity patients and a man of erratic violence, went on the rampage; Renfield could hear him screaming from the other side of the building, and the spreading uproar as the other patients became frightened and took up the din. Renfield shook his head, feeling nothing but pity for those poor weak-minded souls, and indeed for poor Dr. Seward, who looked worn to a rag when he made rounds early in the afternoon.

But shortly before sunset Seward had his rather pedestrian team of brown geldings harnessed to the fly again, and Renfield watched him drive off through the gates and along the London road. And he felt, as the sun sank, the sullen boil of anger that he knew came from outside himself: Wotan waking in his coffin, in the dark of the ruined chapel. Wotan reaching out with his hand, with his mind, with all his dark powers, to take the woman for himself.

Seward did not come back that night, nor in the morning. In his dreams Renfield had seen him, sleeping on the mauve silk cushions of a little couch beside a parlor fire, while visible through the doorway in the next room the shadow of Wotan had bent over the weeping Lucy. And Renfield, too, had wept. When Seward returned late in the afternoon, and made a conscientious round of the patients before dark, he was as white and shaky as if the Traveler had drunk his blood as well as hers.

The thought of this possibility filled Renfield with horror. Would Seward, then, be able to see into his dreams, his thoughts, as Wotan did? Wotan sleeping in his coffin, gorged with blood?

Renfield dared not ask.

Seward drove away the following afternoon, and though he returned that evening, after that Renfield saw little of him, save in the tangled torment of dreams. He saw confused images of Seward operating to transfuse blood from old Van Helsing's arm into Lucy's, Lucy who lay white and gasping, like a corpse already, among a bower of garlic-blossoms twined around the posts of her bed. Saw Lucy sleeping, her blonde hair tumbled about her, the white flowers of the garlic-plant filling the room like funerary garlands. Sometimes Van Helsing, sometimes Seward, slept in the chair at her bedside, and in the darkness of her flower-draped window a black shape beat against the panes.

You must kill him, you know, whispered Wotan in Renfield's ear, as the sun set over London and Renfield stood at his window, wondering what Catherine and Vixie were doing, and how he could accomplish his mission and return to them if he did not go back to eating spiders and flies. So far he'd managed to hold his hunger at bay.

Wotan was angry. Renfield had felt that anger growing, for four days now. In the darkness he'd seen the black bat fly from the window of Carfax chapel; he'd seen it come back, before the breaking day. And Wotan was hungry, frantic hunger that Renfield understood as he understood the hammering of the blood in his neck-vein. Hunger for life, multiplied beyond Renfield's own overwhelming hunger a thousand times.

You must kill him, said Wotan again, and the hazy autumn evening began to blur around Renfield. In his ears throbbed the music of Act Two of *Die Walküre,* Wotan's voice commanding Brunhilde to slay Sigmund, and somewhere in the deeps of his mind he thought he could also hear the wild howling of a wolf. *What other are you, if not the tool of my power, willing and blind?* Then the music faded, and only that terrible whispering voice remained. Without the glory and the beauty, with only hunger and the lust for power. *I will open the way for you, as I open the ways for all my servants.*

You have not been a good master to me, Renfield whispered, and the crimson weight of those alien thoughts crushed him, hurt him. Darkness with teeth.

A master is not a good master or a bad master—he is Master. And he is obeyed. This man must not leave this house tonight.

Renfield whispered, *No, Master.*

And as the sun went down, he dreamed—it had to be a dream, he thought later—that Wotan stood beside him in his cell, formed up out of the gathering shadows, the last gleams of the reflected light burning in his red eyes. And as Renfield knelt to him, Wotan put his hand on Renfield's head, and Renfield felt himself transformed into a wolf, as it was within Wotan's power to transform himself into a wolf. Far away he heard another wolf howling, and when he howled in reply, Simmons came running. With a snarl, Renfield the Wolf sprang on him, knocking him back against the wall.

Fleet as a wolf, hungry as a wolf, Renfield raced along the hallway, down the stair, to Seward's study, where he smelled that the doctor would be. Wild wolf-thoughts dazzled his brain as he slammed the door open, plunged in, knife in hand that he'd snatched from the dining-room sideboard (*No, that's got to be wrong,* he thought. *I'm a wolf and I haven't any hands.*)

Seward was behind his worktable making entries in the day-book and Renfield crossed the room in two strides and sprang straight over the table at him, slashing with his knife. The dream wasn't very clear, Renfield thought later—later when he woke up, in the strait-jacket again and chained to the wall of the padded cell. Seward took a glancing blow with the knife on his left arm, then punched Renfield straight and hard in the jaw with his right hand, sending him sprawling backward. Renfield lay, dazed, trying to work out how a man could punch a wolf in the jaw even in a dream, watching the blood stream down Seward's fingers, splatter to the threadbare and rather vulgar Wilton carpet upon which Renfield lay.

Attendants' voices in the hall. Simmons—*the moron!*—and Hardy. Seward went to the door to speak to them, and Renfield, his hunger overwhelming him, crawled to the side of the table where Seward had been sitting, and licked up the blood.

Drink, and you shall never die, Wotan had whispered to Lucy, as his own blood dribbled down to her chalky lips. *The blood is the life. The blood is the life.*

CHAPTER TWELVE

As he hung on the wall of the padded cell, his brain swimming in a fog of chloral hydrate, Renfield's dream altered. He was a wolf indeed, running through the streets of London, running free and terrified. Smells hammered him, soaked his brain in the stenches of dung and coal-smoke, and the smaller curs of the alleyways fled yowling from his great swift-moving gray shadow.

He knew where he was going. His Master had commanded, and though he did not understand—though terror filled him at this unknown noisy terrible place—still he had to do as his Master said. *What other are you, if not the tool of my power, willing and blind?*

Renfield at least knew the house, for he'd seen it in other dreams. His wolf-self—or that other, genuine wolf whose mind he sensed in his dream—loped along the countrified high road, through the rambling gardens of the little villa, and Renfield saw the house ahead of him and saw no lights, no movement. He was aware, however, of the almost-silent winnowing of leathery wings in the dark behind his head. Was aware of his Master, the Master who had called on him, finally, after weeks of silence . . .

The Master who would not forget him again.

The tall French windows that looked onto the garden were draped with flowers of garlic, as Renfield had seen in earlier dreams, like the decorations of a funeral. He knew their presence enraged his Master, and he knew that he—the wolf whose dream he shared—was sent to open the way into the house, to tear down these fragile poisonous weeds so that the Master could pass through. Renfield's mind was the mind of the wolf, and that mind was clouded with the Master's commands. He smashed through the glass of the French door, saw with his night-seeing eyes the two women lying on the bed, clutching one another in terror, the older in the younger's arms.

The older woman half sat up, white hair streaming down the shoulders of her dressing-gown. Her mouth opened, but no sound came forth but a sort of gurgling gasp. The wolf—Renfield—howled, and howled again, and the older woman fell back, the younger pressing her hands to her mouth, staring with eyes enormous and bruised with loss of blood. As the wolf withdrew its head in pain from the shattered glass, Renfield heard the girl crying, "Mother! Mother!" Her voice was weak, thin, and indescribably fragile in the silence of the dark garden, the empty house.

Before the broken window, shorn of its protective wreaths, the whirling motes of moonlight began to coalesce, Wotan's red eyes burning within the core of their shadow.

In his dreams Renfield began to howl, though so deep was he under the chloral hydrate that even that could not bring him out of his stupor, could not spare him the dream's inevitable conclusion.

* * *

He woke hanging in the straps of the padded room, sick from the chloral hydrate, the taste of blood and filth in his mouth. Footsteps in the hall, Hennessey's sloppy shuffle and another: "'ere, Dr. Hennessey, you know Dr. Seward doesn't 'old with strangers comin' in an' disturbin' the patients."

"Disturbing the patients?" Hennessey's fruity chuckle glinted with a knife of hardness underneath. "My dear Langmore, those poor souls are so disturbed already I doubt they'd know the difference between my good Herr Gelhorn here and yourself, or care if they did know. And there's never been any proof that it does them a particle of harm, no matter what Seward likes to say." His voice lowered. Renfield could almost see the nasty sidelong gleam of his eyes, and smell the reek of gin on his breath. "But if we're going to get into the subject of things Dr. Seward doesn't hold with, I'm sure he has opinions about keepers who help themselves to the laudanum in the dispensary, opinions just as strong as his crochets about students of the human condition being admitted to observe the lunatics."

Keys jangled.

"Now this gentleman, my dear Gelhorn, is a sad case indeed. A true wild man, he spends his days catching and devouring spiders and flies, and sparrows, too, if he can get them. He's a sort of pet of our good Dr. Seward, whom he repaid last night by a murderous attack. When the keepers laid hold of him, he was crawling on his belly, licking up Dr. Seward's blood from the study floor."

That's a lie! Renfield wanted to scream at them, as the door opened to reveal Hennessey and his latest paying "friend," a weedy and anaemic-looking young man clothed in the old-fashioned tailoring typically found east of the Rhine. *Drunken bastard, it is a lie! That was only my dream. How dare you speak of my dreams?*

Young Herr Gelhorn stepped back in alarm, blinking pale eyes behind the square lenses of his spectacles. "How he glares," he whispered. "You are right, Herr Doktor Hennessey. It is a beast indeed." And he licked his pale lips, fascinated.

"He was a nabob, an India merchant," Hennessey went on, with an Irishman's deep delight in telling a tale to an obviously riveted audience. "They say he did murder any number of Hindoo savages over there, in his murderous rages."

Renfield screamed, "Liar!" and Hennessey's red face beamed at having elicited a response.

"When he was brought in here, having been found wandering raving through the streets of London, he never would say where his wife and daughter were, nor what had become of them. His wife's family comes here time and again, begging if he's whispered a word of 'em . . ."

"Lying blackguard!" Renfield hurled himself against the straps that bound him, feeling the red haze of murderous rage surge like an incoming tide around his brain. "You bastard bog-Irish, you keep your tongue off a woman whose shoes you're not fit to lick!"

Both men fell back, but Renfield saw Hennessey's head cock, listening, and a calculating light come into his eyes. *He sees a way to make me speak of Catherine!* thought Renfield, with a sudden and terrible clarity. *He'll tell Lady Brough every word that I say!*

Swallowing his rage brought a physical convulsion, twisting in his bonds and slamming his head back against the padded wall behind him, again and again, trying to blot out Hennessey's satisfied smirk. Instead he brought to mind the image of his own big hands closing on the man's throat, twisting and tearing. Better yet, his own teeth ripping into the man's veins, the gush of blood into his mouth, feeling the buck of Hennessey's gross body beneath his own as the Irishman began to die. Smelling death, hearing him gurgle and gasp as Renfield drank his blood.

Renfield went limp in the straps, gasping himself. He was alone in the room. Voices retreated down the hallway, "Is he ever so?" asked the German hesitantly. "I am a poet, you see, as I told you, Herr Doktor Hennessey, a poet of the Gothic, of madness, of the inner secrets of the mind."

"Ah, you've seen him at his best, laddie! Why, he's attacked me! Torn himself loose from those straps on the wall and leaped upon me like a wolf. I thrust him back, and when he would have attacked me again, I stared him down. I have this gift, you see, of controlling lunatics with the power of my eyes . . ."

Renfield screamed after them, "Liar! Liar!"

If Lucy—and her white-haired mother—had died last night, Seward would be away all the day, maybe more. Hennessey would be back, taunting him about Catherine, trying to force him into rage so intense he didn't know what he was saying. Into revealing where they were hiding.

I must be strong. I must be strong.

But he knew he had not consumed life, gained even those small increments of life, for nearly two weeks.

Without consuming life, he could not be strong.

His pity for the flies, for Lucy, would destroy those he most loved.

He raised his voice in an inarticulate wail of despair, as if his ribcage would burst from the effort to make his cry carry through the padding, through the walls, across the distance to Carfax, where Wotan slept, glutted and smiling, in his chapel.

Help me, Master, for I have need of thee!

R.M.R.'s notes
18 September—evening
1 spider

And a paltry, half-dead creature at that. I had thought that brute Hennessey would leave me strapped to the wall of the padded cell for days, a raree-show for paying customers—yet better that, than to torment me with the aim of enraging me so that I will speak of Catherine, of Vixie. Yet I dare not speak of it to Seward—so low am I brought.

Seward returned tonight, dazed and shaken-looking; exchanged a half-dozen words with me and ordered Langmore to release me and return me to my own room. I could have confessed to murdering the Queen and eating her heart and he would have paid no more heed to the words than he did to those that I actually did say. As Langmore locked me into the room, I heard him ask Seward in the hall, "And how is Miss Lucy, sor?" and to my surprise Seward responded, "She lives, but . . . she is in a terrible way. I must return there tonight, to keep watch beside her."

"Yes, sor."

Of course, Langmore made no mention of Hennessey turning the ravings of those poor souls in the other cells to his profit. With luck, the man will think more of making those little profits—and spending them—than of subjecting me to mental torments, hoping that in my rage I will reveal to him where Catherine and Vixie are hiding.

How long will this terrible game of cat and mouse go on? How long will Seward be away, guarding her with his master Van Helsing and, probably, with the girl's other suitors, those trusted friends of whom I have so often heard him speak?

How long can I hold out against the demon of rage within myself?

19 September
9 flies, 4 spiders
Not enough! Not enough! I must consume more, to make up for the time I have lost in pity and sentiment. I must be strong!

I pray, yet receive no answer. Yet he is there, I know it. I feel him.

Has he forgotten me? Or is this a test of my loyalties, my faith?

20 September
He is gone! He has left me!

Dear gods, what shall I do?

I was watching the last sparrows of autumn fluttering in the garden trees—not with ulterior motive, but merely taking joy in the sweetness of their song—when I saw a cart on the high road, making for the old house at Carfax. It stopped at the gates of Rushbrook House and one of the dirty villains at the reins came up the avenue, to ask the way—stupid bastards could not find their own trouser-buttons without instruction!—yet I knew in my heart that it was Carfax they sought. My anger surged up in me and I began to rate him for the thieving blackguard that he was, anger borne of terror . . . What shall I do, if my Master departs, leaving me here in the power of such as Hennessey and Seward?

When the men had gone, Hennessey came in, asking what I meant by my anger—blind, puling fool!—and with terrible effort I concealed my rage, knowing now how he means to use it against me. He was half-drunk, having consumed his usual pints of gin with his dinner, though even stone sober (which he has not been since the reign of the Prince Regent, I shouldn't imagine) he would believe anything anyone told him, if it would save him trouble. When he was gone, my rage overcame me, and I ripped the latches from my window and sprang to the ground, running up the avenue, desperate to catch the cart that I knew would be returning.

I swarmed over the gate before the porter realized what was happening, leaped down onto the high road just as those monsters, those unspeakable bandits, drove their foul cart past, piled high with the boxes of earth taken from the Carfax chapel. *He* was in one of them, sleeping the sleep that is not truly sleep, for He hears, He knows.

I beat on the side of the box, crying to him not to leave me among my foes. One of the carters cut at me with his whip and I dragged him from the box, blind with rage, knowing only that He must not leave me, He must not go without helping me.

Hardy and Simmons were hard on my heels down the avenue, with Hennessey puffing and wheezing in the rear. As they dragged me back to my cell, I cried out in my despair: "Master, I will fight for you! They shan't kill me by inches! They shan't take you away!"

What shall I do? He has left me indeed.

What shall I do?

20 September—night
It is over.

CHAPTER THIRTEEN

Nightmares.

Light rain pattered on the gabled windows of Rushbrook House. John Seward stared at the ceiling of his bedroom and tried to will himself not to dream.

To sleep, perchance to dream . . . ay, there's the rub . . .

He hadn't slept in two nights now. His body cried for sleep and cried, too, for chloral hydrate—cried, sweated, and shook. But Seward knew from terrible experience that sleep after long waking was particularly fraught with dreams. The thought of the drug holding his eyes sealed shut and his screaming mind in darkness was more than he could bear.

Was this what his patients went through? Emaciated Rowena Kilmer, jerking from sleep a dozen times a night to howl and beat her head on the walls? Frantic Grayson, trying to crowd himself into the tiniest corner of the room, barricading himself behind the bed against the phantoms that only he could see?

Dimly, like the ghostly moaning of the wind, Seward could hear them screaming, somewhere in the house.

It was long past midnight.

I open my eyes and see the ceiling, with stains on its blue-striped paper like old blood.

Blood! Dear God, what happened to Lucy's blood? The drops I took from her that first day of consultation were normal, without the deformed cell-structure of anaemia. It wasn't anaemia she died of, but blood-loss. She bled to death, under our very noses, without a drop being spilled on her pillow.

Through the grief that racked his heart cried the betrayed bafflement of a lifetime of scientific study: *It shouldn't have happened! It couldn't have happened, not logically, not within the bounds of any science I've ever known! This is the modern age—we're almost in the twentieth century, damn it, not back in the twelfth! I should have been able to save her!*

Yet all of them who loved her—young Arthur, and Quincey, and even Van Helsing, with all his wisdom—had been as powerless as he, to prevent her death.

In his mind he saw Quincey Morris bending over Lucy's body, gazing down at her face with mingled pity and bewilderment in his gray eyes, his leathery six-foot-plus seeming desperately out of place in the white and violet of her boudoir; saw the sharp sidelong look in the Texan's eyes when they sat in the breakfast-room. "That poor pretty creature that we all love has had put into her veins the blood of four strong men! Man alive, her whole body wouldn't hold it! What took it out?"

I open my eyes and all those questions crowd in, questions that have no answers. I close them . . .

And throw wide the gates to nightmare.

I have dreams, terrible dreams, Lucy had said, in that same white-and-violet boudoir, but when Seward had asked after them, she'd put him off, hurried to occupy herself with opening the window. What would she have told him, he wondered, if she'd spoken the truth?

Images rose to his exhausted mind, images as vivid as reality, that he could not erase. The cold, alien-looking aparatus of blood transfusion, that he'd operated, not once but again and again in those nightmare days, when they'd enter Lucy's room and find her white and gasping on the spotless bed. The way Van Helsing's breath had hissed, when in adjusting Lucy's pillow he'd dislodged the velvet band she wore around her throat, and revealed those two pale, mangled puncture-wounds above the vein. The smell of the garlic the old man had insisted Lucy wear around her neck and with which he'd draped the windows of the room—draperies and necklet they'd found clutched in poor Mrs. Westenra's hands, when they'd found her dead on the morning of the nineteenth.

Images more disturbing still, as his mind drifted toward the gates of horn and ivory that poets said guarded the Realm of Morpheus.

How Lucy, dying, had smiled up at Art Holmwood—Lord Godalming now, with his father's sudden death. Her flaxen hair had seemed fairer still against the mourning he wore, and she had whispered, *Kiss me,* in languorous passion, her long canine teeth glinting against her bloodless gums. How Van Helsing had thrust Art away like a madman. And how at the funeral Van Helsing had looked sharply at the broken and weeping Arthur when Art had whispered over and over that the blood he'd given to Lucy had been their marriage-bond, since they were denied any other.

Seward recalled Van Helsing's insistence upon leaving a golden cross on Lucy's body, and his rage with the maid who'd stolen it. Remembered his appearance, late on the night of her death, in Seward's room at Hillingham House, whispering of the ghastly ritual he wanted to undertake: to cut off her head, to take out her heart.

Is he mad? Seward wondered dimly. *Or am I?*

You have for many years trust me; you have believe me for weeks past, when there be things so strange that you might have well doubt. Believe me yet a little, friend John . . .

And such was the urgent intelligence in those coldly bright blue eyes, the warm strength of the Dutchman's roughened hands, that Seward did believe. *Credo sed incredulis . . .*

Grotesque interviews with solicitors. Van Helsing's fit of hysterical laughter in the carriage after the funeral. Arthur's face as he gazed down at Lucy in her coffin: *Jack, is she really dead?* And that blithe and golden young man, all the world's darling, weeping brokenly in the arms of their tall Texan friend. *Oh Jack, Jack, what shall I do? The whole of life seems gone from me all at once!*

Quincey's face had been still, like a man bleeding to death inside.

She is gone. She's really gone.

Seward knew he should feel something, and didn't. Only the numbness of exhaustion, and the sweating hunger for chloral hydrate.

Lucy was in her coffin, in her tomb. The quiet tomb of the Westenras on Hampstead Hill, solitary in the twilight groves with the rain pattering softly against the marble, away from the noise of London. Van Helsing had returned to Amsterdam, Art—accompanied by Quincey—to Ring, to bury his father.

And he, John Seward, had only a madhouse to return to, the madhouse he'd once been insane enough to think he could bring Lucy to as a wife. He had worked hard to come to this position of responsibility, he reminded himself. These people were his charge and his study: to learn the nature of madness, to help those lost in its nightmare mazes without the hope of getting free.

But tonight he could only lie here, sweating in the dark, listening to the rain and to the lunatics screaming in the deep silences of the night.

*　*　*

Renfield, too, dreamed of Lucy Westenra, lying in her coffin.

And the dream filled him with horror.

She looked, in veriest truth, as if she only slept. How he could see, he did not know, for the tomb was shut and sealed, the lamps and candles of the mourners long gone. Her lead-lined coffin had been screwed shut, but he could see her in it still, fair hair lying on her shoulders, flesh fine as porcelain and little less white than the graveclothes they'd dressed her in. The bloodless look she'd had, in those other visions during her long crucifixion on the edge of death, was gone. She was relaxed, smiling almost, all her daytime care dissolved, happy in sleep.

There was something about her sleep that reminded him of something, something he would rather not see. That he didn't want to think about.

Then he seemed to be standing in the dark of that stone tomb, looking down at the two coffins—for her mother was buried beside her—hearing the whisper of the rain on the roof of the tomb, smelling old smoke, the clinging remains of incense, the first sickening harbingers of decay. And it seemed to him that at the feet of those two coffins, the shadows began to solidify, coalescing into a column of darkness blacker than the utter night within the tomb. Red eyes burned within that darkness, and a voice whispered, *Beloved.*

Within the coffin, Renfield was conscious of it when Lucy opened her eyes.

*　*　*

He came awake gasping, trembling. Heat and cold flashed through him in waves—shock, terror, despair. Distantly, he could hear the dim howling of old Lord Alyn, but other than that, the room—the house—was utterly silent. It was the dead hour of the night, and still.

Renfield stumbled from his bed, staggered to the window of his room. Hennessey had had the catch replaced on the casement with a stout metal bolt. Beyond the glass, the garden lay in dim spiky shapes beneath the pattering rain.

The trees were losing their leaves, the last of the flowers were dead. *I have been here since April,* thought Renfield despairingly, *and now the year is nearly gone. Oh, Catherine, has it all been for nothing?* He pressed his forehead to the glass, the cold of it like sweet water in his brain. He felt emptier, hungrier, than he could remember feeling in his life.

He rubbed his eyes, blinked, for it seemed to him that fog drifted above the garden, mingling with the fitful glimmer of intermittent moonlight on the rain. For a moment he thought it was only the effect of tiredness, or perhaps advancing age. But after he rubbed his eyes again, they were still there.

Taking shape. Growing more solid as he watched.

A dream, he thought, *a dream I once had . . . When?*

Red eyes gleaming in the darkness. Long hair drifting like seaweed beneath the sea. Pale gowns, and pale forms borne up on the dark air of the night: two dark and one fair.

Valkyries.

Choosers of the Slain.

Graces, goddesses, or the Norns of fate, hanging in the dark air before his window, red eyes looking into his.

"You have only to wish it," whispered the fair-haired girl in German, the tongue of Wagner, the tongue of Goethe, the tongue of Kant. "You have only to wish it, Ryland, and I will come."

Renfield breathed, "I wish it." And returning to his bed, he took the thin pillow and wrapped it around his hand, to protect his fist as he drove it through the glass.

CHAPTER FOURTEEN

Letter, R. M. Renfield to his wife
22 September

Catherine, Catherine, we stand balanced upon the blade of a razor! Either we triumph, or we are utterly undone!

His wives are here! Tonight I have learned much, and the knowledge fills me with terror—with the dread of more terror yet to come!

They came to my room, stepped through a hole in the glass of the window no bigger than my fist, though they seemed not to change shape or size. It was indescribable as the things one sees in dreams.

He is not Wotan, as I saw him in my dreams, but is called Dracula, that was known as The Impaler in his lifetime, four hundred and fifty years ago. A great lord and a great sorcerer, he lives on, vampire, feeding upon the living and making of them the Un-Dead. He has come to London, to England, to hunt, to make for himself a new life, for the countryside of the Carpathian

Mountains that were his home has grown poor, and the few peasants that remain are wary, and employ those things inimical to him and his kind: the flowers of the garlic and the whitethorn, the silver that he cannot touch and the mirrors that refuse to reproduce his image, the Holy things that burn his demon flesh as with fire.

"He has come to make new life here," groused the Countess Elizabeth, the eldest and strongest of his wives, "and left us three, alone, in a crumbling castle in a hostile countryside, without even the service of the Szgany gypsies that are his to command." She is a woman *fair as the moon, clear as the sun, and terrible as an army with banners,* as the Bible says: dark-haired, Roman-nosed, tall and with aquiline features, a Hungarian princess who in centuries past fought at Dracula's side against the invading Turks. "He flees from us, and what does he, before the foam of the sea is even dried upon his clothing, but take for himself another bride, to begin another harem more to his choosing, more apt to his commands? Pah!"

Her long canine teeth gleamed against bloodless lips.

"We have served him," said fair Nomie, in her voice like glass chimes tapped with rods of thin silver. "Surrendered our souls and our wills to him, not once but time and again. For this at least he owes us something." She is the youngest of them, German by her speech, sweet-faced and almost childlike in her thoughtful beauty, her eyes sky-blue and her hair the color of corn-silk.

The third wife, Sarike, only smiled, like an animal with her sharp white teeth.

"He learned to speak English, and how to go on in this country, from a solicitor's clerk whom he had sent out to him in Transylvania," went on the Countess, pacing up and down my narrow room with her long black hair hanging down over her shoulders, her pale clinging dress like a shroud in the moonlight that came and went through the fleeting clouds. "Our kind cannot cross water, save at the turning of the tide. Nor do we have the power to read and influence people's thoughts, nor to come and go as we will—as we do . . ." She gestured with her long hand, pale and ringed in ancient gold, to the tiny hole in the window-glass. ". . . while the sun is in the sky. By day we grow sleepy, and our minds are dulled. We can be taken and killed by those who know who we are, what we are. Only at night are we strong."

"He needs—*we* need—the earth of our burial-place, if we are to rest." Nomie turned to the window, as if she could see through the darkness the thick-clustering trees that surrounded Carfax. "It was an easy matter for *him* to purchase property here in England, to have boxes of the earth from the chapel in the vaults of his castle shipped here. He must sleep in it, and renew his strength as mortal men do, by rest: *that knits,* as your poet says, *the ravel'd sleeve of care.* Sometimes I think your Shakespeare must have suffered sleepless nights himself, for him to write of them so feelingly as he does."

"And sometimes I think you would sooner sit and read your precious Shakespeare than hunt for the blood that keeps us all alive," retorted the Countess, and her deep voice was edged with scorn. She turned back to me. "It is an easy thing for a man to hire servants, to pay solicitors to rent him or buy him houses, to open bank-accounts so that he is not paying in the gold coins of long-dead Sultans whenever he wishes his boots blacked. For women it is otherwise. Especially foreign women."

Her dark eyes fixed upon mine, and had my life depended on doing so, I do not think I could have turned my gaze away.

She said, "You are a wealthy man, I understand, Herr Renfield."

The breath seemed to go out of my body, the strength from my knees.

I stammered, "I . . . I am a prisoner here, a prisoner like the others."

"Not *quite* like the others." They say that tigers purr; I think they speak the truth. "You have house property. Many houses, from what the assistant keeper in this place babbled in drink to our servant Gelhorn. Houses that now stand empty."

"Gelhorn!" I cried. "The German poet Gelhorn, who came here some days ago? He is your servant?"

"He is the servant mostly of opium, and of his own illusions," replied the Countess, with deepest contempt. "He was on a walking-tour of the Carpathians in July, and it took my sisters and I endless nights of singing to him as we combed our hair, to wind our images and our words into his drunken dreams, so that he would find his way—*finally!*—to the castle. We convinced him we are spirits of the mountains and the woods—I never thought I should live to thank Nomie for all those silly romances she reads—and that we must come to England to retrieve magic gold that was stolen so that we could sleep again in peace."

I smiled, and met the girl Nomie's blue eyes. "So he actually believes he is traveling in company with the Rhine Maidens?"

And her eyes twinkled, suddenly very human, in response. "I think he feels safer traveling with the Rhine Maidens than with the Valkyries. But it is a terrible bore, to speak only of matters touched upon by Wagner and the Brothers Grimm."

And I remembered my own dream of speaking to Wotan the Traveler in the hold of the ship.

"Gelhorn is a fool," sneered the Countess. "And fools have

their uses—up to a point. But the man understands nothing of money, has no concept of how to obtain or even rent property in this country. He can barely make sense of a railway time-table and he came close to killing the three of us, through his stupidity, a dozen times on our journey to England in his company. We traced our lord here—"

She gestured again to the window, and I thought I heard the curl of bitter anger in her voice as she spoke of their lord.

"Yet before we confront him, we must have our own place of safety, our own refuge in which we may rest. We could hire no gypsies to fill up box after box with the earth of our *homeland* . . ." She glanced sidelong at Nomie, who cast down her eyes, and I guessed that she, at least, had wed, and died, and been buried in a land far from her childhood home. "We have each a trunk of such earth, and these we must guard as we guard our lives. You will help us, I think."

All this while I had knelt before them, and now I looked up, aghast, into those coal-dark eyes with their red demon gleam.

"These houses that you have . . ."

"Yes, yes, of course!" I cried, springing to my feet. My heart pounded—Catherine, Catherine, forgive me, but if that imbecile Hennessey spoke to their creature Gelhorn about my holding several different properties, who knows what else he might have said? I did not think all those places that you and I bought in secret were known. You were far too clever for that, my beautiful one!

But it has been five months, my darling, five months in which anything can have happened! I think that if you and Vixie had been forced for whatever reason to change your hiding-place, or to abandon the names by which you and I arranged for you to be known, you would have found some way to let me know. I pray that this is so, for I could not risk—I *dared* not risk—this clever and terrible woman beginning to make investigations on her own. The thought of you falling into her power—or into the power of that Thing, that monster, that these women now tell me is the vampire Count Dracula—is more than I can bear!

Forgive me, Catherine, but I told them about the house in Kentish Town, the money we cached there, and the papers that would give them introduction to the bank under the name of Moira Tentrees and her daughter Elaine. I felt fairly certain that you and Vixie would not have had call to use that particular refuge—if you were discovered (may God forfend!) by Lady Brough and her minions, you would likelier have gone to the Cambridge House, or even fled to France (though as I said, I *hope* you would in that event have been able to inform me of it).

Yet I trembled as I gave them the instructions about contacting solicitors and bankers—as I tremble now, at the thought that somehow, the count may learn that I have met with his wives, and taken their side against him.

"What do you fear?" demanded the Countess coldly. "He has deserted you, as you said. He has gone away to London, to be with his new little bride, his little blonde snow-maiden." Her lifted lip showed the glint of a pointed fang. "In a week he will not recall your name."

"If he has not forgotten it already," I said. I took a deep breath, and added, "I trust that you ladies will not similarly forget?"

"Because you know the truth of who 'Moira Tentrees' and her 'daughter' are," asked the Countess, looking up at me with those cold dark eyes, "and who it is who will actually be living at 15 Prince of Wales Road?"

Nomie replied in her soft voice, "Because even as we have the right to demand protection and care of our lord, so now Ryland has the right to demand it of his ladies. Is it not so?"

The Countess Elizabeth raised one brow, black and sharp as a night-moth's antenna, and regarded her sister-wife with speculation, but Nomie did not back down. At length the Countess turned to me and said, "Indeed you shall find that it is so. We shall not forget, Ryland Renfield."

"And you will send me things to eat?" I pressed. "Flies, spiders, sparrows—anything that has life, that I can eat and grow strong, even as you grow strong from the drinking of blood."

She looked startled, then smiled sidelong, like the Serpent in the Garden. "Is that truly your wish?"

I nodded earnestly, and her smile widened, but it was not a pretty smile.

"We will be far from you for a time, my servant, but yes, one of us will come and make sure that you have your heart's fill of the vermin of the earth. Does that content you?"

I said, "It does."

They faded then, dissolving into moonlight, and I dropped to my knees on the floor again and remained there long, shuddering with waves of shock and fear. The thought of going against Dracula, of playing a double game with his rebellious Wives, petrifies me. Yet he has forgotten me, he has not fulfilled any of the prayers I have prayed to him.

And I need strength, my beloved, I shall need strength so badly, if all is to come well for us and for our beloved child! I cannot let her be taken from us, cannot let your mother and your sister drag her away and drink her spirit, vampire-like, until like the victims of the vampires she turns into one of them!

A curse on money, without which those two hags would have

no use for Vixie—without which those three night-hags who stood here in the moonlight would have no use for me!

Yet they were beautiful, and as I write this, their faces swim before my mind again, two dark and one fair, and all perilous as the Angels of Death.

Oh, Catherine, how I long for your advice in this matter! I pray I have done well, and I think that I can control them, can obtain from them what I must have! But I have only done as I must, as I could! How I long only to see your face again, to touch your hands, to hear your voice, the voice of a true woman instead of the cold voices of Dracula's demon Wives!

I kiss this letter, begging all the gods above that it should come to you; praying that when I sleep tonight, it will be your lovely face that I see in my dreams.

Your own, forever,
R.M.R.

CHAPTER FIFTEEN

R.M.R.'s notes
23 September
25 flies, 10 spiders, 6 moths

24 September
28 flies, 4 spiders, 10 moths
-16 flies → spiders
Sparrow—Langmore took it from me. What use has he for a sparrow?

25 September
24 flies, 8 spiders
-18 flies → spiders
Last night as the spiders came crawling from the cracks of the walls, I chanced to look down into the garden and saw Nomie there, golden hair bleached to ivory by moonlight. I think she saw me for she lifted her hand.

When I slept, I dreamed of Lucy, rising from her tomb. Her eyes are blank, and glow from within with the red flame of the demon. She wears her soiled grave-shroud as she moves through the quiet streets around Hampstead Heath in the darkness, as if unconscious of how she would appear were any to see her, and she sings, soft and sweet, to the wretched little children who live in poverty there, whose parents—if they have parents—are too gone in gin to care whether they come in at night or not. She took a child, a boy of six or so, cradled him in her arms as she bit into his throat. When she walked away, leaving him under some gorse bushes on the heath, blood spotted the bosom of her white shroud.

No more moths—Seward has had the broken pane repaired.

* * *

"What is wrong with her?" Renfield asked, when that night he managed to work the window-bolt through the bars, and Nomie walked up from the garden—as light and as casually upon the air as if walking up a stair—and drifted through the slit and into his room. "I see her in my dreams, and she is like a sleep-walker, a revenant. Yet you and your sisters—and your lord as well— you speak, and act, and reason."

"Now I do." Nomie held out her finger, and a huge black-winged moth blundered against the casement, crawled through the gap. She smiled as Renfield took it by the wings and popped it into his mouth. "When first I wakened from death into Un-Death, I was much the same as she. A part of me knew what had happened to me, for during all those terrible months when I was a prisoner in his castle, helpless, separated from my family while he came to me night after night, I knew what would become of me in the end. But my mind went into retreat, like the poor souls here in Rushbrook House. I hunted, mostly children, for they have not an adult's caution and experience to escape. But I do not think I spoke for almost a year."

"It is not then because children are weak?" Renfield wiped a dust of wing-scales from his lip.

For answer, Nomie reached out and casually pulled one of the iron bars from the window, then taking it in her two hands, bent it into a horseshoe. "The living are weak," she said. "But it takes some of us time to learn our strength."

R.M.R.'s notes
26 September
28 flies, 9 spiders
-20 flies → spiders

Dreamed again of Lucy Westenra. *He* walked beside her through the dark of Hampstead Heath, a shadow with burning eyes.

Seward seemed better this morning, a little more of his old self, for which the gods be thanked. One can have only so much of Hennessey's care. Yet just after noon a cab drove up the avenue and Van Helsing sprang out, jaw jutting like a bulldog's and a newspaper clutched in one hand. I felt cold to see it, cold with apprehension, knowing what it would mean. When Seward made his afternoon rounds, he seemed like a man stunned, struck over the head, as if like poor Lucy he had been wakened into a world and a manner of life that he could not comprehend.

"Gor blimey, what'd that Dutchman tell him?" I heard Simmons whisper in the corridor to Hardy, and Hardy replied, "Not the foggiest. They was shut up in his study and I heard the Doc hit the table like a gunshot and yell, 'Are you mad?' but I guess after a little discussion they come to the conclusion he weren't, 'cos they're off to town this evenin'. Good job, too, 'cos old

Hennessey's got a couple of payin' customers comin' in to have a look at the loonies at eight." And their voices drifted away.

Later I saw Seward's fly brought round to the front of the house, and Seward and Van Helsing get in, their faces like stone.

27 September
25 flies, 13 spiders, 1 moth

* * *

Seward whispered, "My God," as the coffin lid was removed and the pale afternoon sunlight fell through the half-open door of the tomb and across the face of the girl within.

Yesterday, he recalled—the day Van Helsing had brought to him the newspaper, had told him that fantastic tale of the Un-Dead—had been Lucy's birthday. She would have turned twenty.

He breathed, "Is it a juggle?" For last night, when Van Helsing had brought him here, the coffin had been empty. Van Helsing had claimed that the white figure they'd seen among the yew trees at the edge of the cemetery had been Lucy, and of a certainty they'd found a four-year-old Italian girl asleep and half-frozen under the bushes where the white figure had cast its burden aside. But there had been on that tiny neck no such puncture-wounds as had been found on the throats of the other children that had been attacked over the past week.

No such puncture-wounds as he had seen on Lucy's throat, in the weeks before she'd died.

They had taken the child to Northern Hospital, and returned to Hampstead Hill Cemetery only in the golden light of the following afternoon.

"Are you convinced now?" asked Van Helsing softly, and when Seward did not reply, reached into the coffin and drew back the young woman's delicate lips. "See," he said, "the teeth are even sharper than before. With this and this" —the blunt brown finger touched those long canines, upper and lower, like a wolf's or a cat's— "the little children can be bitten. Are you of belief now, friend John?"

Seward backed away, shaking his head. The newspaper had spoken of children being attacked. Van Helsing had said it was Lucy. *Lucy!*

Van Helsing whom he trusted, whom he knew to see farther and deeper into the shadows of the human mind than any scholar of his acquaintance . . .

"She may have been placed here since last night."

"Indeed? That is so, and by whom?"

"I don't know. Someone . . ."

"And yet she has been dead one week. Most peoples in that time would not look so."

No, thought Seward numbly. *Most peoples in that time would not.* Already, despite its lining of lead, the body of Lucy's mother in the coffin beside hers had begun to faintly stink.

His mind raced back and forth against the truth that he could not look at, like a rat thrown into a rat-pit, before the dog is turned loose. Beside him, Van Helsing continued to look down at the girl in the coffin, with grief and a kind of curious, hungry longing in his eyes.

Other than the fact that her breasts did not stir with life's breath, she looked absolutely as if she were peacefully asleep. The drawn whiteness of her last few days had vanished. Her lips were red, her cheeks faintly stained with pink. Still living, she had resembled a corpse. It was her corpse that had the appearance of a living woman.

Dear God, did we bury her alive?

But Seward had seen those bodies, too, after a week. Few medical students hadn't had some dealings with the men of the resurrection trade. They "did not look so" either.

"She was bitten by the vampire when she was in a trance, sleep-walking," murmured Van Helsing, and Seward glanced sharply at him, startled that he should know this. "In trance she died, and in trance she is Un-Dead, too. Usually when the Un-Dead sleep at home . . ." His gesture took in the plastered walls of the little tomb, the sealed niches with their marble plaques. ". . . their face show what they are. But this so sweet that was when she not Un-Dead, she go back to the nothings of the common dead. There is no malign there. It make it hard that I must kill her in her sleep."

Seward drew a deep breath. The words hit his brain like a chisel on rock, with a cold sound and a sharp pain that changes forever the shape of what has been.

If she were dead already, what would it matter if Van Helsing mutilated her body, as he had proposed to mutilate it before the funeral—after the cleaning-woman had stolen the golden cross that he had placed on Lucy's lips "for protection."

"I shall cut off her head and fill her mouth with garlic," Van Helsing continued, in answer to Seward's whispered question. "And I shall drive a stake through her body." That at least Seward remembered from the night before the funeral, the night when Van Helsing had searched Lucy's room and asked that all her papers and her mother's be sealed, for him to read. This morning, when he'd met Van Helsing in the lobby of the Berkeley Hotel, where both had spent the night, he'd seen his old master had a satchel with him.

But to do this to Lucy . . .

He looked back at that radiant face, sleeping so gently. So

beautiful was she that he had at first not seen the dirt and moss-stains that marked her white grave-clothes, the small brown spots on its bosom.

Then his gaze returned to Van Helsing's face. To those clear light-blue eyes, filled with tenderness, pity, longing . . . and something else.

Van Helsing tore his gaze from Lucy's face, turned to Seward with an air of decision. "If I did simply follow my inclining, I would do now, at this moment, what is to be done." He wet his lips. "But there are other things to follow, and things that are a thousand times more difficult in that them we do not know. This is simple."

He glanced, quick and sidelong, at Lucy's face again, as if his eyes were drawn to her against his will.

"We may have to want Arthur," he said, "and how shall we tell him of this? If you, who saw the wounds on Lucy's throat, and saw the wounds so similar on the child's at the hospital; if you, who saw the coffin empty last night and full today with a woman who have not change only to be more rose and more beautiful in a whole week, after she die—if you know of this and know of the white figure who brought the child to the church-yard, and yet of your own senses you do not believe, how can I expect Arthur, who know none of those things, to believe?"

He tore himself as if with physical force from the side of the coffin, paced to the door, shoes crunching the brown leaves they had tracked in from outside. "He doubted me when I took him from her kiss when she was dying," he said, as if speaking to himself, and Seward shivered at the memory of Lucy's face then, the way her lips drew back from those long, sharp teeth, the gleam of unholy greed in her eyes. "I know he has forgiven me because in some mistaken idea I have done things that prevent him say good-by as he ought; and he may think that in some more mistaken idea this woman was buried alive; and that in most mistake of all we have killed her. Yet he never can be sure, and that is the worst of all."

Yes, thought Seward, looking down at the moss-stain on Lucy's sleeve, the blood-spot on her breast. *Not to be sure...* Not to ever be sure who or what that white form was that he'd glimpsed last night, flitting among the graves with the sleeping child in her arms.

A part of him thought, *But Art will never know...*

But he'd nursed troubled minds long enough to be aware that there was no certainty whatever that Arthur wouldn't come to this tomb himself. Would sneak here, drawn as if against his will, too ashamed to breathe a word of his secret to his friends . . .

And find what?

And what would that do to him, make of him, thereafter? Especially coming, as it did, in tandem with his father's sudden death from stroke?

All that awareness was in Van Helsing's voice, too. "I know that he must pass through the bitter waters to reach the sweet," said the old man softly. "He must have one hour that will make the very face of heaven grow black to him; then we can act for good all around, and send him peace."

Seward helped Van Helsing fold the coffin's lead lining back over Lucy's face and upper body; helped him replace the heavy lid. He felt numb and strange, as if everyone around him had suddenly begun speaking a foreign language, and wondered if this was what it was like for the men and women in his charge, when first they began to go mad. Since his smallest childhood he had quested to know Why, and had followed those longings down the road of logic and science. Indeed, only on meeting

Lucy had he begun to doubt that all things could be explained in terms of matter, logic, and the physiology of the nervous system.

Could the Un-Dead be some physical phenomenon unknown as yet to science? Some illness, some condition of the flesh or the brain?

Van Helsing didn't seem to think so.

Was Van Helsing mad? Seward wondered again.

Was he himself?

Chapter Sixteen

Through the night as Van Helsing kept watch in the graveyard, he asked himself the same question.

Am I mad?

He'd asked himself that at intervals throughout his long life, and had never come to a satisfactory conclusion.

He leaned his back to one of the pale-barked sychamores that grew near the Westenra tomb in Hampstead Cemetery, touched with uneasy fingers the thick links of silver chain he'd wrapped around his throat. He wore them on his wrists as well—a woman in Thibet had instructed him in this—and in his hand he carried a rosary twined with garlic flowers. He did not fear Lucy Westenra so much, for he had carefully chinked up every crack in the tomb's door with a paste of flour and water, mixed with fragments of a consecrated Host, and had hung another crucifix over the keyhole of the door.

But he guessed that Lucy did not always hunt alone.

He shuddered, as Lucy's sweetly beautiful face returned to his mind.

He had encountered the Un-Dead before, in Egypt, in Constantinople, and in Paris; had heard of them in India and Thibet. Three times had he found himself, looking down into their faces as they slept after their kills—one of those had been a woman he'd known in life. And always it was the same.

They were so beautiful.

He knew what they were. He had seen them kill, and seen the chaos of horror and doubt they left in their wake. He had seen them prey on those closest to them, those whose grief made them willing to believe whatever their returning beloveds told them. He had seen them make others of their own kind, through an exchange of blood with chosen victims, victims who did not merely die but became predators in their turn. He had seen their callousness and absolute selfishness as they chose the death of others over their own discomfort, their own craving for blood.

It was unspeakable, that he should look on the faces of vampire women, and feel what he felt.

Desire so overwhelming as to almost blot out thought.

He closed his eyes, then opened them again almost at once. *Fool, these thoughts will only weaken you. You close your eyes, you open them to see Him, to see Dracula, this Dracula that Jonathan Harker write of, Jonathan Harker that marry the sweet Madame Mina, who share with me the letters Miss Lucy write.* He tried to push from his mind the admission of wanting Lucy, to bury it under loathing of what she had become, under ironic amusement at the recollection of poor Arthur Holmwood's passionate ramblings about how the transfusion of his blood into Lucy's veins had made them husband and wife in the sight of God.

And am I, then, too, her husband? And your friends John and Quincey? Are we all co-husbands together in a harem?

He tried to picture Lucy as he knew she must be now, a beautiful body inhabited by a demon, a damned soul, that lured children to her and drank their blood. That would not stop with children; that was growing stronger each night.

It did not drive from his mind the white-hot flash of desire that had pierced him like a swordblade, when she'd opened those smoky demon eyes and smiled at Arthur on her deathbed: *Oh my love, I am so glad you have come! Kiss me . . .*

It did not drive from his mind his utter loathing at himself.

It did not root out his fear that one day that blind lust would prove too much for his strength, and would lead him, too, in spite of all he knew, into the red nightmare of Un-Death.

And that he would enjoy it.

He drew in deep breaths of the cold air. It was autumn, the threshhold of winter. Though Hampstead Hill lay far from the Thames, the sooty reek of its fogs drifted through the graveyard, and through the trees southward he could see the dull glow of the city's gas-lamps. Here in the cemetery it was quiet, the birdless quiet of winter, save for the soft, terrible scratching at the marble door of the tomb.

Man is born to Sin, as the sparks fly upward. His friend and student John, who did such good work among those troubled in their minds, might have been able to explain this curious, desperate lust that seemed to operate in tandem with his genuine affection for Lucy and for her friends, his deep horror and pity for the situation in which they all found themselves. John had proclaimed often that he held no belief in Sin, nor in the doctrines of Predestination and Fate.

Charcot was his god, and Bernheim and that young Austrian Freud. In them he would doubtless have found some rational explanation for the feelings that, despite all he could do, scorched Van Helsing with shame.

Or perhaps, he thought, *I am only mad.*

But mad or sane, it did not change what he knew to be facts, which others these days ignored, or walked in ignorance of.

That humankind was not alone upon the Earth.

That there were indeed more things in Heaven and Earth than were dreamt of in the philosophy of Hamlet's friend Horatio or of anyone else: hidden powers whose aims and perceptions were as different from those of humankind as humans' were from those of the sponges beneath the sea.

That the Un-Dead walked, as they had long walked. And that their bite would spread their condition to others, if they were not stopped.

R.M.R.'s notes
28 September
27 flies, 9 spiders, 4 moths, 1 mouse
-19 flies, 4 moths → spiders
-12 spiders → mouse

Seward back, but so distracted as to be completely unaware of the mouse (a gift, I am sure, from Nomie, my faithful little Norn). He is gray-faced and shaken, like a man who has looked down into Hell.

How can Hell have shaken him? He rules one of its tinier Circles. Does he not yet know this?

28 September—night
Seward departed shortly before nine.

* * *

In the darkness of his dream, Renfield saw again Lucy West-enra's tomb. Night lay thick on London, thicker still on this sub-urban wilderness of headstones and tombs. He could smell the soot-laden fog, hear the whooping screech of the owl, the fran-tic squeak of the mouse it seized. Taste the blood.

Four men came over the cemetery wall, Seward and old Van Helsing and two others. The younger of these two—the youngest of the four—followed hard on Van Helsing's heels as the old man unlocked the marble door of that ghostly pillared sepul-chre, a golden-haired godling in black, like a young Siegfried. He looked inquiringly at the old professor as they gathered around the twin coffins, then at Seward. To Seward, Van Helsing said, "You were with me here yesterday. Was the body of Miss Lucy in that coffin?"

"It was."

"You hear." Van Helsing turned to the other two, Siegfried and a tall, stringy man with the faded remains of a deep tan on his long-jawed face, a long sandy mustache and a rough blue greatcoat such as Renfield had seen Americans wear, who got them second-hand from their Army. "And yet there is no one who does not believe with me." With that rather confusing dou-ble negative, Van Helsing took his screwdriver, and unfastened the lid of the coffin. Siegfried—who was, Renfield guessed, Sew-ard's good friend and successful rival Arthur Holmwood, the new Lord Godalming—and the American both backed away a step, and in the glow of the dark-lantern the American bore, Renfield could see they were steeling themselves for the stink of a body ten days dead.

He could see their faces change when they smelled no such thing, even before they stepped forward to look.

"Professor, I answered for you," said the American. "Your word is all I want. I wouldn't ask such a thing ordinarily—I wouldn't so dishonor you as to imply a doubt; but this is a mystery that goes beyond any honor or dishonor. Is this your doing?"

Van Helsing replied, with no more emotion in his voice than if the question had been one of hat-size rather than honor, "I swear to you by all that I hold sacred that I have not removed nor touched her." And he explained, with the calm of a man in the witness-box, the events of two nights before. "Last night there was no exodus, so tonight before the sundown I took away my garlic and other things. And so it is we find this coffin empty. So" —he shut the slide of his lantern, leaving them in the dark— "now to the outside."

Renfield turned in his sleep, whimpered with fright. Someone was watching, someone was listening, someone standing very near them in the darkness. Someone who could smell the blood in the veins of the four men, who could see them clearly, even when the heavy scudding clouds concealed the moon.

Someone who drew back, even as Godalming and the American leaned forward to see what Van Helsing was doing as he worked his flour paste through his fingers again, caulked up the chinks in the door. "Great Scott," said the American, pulling a foot-long bowie knife from a sheath at his belt to cut tobacco for himself, "is this a game?"

"It is."

"What is that which you are using?" asked Godalming, and Van Helsing reverently lifted his hat as he answered.

"The Host. I brought it from Amsterdam. I have an Indulgence."

You mean you have a priest who believes, like you, in the power of the Un-Dead, thought Renfield. He knew perfectly well that no Pope, nor any member of the organized Church, would issue an Indulgence for such use of the consecrated wafer. By their silence—Godalming, as a true-blooded scion of an English noble house, was by definition Church of England, and most Americans couldn't have described the difference between a Catholic and a Druid—both men were struck dumb with superstitious reverence: the American even endeavored to spit his tobacco in a quiet and seemly manner. In the darkness the watcher—watchers, Renfield could feel their minds—stirred, then stilled. They could feel Lucy's approach long before Van Helsing whispered, *"Ach!"*

Moonlight flickered on something white in the avenue of yews. A child cried out, in fear or pain. Or perhaps, thought Renfield, deep in the well of sleep, it was his own cry that he heard. The light of Van Helsing's lantern fell on Lucy's face, on the crimson glisten of blood on her mouth, which trailed down to dribble her white gown.

"Arthur." With a casual motion she threw to the ground the child she had been carrying in her arms, held out her hands. The men standing ranged before the tomb might have seen only the demon fire in her eyes, but Renfield thought, too, that she was still a revenant, still tangled in the madness of new death and animal hunger.

His own mouth burned with the memory of the spiders he'd eaten—each sweetly charged with the flickering energy of the flies—with the murky deliciousness of the blood he'd sucked out of the mouse that morning. Had Langmore come then and tried to take it from him, he thought he, too, would have turned on him, with just such wildness in his eyes.

"Come to me, Arthur," she whispered, and moved forward, her bare arms outstretched. "Leave these others and come to me. My arms are hungry for you." The words whispered like a half-heard echo of dreams of passion, never filled . . . Never filled by Arthur, in any case. "Come, husband . . ."

With a desperate sob, young Lord Godalming opened his arms for her, but Van Helsing—as Renfield knew he would— stepped between them, holding out a small gold crucifix upon a silver chain. Lucy drew back with a cry, and Renfield felt it again, the minds of those who watched from the darkness beyond the tomb. The shiver, at the burning energy that focussed in sacred things. It was as if, seeing with their eyes, he saw the deadly glow that could sear otherworldly flesh, shining forth not only from the crucifix but from the caulking that sealed the door of the tomb.

Lucy swung around a few feet from the door, mouth open in rage to show blood on the long white teeth, trapped and furious. In a quiet voice Van Helsing asked, "Answer me, o my friend! Am I to proceed with my work?"

Godalming slipped to his knees to the damp gravel of the path, buried his face in his hands. By the light of Van Helsing's lantern Renfield saw Seward's face, as he looked down on the golden head of the younger man. Godalming's voice was barely audible. "Do as you will, friend. Do as you will."

It was the American—Morris, Renfield remembered his name was, Quincey Morris—who helped bring Godalming back to his feet, while Van Helsing moved cautiously past Lucy to un-caulk the putty from the door. In Lucy's place, Renfield sup-posed he would have simply fled, yet where could she go? If, in fact, she could find no rest other than in the place where she had been buried, where could she fly?

Like Catherine, he thought, before he and she had bought those other houses for her and Vixie to disappear into. Before they'd set up bank accounts, and papers, proving that she and her daughter were people other than the women Lady Brough was looking for, to take their money back for her own.

Lucy slipped through the chink in the door like smoke, like the figure in a dream, as Nomie, Elizabeth, silent Sarike had come through the broken pane of glass into Renfield's room eight nights ago. Van Helsing prodded the putty back into place, then went to where the unconscious child still lay in the moonlight of the path.

"Come now, my friends." He lifted the little boy in his arms. "We can do no more 'til to-morrow. There is a funeral at noon, so here we shall all come before long after that. The friends of the dead will all be gone by two . . ."

So intent were the men, grouped around Van Helsing, that they glimpsed nothing of the three shadows that followed them along the avenue toward the low point in the wall. The three Wives had, Renfield noticed—seeing them clearly in his dream for the first time—disposed of their own pale old-fashioned gowns and wore now dark modern walking-dresses, stylish and nearly invisible in the thick gloom of the gathering clouds.

"As for this little one, he is not much harm, and by to-morrow night he shall be well. We shall leave him where the po-lice will find him, as on the other night; and then to home."

Darkness drifted then into Renfield's mind, and his dream

segued into the thick heat of India, the stink of the Hoogly River, and white ants crawling in armies up a tree in his garden in Calcutta . . .

But he thought, as Van Helsing laid the sleeping child down against the cemetery wall, that he heard the Countess Elizabeth laugh.

Chapter Seventeen

They killed Lucy at a little after two.

Renfield felt it, like the distant memory of pain, stabbing his chest and darkening his eyes. Far more clearly he felt Dracula's fury, like the mutter of thunder and the taste of ozoneous storm-winds sweeping down the mountains, to tear the valleys to pieces in their wrath.

He sank onto his bed and crushed his hands over his ears, then over his eyes, then over his heart, trying to blot out what he heard and saw and felt. Mostly what he was conscious of was terror.

He'll find them—Elizabeth, Sarike, Nomie. He'll say Lucy's death was their doing.

He'll say I helped, or kept my silence, of my own accord.

The Wives are too powerful for him to hurt, and the men—Van Helsing and Seward and the others—too wary now, and too prepared.

But within the coming growl of that terrible storm he knew

that Dracula would massacre someone in his revenge, and would not much care who it was.

In a frenzy of terror Renfield scrambled to his feet and ran to his boxes, to devour every spider, every fly, every moth, and even the second mouse that Nomie had caused to crawl under the door of his room early that morning.

None of it helped.

* * *

Late in the afternoon Seward returned from London, with a sweet-faced, pretty, dark-haired woman whom Renfield, watching the driveway from his window, recognized as Lucy's friend Mina. She seemed both smaller and older than she had appeared in his dreams, more delicate and yet stronger than steel. She had come a long way, he thought, since she'd giggled and hugged Lucy and Mrs. Westenra in the Whitby train-station, saying good-by to them for what turned out to be the last time. Like her other clothes, her mourning-dress was worn and a little out of fashion. She carried a small traveling-bag, and as Seward helped her down from the carriage, he took from beside her feet a small, heavy square box which Renfield recognized as the case of a portable typewriter. As they passed around the corner of the house toward the shallow front steps, Renfield heard old Lord Alyn in his barred front bedroom begin to howl, the others along the hallway taking up the din, until the cacophony blew around the eaves of the house like the screech of storm-winds in the dead of night. Mina—Renfield wished he knew her surname, for the sake of good manners—broke stride with a shudder, then steeled herself and followed Dr. Seward out of sight around the corner, and into the house.

As usual, Seward gave no sign of having heard a thing.

Like Seward, like Lord Godalming, like the American Morris, this young woman had been Lucy's friend. She must still have been abroad in Europe—with her ailing husband?—when Lucy was taken ill, for Renfield couldn't imagine Catherine, for instance, not being constantly in the house of a friend who was slowly dying as Lucy had died.

Yet what was she doing here?

Seward will tell her, thought Renfield, pressing his forehead to the iron window bars. They were cold, like the day outside. Wind jerked and twisted at the bare branches of the garden trees. *Seward will tell her of the scene in the graveyard, of the bitten children.*

And what then?

Seward was pale and silent as he made his rounds, and did not seem to notice that Renfield had devoured his entire stock of spiders and flies. As the house grew quiet that night, Renfield thought he could hear, in the study downstairs, the rapid clatter of typewriter keys, hurrying and pausing, hurrying and pausing, as if to keep up with some unheard dictation, far into the night.

R.M.R.'s notes
30 September
25 flies, 10 spiders

Nomie my friend, you are the only one who has offered me the smallest actual assistance in this terrible time!

Has it not occurred to Seward to wonder at the continued presence of so many flies in this chilly weather? Yet it is typical of the smallness of the man's scope.

Another visitor today, Madame Mina's husband Jonathan Harker, Langmore tells me. A tallish thin man whose black clothing hangs loose on an emaciated frame, the souvenir of those weeks of brain-fever in Buda-Pesth. The brim of his hat hid his face as he passed around the corner of the house, but he moved like a young man, and looked around him with a kind of nervous alertness: another echo of brain-fever as well? There is something that troubles me about the sight of him, something familiar in his walk and his frame, as if I have seen him somewhere before, and I have a terrible sense of urgency about the lost memory. Could it be that he is one of Lady Brough's creatures, or one of her vile elder daughter's? Langmore says he is a solicitor.

Later—Indeed the eagles gather! I have just seen young Lord Godalming and the American Mr. Morris descend from the Godalming brougham (with a team in harness at five hundred guineas the pair, if they were a shilling!). Morris wore a perfectly respectable derby hat in place of the wide-brimmed American slouch he had on last night, his long sandy hair sweeping out beneath it. Curious, to see these men in the flesh whom I recognize from dreaming—could I have seen Jonathan Harker in dream?

But when? And why?

The sight of them gathering fills me with dread, for as the sun sinks I feel, stronger and stronger, Dracula's growing anger, as he lies within his coffin. Like mine, his mind was touched by Lucy's agony this afternoon as that handsome young lordling drove a stake into her heart. Wherever he now lies—in some hideaway in London to which he transported his boxes of earth—in his sleep he heard her screams, tasted her blood, felt her death. Like me, he saw the faces of her killers in his dreaming.

Did he love Lucy Westenra? Perhaps, as he understands the word, he did. But what I feel in his dreaming is not grief, but rage.

He had claimed her by his blood, and she was *his*.

In life he was not a man to forgive the smallest slight: Nomie told me that men who broke his law, in the smallest degree, were impaled upon iron stakes on the roadsides, and left to slowly die: thus he had his name. Four hundred years of hunting humankind has not taught him either mercy or tolerance.

His rage is like the storm that builds above the Himalayas in the summer heat, lightning hoarded in murderous dark. I feel it coming. When the storm strikes, God have mercy on us all!

* * *

"Renfield?" The tap on the door had to be Seward. He was the only one in Rushbrook House who ever knocked, and he not always. And indeed, he did not wait to be invited to unlock and enter the room.

Renfield turned from the window, beyond which the hazy red sun was burning itself out in the sky above London's lurid smokes.

"There is a lady here, who would like to see you."

Renfield had caught a glimpse, through the door as it opened, of Mina Harker's black dress. Indeed it would have been far too much to hope, that Catherine would have come at this time. He kept his voice steady with an effort. "Why?"

"She is going through the house, and would like to see everyone in it."

Renfield wondered if Seward had any idea just how many other people went through the house and saw everyone in it, behind his back. "Oh, very well. Let her come in, by all means. Just wait a moment while I tidy up." He gulped down the spiders and the flies hastily, without the joy of savoring them. He had a feeling he would need all the strength he could get. "Let the lady come in."

He went to sit on the edge of the bed, so that he could see Mrs. Harker as she entered the room. Seward kept within striking-distance—*as if I could not knock his brains out against the wall if I wished it!*—but Mrs. Harker walked in without either fear or hesitation, and held out her black-gloved hand.

"Good-evening, Mr. Renfield. Dr. Seward has told me of you."

Renfield studied her face for a few moments, taking in the frank dark eyes, the firm set of her mouth, the air of compe-tence she had exuded even hunting for her friend in the moonlit churchyard. He almost said so, then remembered he was never supposed to have seen her before in his life. "You're not the girl the doctor wanted to marry, are you? You can't be, you know, for she's dead," he added, and saw Seward start.

"Oh, no! I have a husband of my own, to whom I was mar-ried before I ever saw Dr. Seward, or he me. I am Mrs. Harker."

"Then what are you doing here?" He thought he sounded sufficiently genuine.

"My husband and I are staying on a visit with Dr. Seward."

"Then don't stay."

"But why not?"

"And how did you know I wanted to marry anyone?" asked Seward, a little miffed—as if, thought Renfield, he didn't know that it was common knowledge throughout the asylum.

He rolled his eyes. "What an asinine question!"

"I don't see that at all, Mr. Renfield," said Mrs. Harker, as if the conversation were taking place in a drawing-room instead of a bare cell with bars on the window.

"You will understand, Mrs. Harker," said Renfield, "that

when a man is so loved and honored as our host is, everything regarding him is of interest in our little community. Dr. Seward is loved not only by his household and his friends, but even by his patients, who, being some of them hardly in mental equilibrium, are apt to distort causes and effects. Since I myself have been the inmate of a lunatic asylum, I cannot but notice that the sophistic tendencies of some of its inmates lean toward the errors of *non causa* and *ignoratio elenchi*."

The relief in having an actual conversation, with a young woman whom he was coming to like and respect, was unbelievable. He felt a flash of regret that he hadn't saved out a single fly to offer her.

She would need them, he knew, as much as he.

"It may be that they cannot help it," said Mrs. Harker. "I myself have not your experience, so I cannot judge, but even among the so-called sane of my acquaintance I have encountered some very curious beliefs."

Renfield laughed—the first time, he realized, he had laughed since coming to Rushbrook House. "And I'll wager you would think them a very college of sanity, compared to some of the queer nabs I ran across in India. Why, I am myself an instance of a man who had a strange belief. Indeed, it was no wonder that my friends were alarmed, and insisted on my being put under control. I used to fancy that life was a positive and perpetual entity, and that by consuming a multitude of live things, no matter how low in the scale of creation, one might indefinitely prolong life. At times I held the belief so strongly that I actually tried to take human life. The doctor here will bear me out that on one occasion I tried to kill him for the purpose of strengthening my vital powers by the assimilation with my own body of his life through the medium of his blood—relying, of course, upon the Scriptural phrase, 'For the blood is the life.' Isn't that so, Doctor?"

"Er—indeed it is." Seward looked completely disconcerted, and glanced at his watch. "I fear it is time to leave, Mrs. Harker."

"Of course." Mrs. Harker smiled, and took Renfield's hand again. "Good-by, and I hope I may see you often, under auspices pleasanter to yourself."

Renfield rose, and bowed. "Good-by, my dear. I pray God I may never see your sweet face again. May He bless and keep you!"

As the door was closed, the lock clashing harshly, Renfield knew without turning that the sun had disappeared behind London's black sullen rooflines. He felt it: the flowing horror of bitter-cold air that precedes the storm like a moving wall, the inevitable terror of the lightning.

Somewhere in the dark of London, Dracula woke.

He knows they are here. That awareness went through him like a killing spear, dropping him to his knees, his breath laboring and sweat standing out on his face like a dying man's.

He is coming.

CHAPTER EIGHTEEN

From the window of his room Renfield watched the glow of Dr. Seward's study lamp, the shadows that moved back and forth across it on the laurels of the garden. Once the men came out into the dark garden, and Renfield saw Seward point across the lawn and through the leafless trees, to the wall of Carfax.

So they know.

He didn't know how they'd learned of it, but in his bones he was sure of it. They were on Dracula's trail.

And Dracula was on theirs.

Renfield clung to the bars, watching the moving white blurs of shirt-cuffs, collars, the golden glint of the study lamplight on Lord Godalming's hair. Heads nodding. Seward pointing in the direction of the shed, where the ladder was kept.

Dear God! Dear God, save me!

One by one, the other lights in the house went out. Seward made his rounds, pale and distracted. A little later Renfield heard Langmore come off duty at midnight, heard Hardy settle into the chair. Renfield paced the room, sweating. *They are going to Carfax tonight.*

They are leaving Mrs. Harker here alone.

Christ had prayed in the Garden, *Let this cup pass from me.* Renfield pressed his face to the bars, staring out into the darkness, then turned to pace again. He remembered the wolf, broken from its home in the Zoo and sent loping through the streets of London, to force a way into the house that Dracula could not enter on his own. *I open the ways for all my servants,* Dracula had said to him, but it was the servant—the wolf whose mind Renfield had felt in his dream—who had opened the way for the Master. *He will hang in the darkness before my window, materializing out of the moonlight and fog.*

He will whisper to me, Let me in.

Renfield knew that it was physically impossible for him to do other than say, *Come.*

What other are you, if not the tool of my power, willing and blind?

The study lamp was dimmed down. A brief bar of very faint light, like a lantern's, shone out as the front door opened, shut. No one emerged, but in a moment they would . . .

Renfield flung himself against the door of his room. "Hardy!" he shouted through the judas. "Hardy, send for Dr. Seward! Bring him here, at once, this moment! I must see him!"

The big guard's whiskery face appeared in the judas. "Wot, at this hour? It's two in the morning!"

"If I'd wanted a report on the time, I'd have sent for the town crier! I have something urgent to tell Dr. Seward, something desperate! He's awake, he and his guests, I've just seen their lights. Please fetch him. Please." Renfield clutched at the bars, as if he could reach through them and wrest the promise from the guard. He fought to keep from shouting. "Please."

Shaking his head, Hardy withdrew. Renfield pressed his face to the judas and saw him walk downstairs, then sank to the floor before the door.

He will know. He will guess, and he will punish.

He will come here tonight. He will use me, use me to destroy Mrs. Harker, use me as a cat's-paw as he tried to use me before. The one person of all of them, who treated me as a man and not a beast.

Footsteps in the corridor. Renfield scrambled to his feet.

The clank of the lock.

"What is it, Renfield?" Lamplight in the cell, the lamp held aloft by the tall Quincey Morris in his blue American Army coat. Van Helsing, Jonathan Harker, and Lord Godalming were with Seward also, all five men dressed rough, as if they were going burgling, which Renfield guessed they were.

"Dr. Seward." Renfield spoke in his most calm and careful voice. "I have a most special favor to ask of you. You must have been aware, in the past day or two, of my return to sanity. I'm certain that only the press of your duties as host to your friends has prevented you from fulfilling the legal and medical technicalities of my release. Though I hesitate to seem impatient or importunate, still I must request, as a matter of considerable importance, that you release me tonight. Now, in fact. Release me, and send me home."

To Catherine, he thought, trying to keep the wild elation from his face, *to Vixie. I can take them and be gone from this country, from my dread Master's awareness, before morning. He cannot cross water, we can flee to France.*

"I'm afraid," said Seward calmly, "that even did I judge you restored to complete sanity, those technicalities could not be dealt with at this hour, and in this fashion. We could not . . ."

"I appeal to your friends," coaxed Renfield, reminding himself that screaming at Seward and knocking him against the wall would probably not serve him well. "They will, perhaps, not mind sitting in judgement on my case. By the way, you have not introduced me."

"I beg your pardon." Seward beckoned the others forward. "Lord Godalming; Professor Van Helsing; Mr. Quincey Morris, of Texas; Jonathan Harker—Mr. Renfield."

"Lord Godalming." Renfield shook the young man's hand. "I had the honor of seconding your father at the Windham; I grieve to know, by your holding the title, that he is no more."

His young lordship blinked at the incongruity of Renfield's small-talk in the barren cell, at two in the morning, but made a polite bow.

"Mr. Morris, you should be proud of your great state. Its reception into the Union was a precedent which may have far-reaching effects hereafter, when the Pole and the Tropics may hold alliance to the Stars and Stripes."

Morris inclined his head, throughly imperturbable. Renfield guessed he'd encountered stranger situations.

"What shall any man say of his pleasure at meeting Van Helsing? Sir, I make no apology for dropping all forms of conventional prefix. When an individual has revolutionized theraputics by his discovery of the continuous evolution of brain-matter, conventional forms are unfitting, since they would seem to limit him to one of a class. And Mr. Harker, I can only congratulate you upon having the wisdom and discrimination to find, in all the wide world, that pearl among women who is your beautiful wife."

He hesitated, looking into the young solicitor's face in the huge shadows, the upside-down lantern-light, seeing it . . . when? By firelight? In a dream? Why did it look so familiar?

Not wanting to be seen staring, he turned quickly back to the others. "You, gentlemen, who by nationality, by heredity, or by the possession of natural gifts, are fitted to hold your respective places in the moving world, I take to witness that I am as sane as at least the majority of men who are in full possession of their liberties. And I am sure that you, Dr. Seward, humanitarian and medico-jurist as well as scientist, will deem it a moral duty to deal with me as one to be considered as under exceptional circumstances."

"Indeed at all times I attempt to so deal with you, and everyone under this roof," agreed Seward. "And indeed, you do seem to be improving very rapidly. But it requires a longer interview than this, to even begin to think about taking steps to meet your wish."

"But I fear, Dr. Seward, that you hardly apprehend my wish," said Renfield. "I desire to go at once—here—now—this very hour—this very moment, if I may. I am sure it is only necessary to put before so admirable a practitioner as Dr. Seward so simple, yet so momentous a wish, to ensure its fulfillment."

Seward's face was like wood. Renfield looked past him to the others: Godalming, Morris, Harker, Van Helsing. *Imbeciles, do you understand nothing?* "Is it possible that I have erred in my supposition?"

"You have," said Seward.

No pleading on Renfield's part would move them. He felt

frantic, hampered by his terror of Dracula's reaction should he guess Renfield's attempted defection; hampered, too, by his sense of the vampire's approach, stealing like a dark cloud down the silent river, across the Purfleet marshes, a cloud filled with malice and wrath.

"Can you not tell frankly your real reason for wishing to be free tonight?" asked Van Helsing, speaking like Mrs. Harker as an equal, and Renfield could only shake his head.

"If I were free to speak, I should not hesitate a moment, but I am not my own master in the matter. I can only ask you to trust me. If I am refused, the responsibility does not rest with me."

"Come, friends," said Seward, who seemed, Renfield thought, to have a fairly small repertoire of closing remarks. "We have work to do. Good-night."

He turned from the room. Renfield cried, "Please!" and threw himself to his knees before him. "You don't understand what you're doing, keeping me here! Let me implore you, to let me out of this house at once! Send me away how you will and where you will; send keepers with me with whips and chains; let them take me in a strait-waistcoat, even to a jail, but let me go out of this! You don't know what you're doing by keeping me here!"

Seward's face hardened, as if this outburst was something expected and much more in line with his ideas of how small-hours interviews with lunatics should be conducted. Renfield wanted to take him by the shoulders and shake him. But that, he knew, would only result in the strait-jacket, and the thought of being so bound when Dracula came was more than he could bear.

"By all you hold dear—by your love that is lost—by your hope that lives—for the sake of the Almighty, take me out of this and save my soul from guilt!" Tears of frustration and despair rolled down his face. "Can't you hear me, man? Can't you understand? Will you never learn? Don't you know that I am sane and earnest now; that I am no lunatic in a mad fit, but a sane man fighting for his soul? Let me go! Let me go!"

Seward caught the hand Renfield raised in pleading, pulled him to his feet. "Come! No more of this; we have had quite enough already. Get to your bed and behave more discreetly."

"*Discreetly?*" Renfield bit back a crack of hysterical laughter. For a time he stood, looking into Seward's eyes in the glow of Quincey's lamp, seeing in them the man's blind grief, his blind pride in being the doctor, the keeper, the Man Who Is Sane. He felt, suddenly, exactly as he'd felt while trying to argue with Lady Brough, with Catherine's sister the obnoxious Georgina, trying to convince them that to take Vixie away from him and Catherine, to lock her into one of their "select young ladies' academies" would be the death of that fragile, lively, passionate girl's soul.

To do otherwise was simply Not Done.

Without a word, Renfield walked back to his bed, and dropped down to sit on its edge.

He saw Seward's shoulders relax, as if, though he did not smile, all things had been restored to the way he knew they should be.

The other men filed out. As Seward turned, last of all, to shut the door, Renfield raised his head. "You will, I trust, Dr. Seward, do me the justice to bear in mind, later on, that I did what I could to convince you tonight."

* * *

From his window Renfield watched the hooded yellow blink of the lantern bob its way across the abyss of the garden. Watched it ascend what he knew to be the wall, invisible beyond the leafless trees. Watched it vanish.

Pallid moonlight outlined the nearest tree-trunks, slipped away. Returned, to show the thin streak of white mist that had begun to steal across the garden, mist that glittered in the faint reflections of Seward's study lamp, and from another window where the gas was also turned down low. Somewhere a dog was howling, and Renfield pressed his face to the bars and cried "Dear God! Dear God!" though he could not have said whether he prayed to the disapproving God of whom he'd been taught in childhood, or to Wotan, whose red eyes he saw flickering, flickering in the heart of the mists.

As the black form took shape, hanging in the darkness outside Renfield's window, he thought, *That is where I saw Jonathan Harker. In my dream of the Valkyries. It is he who was the prisoner.* He could even now hear Nomie's silvery voice: *I am called Nomie, Jonathan . . .*

But it was not Nomie and her sisters who took shape outside the window now, but Wotan—Dracula—with his red eyes burning through the mist like malign spots of flame.

Black moths beat against the window, crawled through the narrow slot of the nearly shut casement, flopped limply on the floor in the moonlight around Renfield's feet. Though it was night, and chill, big steely black flies swarmed with them, and spiders crawled from the cracks in the paneling, and still the black form took shape in the darkness outside the window.

I am here.

Renfield whispered, "Master."

I am here. You have sworn your love for me; lo, I have brought you good things. Will you not bid me welcome?

The grip of his mind was like iron and ice, crushing and freezing at once. Renfield thought despairingly of that lovely young woman who had spoken so kindly to him, sleeping alone in this terrible house; thought of the long horror of Lucy's death; of the three sisters and their power. He wept, but his voice choked on the name of God as if Dracula's steel grip closed about his throat. In that moment he could have called upon neither God nor man.

"Rats," Wotan whispered—Dracula whispered—the leitmotif of the Traveler God beating in Renfield's brain, and across the lawn Renfield saw a dark mass creeping, like water spreading toward the house, a dark mass prickled by a thousand paired crimson flames. "Rats . . ." With a gesture of his long-nailed hand, Dracula brushed aside the mists that surrounded him, and Renfield saw them, smelled them, the sweet filthy unmistakable mustiness of their bodies. "Every one of them a life. And dogs to eat them, and cats, too. All lives—all red blood, with years of life in it, and not merely buzzing flies!"

Lives, thought Renfield. *Strength. Strength for my great work.*

"All these lives will I give you. Ay, and many more and greater, through countless ages, if you will fall down and worship me. Will you not bid me welcome?"

With a sob, Renfield stumbled to the window, pushed at the casement through the bars. "Welcome, Master," he breathed. "I bid you come in."

The black shape before the window dislimned; the moonlight all but disappeared. White mist poured through the inch-wide crack in a thin stream that flowed down the wall, across the floor, and under the door of the cell. Then it was gone.

Renfield sank to the floor of his cell and wept.

Chapter Nineteen

Van Helsing came to see Renfield next morning, cheerful—cock-a-whoop, Renfield thought, observing the old man's springy step and bright eye with a kind of numb bitterness. They must have found some of the Count's crates of earth at Carfax. Of course, it would be Jonathan Harker who'd told them the Count had bought the old house, and shipped his crates of earth there, so that he could have a place where he could rest in this foreign land.

Renfield saw it all now. Harker was a solicitor. It must have been he, whom Dracula hired as his agent, as the Countess Elizabeth had said. Harker must have somehow escaped Dracula's castle in the Carpathians.

Renfield shuddered at the thought. Enough to give one brain-fever indeed—he couldn't imagine how anyone, mortal or Un-Dead, could escape the Count. There must be a great deal more to that young man than met the eye.

Yet for all their cleverness, he thought despairingly, for all their smug self-satisfaction, neither Van Helsing, nor Seward, nor His Handsome New Lordship Godalming, nor any of the others had seen the danger of the Count coming in behind them, taking Mrs. Harker while they were away counting earth-boxes and congratulating themselves. Mrs. Harker who was innocent and kind, who had gone walking through the midnight streets of a strange town to save her friend from social embarassment and chill. The Count must not have killed her—Van Helsing showed no sign of even suspecting that a thing might be amiss. So there was to be another slow crucifixion, another tortuous game of cat-and-mouse, such as he had played with Lucy.

And with Nomie, a hundred and ten years before.

"Don't you know me?" Van Helsing asked, clearly fishing, Renfield thought, for more compliments about revolutionizing theraputics by his brilliant theories.

"I know you well enough," snapped Renfield. "You are the old fool Van Helsing. I wish you would take your yourself and your idiotic brain theories somewhere else. Damn all thick-headed Dutchmen!"

Are you all blind?!?

Evidently they were, for when Seward came in a little later, and tried to engage him in a long discussion of devouring life and consuming souls, he, too, seemed blithe and cheerful, more cheerful than Renfield had seen him since the night of his disastrous dinner for Lucy and her mother, as if the problem of Dracula were well on the way to being solved.

He will come back! Don't you understand that he will come back?

Renfield was hard put to keep his voice normal, to keep from shouting at Seward or striking him in sheer blazing frustration, as the doctor talked of lives and souls as if he knew the slightest thing about them. But at the stroke of noon—the brief period at which the vampire could move and have power—flies began to buzz in at the window again, and spiders creep out of the wall.

Maybe I have to sacrifice poor Mrs. Harker, thought Renfield, chewing wearily on a bluebottle, *to save Catherine, and Vixie. It is after all for their sakes that I am doing all of this.* Mrs. Harker's kindness had touched his lonely pain, reminding him of how long it had been, since any woman had spoken kindly to him . . .

Any living woman.

Oh, my darling, Renfield whispered, *the time is coming. When this is done, and poor Mrs. Harker is his, I shall ask that he let me out of here as a reward, that he let me go. Then I will return to you, and we will all three of us be free.*

The thought brought him comfort for a time. He returned to catching flies with a lighter heart.

* * *

Seward put an extra guard in the corridor that night. Renfield saw Harker return late, and prayed that the presence of Mina's husband would be enough, to keep the Count away. Yet he watched by the window in the deeps of the night, and saw the thread of mist creep across the garden, crawl like a vaporous serpent up the wall, through the chinks in the window casement. Out in the corridor he could hear Hardy's snoring deepen— Nomie had told him of how the Count could command sleep, paralyzing the limbs of his victims or those who sought to guard them. He remembered his dream, of Seward sleeping like a dead man on Lucy's mauve satin sofa, while through the open door in the dim firelight the Count drank Lucy's blood.

The Count neither materialized, nor troubled to speak to

him. Only the mist flowed across the floor, and beneath the door of Renfield's cell, while Renfield crouched on the bed watching it in sickened silence. When it had passed, he fumbled open his boxes, devoured every spider and fly within them.

Catherine, he thought, *oh my beloved, forgive me! And Mrs. Harker, my dear sweet Madame Mina, forgive me, too!*

The cold deepened. The little camel-back clock in Seward's study spoke three sweet tones. But sleep would not come, and instead of lessening with Dracula's departure from the house—as surely he must have departed already?—Renfield's agitation grew.

Mist gathered in the garden, before his window.

Dear God, has he come back for me? Come back to give me my reward?

The red glint of eyes.

Six of them.

Renfield flattened against the wall in terror.

They took shape, and seeped around the casement of the window like a mist.

"So this is how you say, 'help'?" The Countess Elizabeth strode forward in a towering rage, and Renfield buried his face in the meagre pillow of his bed. "We say, that our erring husband is not to go about England taking other wives who please him better, and this is how you go about serving us? By saying, 'Come,' when he comes knocking at your window like a lover singing a serenade? Get your face out of your bedclothes and sit up like a man!"

Renfield obeyed. The Countess's eyes blazed red as fire, her lips were drawn back over fangs like a wolf's. Sarike, at her shoulder, grinned though she probably couldn't understand the Countess's thick-accented German, and licked her sharp teeth.

There was blood on the dark ruffles of her walking-dress, both dried and fresh.

"What could I do?" whispered Renfield. "He would kill me!"

"He will kill you, once he can come into this house!" retorted the Countess. "But until you invited him in, you were as safe as if you sat on the altar of a church!"

"There are a dozen madmen whose minds our husband could have touched in dreaming," broke in Nomie. "You know what he is, with those who pledge their word and then betray it."

"Coward!" The Countess's voice was like the hiss of a serpent. Her red eyes narrowed, and she reached to Renfield with her clawed hand, and picked the wing of a fly from the corner of his mouth. "Glutton. You would betray us for pottage."

For lives, thought Renfield, too paralyzed with terror even to whimper. *For Catherine.*

"So now he drinks the blood of this—this *Englishwoman*. This *schoolmistress*. This type-writer lady whose husband leaves her alone, like a fool, to be cuckolded by the Lord of Darkness! He of all men should know better than that."

Sarike's smile widened and her eyes gleamed with demon evil, and she said, "Jonathan," in her sweet crystal voice.

The Countess sniffed. "He'll be her first kill—I'll bet you my pearl earrings on that." Her eyes slid sidelong to Nomie. "And I'll further bet that the bitch won't share."

Then she looked back at Renfield. "*If* he completes his kill. Pah! He fools with them and fools with them, whispers to their dreams, until they come willingly, swooning at his feet."

Nomie looked away.

The Countess went on, "You know, do you not, that it is only those who drink the vampire's blood in their turn, who become vampires—and then only those who have the strength, the will, to hold on as death rolls over them; to hold on to the will of their master. That is why he seduces them. He makes them love him too much to let go of their lives."

In the silence that followed these words, Nomie gazed out the window as if she were enduring a beating; only once, very quickly, she pressed her hand to her mouth.

"She has a core of steel in her, that one." The Countess's deep voice was hard. Her black hair, where it trailed in tendrils from her chignon, made streaks of night across a face white as the waning moon. "He will use her against me—against us," she added, with a glance at her sisters. To Renfield she said, with an outstretched finger of command, "Stop him."

Renfield gasped. "How?"

"By doing what you should have done last night. By raising an alarm. By showing some courage."

"I am a madman, in case you haven't noticed!" protested Renfield. "I am locked in a cell! I did everything I could, everything!"

"You did what you could to be taken out of the house," retorted the Countess. "I notice that not one word passed your lips concerning the precious *Madame Mina's* being taken out of the house." Renfield reflected that this business of seeing things in dreams obviously worked both ways. "That imbecile poet Gelhorn could have done better."

"Then why didn't he?" Renfield straightened up a little from his crouch. "Why don't you send *him* to rescue Mrs. Harker, or to warn her husband of the danger in which she stands?"

"If you'd ever seen him trying to get his luggage back from a railway porter, you wouldn't be asking that."

"Because you are the braver man," said Nomie softly, and turned back from the window to look at him. "And the more intelligent one, I think. Do this for us, and we will do what we can—*I* will do what *I* can—to have you released, or to sunder these bars and spirit you away."

"Fail," added the Countess grimly, "and it will be the worse for you, to a degree that you cannot even imagine."

And Sarike, like an animal, only smiled again and licked her lips.

Then they were gone.

* * *

Renfield saw Mrs. Harker briefly the following day, pale and thin, like tea after too much water has been added to the teapot. Her eyes were sunken and bruised-looking, as if from too much sleep or too little. Other than that brief glimpse, as she stood on the gravel driveway bidding farewell to Lord Godalming and Mr. Morris—God knew where they were off to, Harker had left early in the morning—he saw none of the little band of conspirators against the vampire Count. According to Dr. Hennessey, who made Seward's rounds for him, Van Helsing had gone to the British Museum. Seward himself was closeted in his study, making preparations and plans of his own.

Somehow, Renfield couldn't bring himself to tell Hennessey of Mrs. Harker's danger: Hennessey who reeked of gin and whose smutty-minded speculations about the female patients had been audible to Renfield night after night when the Irishman had chatted with the keepers.

In any case, there was no telling what he'd do with that information.

Though the day was chill, flies swarmed to the little sugar he put out. He didn't even trouble to put them in boxes, simply caught them and ate them, desperate to increase his strength, to build up the forces of his own life to meet what he knew would come.

Seward has to make evening rounds, thought Renfield. *I'll tell him then. That will be time to get her out of the house.*

But Lord Godalming and Morris arrived just at sunset, met by Seward in the avenue. *He must have been watching from his study window.* An hour later Van Helsing's cab pulled up at the door, and some time after that, Hennessey came again on Seward's rounds: "Very took up with Dr. Van Helsing, he is," the Irishman reported. "As well he might be—great man like that. And he was most kind, most kind indeed, when I told him at supper last night of my own observations and experiments with training the demented to behave themselves. Why, he said he'd seldom encountered a system as original as mine!"

Renfield could almost feel pity for the elderly Dutchman, trapped at the supper-table with Hennessey in full cry.

"If you would, Dr. Hennessey," said Renfield, "could you please tell Dr. Seward that I must see him. As soon as may be, this evening certainly, before the house retires to bed. It is vital."

"'Course I'll tell him," agreed Hennessey. "'Course I will." He unscrewed and sipped his flask as he went out the door. Renfield could hear him trading a crude joke with Simmons in the hall. *I might just as well,* Renfield reflected wearily, *have asked one of my spiders to take a message.*

Seward didn't come. Harker arrived at nine, springing up the steps like Sir Lancelot after dispatching a not-very-fearsome dragon. Renfield waited at the window, watching the reflected splotches of golden light from the asylum's windows perish one by one against the night-shrouded laurels, until only one remained.

Somewhere in the darkness, a dog began to bark. Other dogs,

everywhere in the neighborhood, took up the cry, and in the padded room, muffled by the coir mats of the walls, Lord Alyn howled as if in response. Like the dogs, the other patients added their voices to his, Renfield picking them out as Cockneys pick out the voices of the City's churchbells.

> *Oranges and lemons,*
> *Say the bells of St. Clemmons.*
> *Demons scratch at my door,*
> *Screams Emily Strathmore.*
> *How the dark night has fall'n,*
> *Howls Andrew, Lord Alyn.*

Mist began to creep over the garden wall. In the veiled sky, the moon was barely more than a fingernail, yet Renfield saw clearly the slow seep of those winding vapors toward the house. Terror filled him. He rushed to the door, pressed his face to the judas, but Simmons was gone from the hall; it seemed every man on the wing had begun to scream and pound the walls, and Renfield's cries were swept away in the not-uncommon torrent that Seward and Hennessey had long since ceased to hear.

"Dr. Seward!" Renfield screamed. "He is coming! He is coming! Get Mrs. Harker out of the house!"

The gas-lights showed him a hallway blank and empty as if it were a thousand feet underground.

Chill touched him, like an evil wind. Turning, Renfield saw the first curls of mist seeping under the casement, flowing down the wall.

He turned back to the window, spread out his hands. "Get out! I forbid you to enter this place!"

Outside the window, the mists congealed in the thin glow of

the moon. Renfield saw the glaring red eyes, the red mouth open and laughing, a terrible laugh. Saw the sharpness of the white teeth.

"Get out, I tell you! I renounce you and all your works! Begone, and trouble this house no more!"

And in his mind, Wotan's voice whispered against the pounding leitmotif of Wagner, *It is too late for that.*

The mists pooled, where the small glow of the gas-light from the hall fell through the judas. Flowed upward in a column, in which burned two crimson eyes.

Renfield shrieked, "Leave her alone, for she has never harmed you!" and threw himself at the shadow that was forming within those mists, behind the burning eyes.

Chapter Twenty

In agony, Renfield dreamed.

He saw Mina Harker in her room—it had the same wall-paper as Dr. Seward's study and the hall in the men's wing of the house—and the sickly light of that fingernail moon barely touched the edges of the window-frame, the bedposts, the china ewer on the dresser. Jonathan Harker lay beside her, so deeply asleep that Renfield thought the Count must have broken his back, as he had broken Renfield's . . .

. . . broken it and left him lying in agony, dying in a pool of blood on the floor of his cell.

From a great distance Renfield was aware of himself, of pain like a thousand sawing red-hot knives. He was aware, just as vividly, of the Count, standing beside the bed in the guest-room downstairs.

The Count held Mina Harker in the iron circle of his arm, the black of his clothing and his cloak like enfolding storm-cloud around the simple white linen of her night-dress. Her head lay back against his shoulder, her black hair, escaping from its braid, a marvelous inky torrent flowing to her waist. She made no sound, raised no cry, but her dark eyes were open, staring up at the Count's face in revulsion, horror, fear that had nothing in it of panic blankness.

She knew what was being done to her.

The Count's head was bent over hers, his mouth pressed to her throat. Blood ran down her breast onto her night-dress.

* * *

More pain. The dream splintered as if every bone in Renfield's body were shattering with it. Renfield opened his eyes, saw Van Helsing's face.

He couldn't breathe. His whole body felt as if every joint, every muscle were locked in vises of incandescent iron. Tangled memories of Dracula hurling him to the floor, beating his head on the boards.

He tasted blood in his mouth, smelled it everywhere in the room. Lamplight burned his eyes. Quincey Morris had a lamp, so did Lord Godalming, both men tousled in pyjamas, hair hanging in their eyes. Van Helsing was dressed, in shirtsleeves, Seward likewise. There was blood on their sleeves, glaringly dark in the orange light, like Mrs. Harker's, trickling down her night-dress.

"I'll be quiet, Doctor," Renfield whispered. "Tell them to take off the strait-waistcoat. I have had a terrible dream."

I dreamed I was insane.

I dreamed that I was locked in a madhouse, from April to the threshhold of bitter winter, with no one to care for me, no one to love me, no one to touch me or talk to me in the deep of the night.

I dreamed of Catherine, lying asleep in the moonlight of our room . . .

He blinked. "It has left me so weak that I cannot move. What's wrong with my face? It feels swollen . . . smarts . . ." He tried to move his head, and darkness came over him.

"Tell us your dream, Mr. Renfield," said Van Helsing softly.

"Van Helsing," Renfield whispered. "It is good of you to be here. Water . . ."

Darkness again. Darkness and pain, and the yawning abyss where more pain waited for him—pain and the horrors of things he could barely see and didn't want to. Then brandy burned his lips, and he opened his eyes again. Van Helsing was still there.

"No," Renfield whispered. "It was no dream."

He was dying, and the knowledge gave him a kind of exhilaration, a lightness. There was nothing further that Dracula could do to him. *Catherine,* he thought, *Catherine, I have failed you.*

But Mina, at least . . . Mina—Mrs. Harker—could be saved.

Freed by the knowledge of coming death, he told them of Dracula's visits, stammeringly at first, then with greater confidence. Of the flies, of Dracula's promises; of the Count's coming that night and of how he had tried to stop him, to save Mrs. Harker who had been so kind. *Surely,* he thought, as he tried to gather breath and strength to speak again, *surely now one of them—Van Helsing—will understand, and will go to Catherine, will understand the danger she and Vixie are in, will save them.*

But as he was trying to form the words, Van Helsing straightened up away from him: "We know the worst now," he said to the others. "He is here, and we know his purpose! It may not be too late! Let us be armed . . ."

Renfield whispered desperately, "Catherine . . . Promise me . . ."

But they were already rushing to the door, crowding one another in it in their desperation to go, the lamplight jostling their shadows wildly over the walls.

"Please . . ." Renfield breathed.

But they were gone. He heard their footsteps thudding down the hall, felt the jarring of their race down the stairs. The gaslight of the hall fell through the open door over him, the thin distant howling of some of the women patients sweeping through the building like the whistle of wind.

He thought, despairingly, *Catherine, forgive me! I've botched it all up! I only did it for you. It was all for you. And now I will never see you again.*

He could not move, and the tears that flowed from his eyes ran down the sides of his face to the bloodied boards of the floor.

Catherine . . .

Mist curled before his eyes.

Dracula, he thought. *Wotan. He has done with Mrs. Harker and he has come to drink my life. Come for the final insult, the final triumph . . .*

Red eyes glowing in the mist.

Then the pale oval of a gentle face, materializing out of the reflected gas-light of the hall. Fair hair like the sunlight that beats on the yellow rocks of the Khyber Pass. The red light died, leaving the eyes that looked into his as blue as pale sapphires, like the deeps of the up-country sky above the Simla Hills.

She asked, "Will you stay, or go?"

Renfield's tears flowed harder, grief and guilt and pain. He managed to whisper, ". . . work yet to do. I must . . . save them. Help me."

Without another word, Nomie bent her slim body down, and like gentle kisses drank the blood that was still trickling from the gashes Dracula's nails had opened in Renfield's face, from the open wound where Van Helsing had trephined the skull to relieve the haemorrhage inside. Then she undid the pearl buttons of her sleeve, pushing the fragile figured lawn up to reveal an arm no less white than the fabric, and with her long nails slit open the veins.

Somewhere in the house came the rending crash of a door being broken open, men's voices shouting. Nomie turned her head, listening for an instant, then pressed her bleeding arm to Renfield's lips. "Trust me," she breathed, "and drink."

Her blood tasted coppery on his tongue, sweet and salt at once, like the blood of the men who'd died in the Mutiny, all those years ago under the broiling Indian sun.

"He is ours," whispered the Countess's voice, and opening his eyes again, Renfield saw the other two standing behind her. "If he will be so, he will be of us all, my sister." Kneeling, she ripped the black silk sleeve of her dress, and opened the flesh beneath; while Renfield drank of the blood of her arm, she pressed her lips to his throat. He felt her teeth tear into his flesh, but the sensation was distant, as all sensation was failing.

Sarike opened her bodice, tore the vein above the dusky satin of her breast; lapped the blood off his face like a greedy cat.

"You are ours now," whispered the Countess, kneeling above him, her uncoiled black hair hanging down to brush his face. "We will carry you through the dark of death. Your soul will be cradled within ours, until such time as it returns to your death-changed flesh. But a portion of that soul will remain forever in our keeping, so long as we ourselves inhabit this world. Do you understand?"

Renfield's lips formed the words, *I understand.*

Somewhere in the house a woman screamed, the frantic

scream that had nothing in it of insanity, but of too-clear awareness. *Mrs. Harker's voice,* thought Renfield, drifting on the bor-
derlands of oblivion. Men's voices clamoring, then Mrs. Harker's
crying above them, "No! No, Jonathan, you must not leave me!"

Cold began to seep into the room. At first, Renfield thought
it was only his own body sinking into death, but the Countess
turned her head sharply, whispered, "He is coming." She and
Sarike stood. Nomie remained kneeling beside Renfield, and the
Countess reached down and dragged the girl to her feet. For a
moment Nomie's eyes met Renfield's, before all three women
faded into the thready glimmer of the moonlight.

The next moment, the Count was in the room. His face was
like a steel mask, with blood smeared down his mouth and
streaking the front of his shirt. Shirt and the black silk waistcoat
above it were open to the waist, and a bleeding gash on the pec-
toral muscle showed Renfield where Mrs. Harker's mouth must
have been pressed, to drink of the vampire's blood. In his cloak
Renfield could smell the clinging remains of her dusting-powder,
vanilla and sandalwood mingling with the reek of gore.

"And as for you," Dracula whispered, standing over him, a
towering shadow, like Satan rising up from the floor of Hell.
"Judas. Are you like them now, who pit their puny brains against
me? Who would go against me, with their weak mortality? Who
would separate me from what is my own? See how I deal with
those who would betray me!"

He bent down and lifted Renfield as if he were a child, raised
him over his head. In final despair, Renfield blocked his lips, his
mind, from screaming Catherine's name as he was hurled down
into darkness.

CHAPTER TWENTY-ONE

Catherine!

Renfield's eyes opened in panic. He saw only darkness, felt the close bounds of the coffin against his arms and his thighs, but that didn't trouble him. *Trust,* Nomie had said, and he had trusted.

It had all taken place, exactly as the Countess Elizabeth had promised: the dark terror, the horrifying agony of separating from his dying body, the dark and hideous intimacy of those three minds cradling his soul among them . . .

And then the dreams.

Dear God, the dreams!

Catherine . . .

Renfield brought up his hands to the coffin-lid just above his breast, and thrust. In life he had been a strong man. The lid gave way like cardboard, with a sound that was shocking in the deep silence.

The damp melancholy smell of dying leaves, of turned earth,

came to him above the mouldy stink of mortality and wet stone and rats.

Renfield was a little surprised. He was in the family tomb at Highgate. He recognized it, from when they'd buried his parents. He'd have bet money Lady Brough and Georgina would have given instructions that he be sent to a medical college for dissection.

Or was it beneath the dignity of the Brough family to have even a disgraced in-law anatomized by such low creatures as students?

Looking back, with a sense that was not quite sight, he saw that the coffin was of cheap pine. Apparently they drew the line at putting forth a single extra penny on a mere tradesman, an India-merchant who'd had the temerity to refuse their advice about how his daughter should be brought up. As a living man he could have ripped his way out of it, never mind one of a vampire's preternatural strength. The clothes he wore were those he'd been found in, wandering the streets of London raving last April. They hadn't even cleared out the pockets: his handkerchief, a few bus-tickets, an old key.

The lingering smell of parafin within the tomb, and the freshness of the tracked mud near the door, told him he'd been put there that day. Even in total darkness he knew it was sundown that had wakened him. His back no longer hurt, nor his face. He raised his hand to feel his skull above the right ear, where Van Helsing had trephined to relieve the pressure of the blood, and the skin was smooth.

Had they even noticed? he wondered. Or had Seward been so shocked and disoriented by Dracula's assault on poor Mrs. Harker that he'd simply signed the death certificate and left that drunken imbecile Hennessey to take care of the details?

All this went through his mind in a few distracted moments, as he stood before the tomb's marble door. None of it mattered to him, nor formed more than a candle's weak glow against the blazing sun of the thought: *I must get to Catherine.*

The horror of his dream hammered in his mind.

The door of the tomb was locked. Renfield thought he could have broken it, but he'd seen the other vampires pass through tiny cracks, keyholes and slits, in the form of mist. If they could do it, surely he could, too.

It was a most curious sensation.

He was, as he'd thought, in Highgate Cemetery.

Catherine, he thought again. *I must get to her. I must tell her . . .*

He began to run.

*   *   *

He had dreamed about Catherine, dreamed terrible things. Georgina and Lady Brough were going to take Vixie, take her and lock her up, send her away. Teach her shame and squeamishness. Teach her that everything she loved and felt and cared about was wrong.

He had dreamed about Catherine weeping, weeping until she was ill, by the glow of the lamps in the bedroom of the house they'd taken in Kensington, under the name of Marshmire. Renfield had pleaded with her, pointed out again and again to her that they'd covered their tracks well. They'd made provisions, taken other bank accounts, established still other names, other identities . . .

They'll never find us, he said to her, and she'd only shaken her head, her long red hair shining in the soft glow of the gaslights:

They will. They will.

The dreams turned to horror after that.

He had dreamed he'd gone mad, had been locked up in an asylum full of fools, only the fools weren't in the cells, but running the place. Drunken fools like Hennessey, or stubborn small-minded hidebound ones like Seward. Fools who couldn't see the larger world if it loomed before them and bit them and drank their blood.

Catherine, he whispered, as he ran—ran lightly, half-invisible, like a great jumble of flying newspaper whipped along by the wind, as a man would run in dreams. Homebound clerks turned to stare at him as they clambered aboard omnibuses or clustered on the dark wind-swept corners; costermongers and tattered women in black shawls shrank back into the glare of lights from the public-houses and cafés. *Catherine, I'm coming!* He passed through the dark of Regent's Park, the bright-lit streets of the West End, dodging hansoms and growlers, omnibuses and carriages. In Hyde Park the cats fled from him, and dogs barked wildly at his passing shadow.

Kensington. Abingdon Road. The dark brick face of the house that belonged on paper to Mr. Marshmire—"Oh, pick a gloomier name, why don't you?" Catherine had teased, laughing. Lightless windows. Locked doors.

She was inside. Renfield knew they were both inside.

On either side the tall pleasant houses were gas-lit. The autumn evening, still early, was cold. Renfield was conscious of the chill without particularly minding it, though he remembered how cold he had found England, how bone-gnawingly damp, after the languid heat of India. He had heard it said—by the Countess?—that vampires could not enter any place unless and until they had been invited, but it was his house, he had bought it.

Was that why vampires generally started their feeding on their own families?

He stood on the steps, looking down at the windows of the kitchen areaway and up at those of the drawing-room above, dark as the eyes of a dead man. He had run from Highgate across London to Kensington, close to five miles. Yet he felt no weariness.

Only enormous hunger.

He passed into the house.

It was as he remembered it, that last night he'd been there. They'd bought it furnished from its previous owners, lest Georgina or Lady Brough grow suspicious. Vixie had whooped with laughter over the old-fashioned furniture, the stuffy Biblical oleographs on the walls. To Vixie it had all been a giant adventure, a gamine delight in outfoxing the grandmother and aunts she had always loathed.

Renfield called out, "Vixie!" into the stuffy silence of the dark house, but received no reply. "Catherine!"

Only the smell of dust, and of mice, and of rooms unaired.

Renfield climbed the stairs. On the second floor, Vixie's water-colors hung in the drawing-room, her sitar propped on the window-seat where she'd used to practice it. The bright cushions Catherine had made bloomed like incongruous flowers on the black slick horsehair of the previous tenant's chairs. On the third floor, Catherine's yellow silk kimono lay across the foot of the unmade bed, and Renfield knelt, pressed the sheets to his face, then the silk, inhaling the lingering scents of her perfume, her body, her hair. It was as if she had lain there only last night. But he knew it had been longer than that.

On the third floor, Vixie's bed was likewise disordered in the small room that had been hers. Her brush still lay on the little dresser, and the jeweled combs she'd used to put up her hair. Lavender kid gloves, like withered flowers. The torn-up pieces of the letter that Bolton, Renfield's solicitor, had delivered to her from her grandmother Brough, still on the floor where she'd left them.

Renfield picked one up, saw in the hated handwriting the name of Madame Martine's Select Academy for Young Females, in Lausanne, and the phrase, ". . . Wormidge will be by in the morning to take you to the station . . ."

Slowly, Renfield descended the stairs.

The other papers Bolton had delivered from Wormidge lay where he'd left them back in April, on the marble-topped dresser in the hall.

He called out softly, "Catherine?" and only the rustle of mice answered him, from the open pantry door.

Through the pantry he descended to the kitchen. *It's a cold night,* he thought. *The servants might have the night off. They'll be keeping warm in the kitchen.*

Mice scattered at his tread; the stink of them rose to him like a cloud. Split bins, chewed-open sacks, apples and cheese long spoiled, the nasty stink of the mortality of all things. Renfield looked about him at the dark clammy room, the unwashed dishes piled on the counters—had Catherine fired the servants altogether? His gaze went three times past the little door that led to the sub-cellar, because of course there was no reason for them to go down there.

But it always came back.

It was locked. The key was in the pocket of his jacket, with the handkerchief and the bus tickets. He could have passed through the keyhole or under the door in a mist, but he unlocked it, and descended the slippery damp steps.

They didn't want to be found, he told himself. *They don't dare be found. That's why they're sleeping in the sub-cellar.*

So Georgina won't find them.

So Lady Brough won't find them.

So they won't take Vixie away.

"Catherine?" he said softly, hoping against hope that his dream had been, in fact, only a dream.

But it hadn't.

He'd known that, from the moment he'd opened his eyes in the tomb.

They were where he'd left them. There was a table in the middle of the room where boots or silverware could be cleaned, or wine transferred from bottles to decanter. That night back in April he'd laid every tablecloth he could find on it, before bringing them down there to sleep, and the damask cloths were brown and crusted with the fluids of their mortality. The whole hot summer's worth of dead flies crunched like little curls of parched paper beneath his feet. It had been six months, but he could still distinguish between them, by Catherine's beautiful red hair, and Vixie's dark curls.

Renfield knelt at his wife's side, gathered up a double-handful of her hair, and kissed it. "I'm sorry, Catherine," he whispered. "I'm so sorry."

Standing again, he took off his jacket, pushed up his shirt-sleeve, to tear open the vein of his arm with his nails, as Nomie had done, and Dracula. He held his arm over Catherine's mouth and let the blood drip down onto her lips—or what was left of her lips. The coroner had taken away his notebooks, but he knew exactly how many flies he'd consumed—three thousand, four hundred and eight—plus nine hundred spiders, six hundred and fifteen moths, seven sparrows, and four mice, and a little tiny bit of Dr. Seward's blood, though that probably didn't count. Surely life enough?

Wasn't it?

Please?

He didn't know how long after that it was—not midnight, he didn't think—when he felt the cold whiff of mist flowing down the sub-cellar stairs. He was still weeping, and did not turn around. He knew it was Nomie.

She said, "I am sorry, Ryland."

"I hoped it was a dream," he said, after some time. "Just a dream I had. Part of my madness, like the letters I wrote her. Six months now I've hoped." He turned then and looked at her, a blurred pale shape through the blindness of his tears. "Can you do it? I've only eaten flies—mice—moths . . . You've consumed life, real life, men and women. You are strong . . ."

"No one of us is that strong, Ryland. Not my lord Dracula, not those dark ancients that haunt the mountains of Thibet and the deserts of Egypt. We are the Angels of Death, and the Angels of Un-Death—the Choosers of the Slain, you have called us. We can avert death, but we cannot bring them back through the Gate, once they have passed through to the Other Side."

She laid her hand on Renfield's as she spoke, and turning, he caught her in his arms and clung to her like a drowning man, weeping against the golden silk of her hair.

"They were going to take Vixie," he stammered, his body shaking with sobs. The words came out of him as if, like a sick man, his body had to expel them or die. "Lady Brough—her vile solicitors—Catherine's hag of a sister . . . They dug up old scandals, old rumors about me when I was in India. They were having me declared unfit to care for my own daughter! And because Catherine was a free soul and had lived an unconventional life, long before she met me, she, too, was to be disbarred from ever seeing Vixie, was to be cut out of the family. That was what they wanted. Her money, and control of mine! I did it only to keep Vixie from them, to keep them from killing her by inches, smothering her spirit, turning her into one of them and worse in their damned Select Academies! *I would rather be dead, Papa,* she said, the night those damned letters came, those damned papers . . . The night Bolton brought them to the house. *I would rather be dead.* Those were her very words."

"And you killed her?"

Renfield nodded. "I was in red rage. Bolton had the temerity, the nerve, to follow me to this house. I knocked his brains out with the fire-shovel, there in the hall. My mind was swimming with the smell of his blood. Blood has always . . . had that effect upon me," he added, a little hesitantly. "In India I used to kill . . . kill . . . snakes, and . . . and mongeese . . . and drink their blood. I came upstairs and she was weeping, weeping herself sick on her bed, and I . . . I did it very gently. Broke her neck . . . held her against me as she died, as she . . . she passed beyond where they could get her, change her, make her what she would hate to be. She was such a free soul, Vixie. Such a beautiful soul. Then Catherine came in, and screamed . . ."

His arms tightened around Nomie, and he wept afresh. "I thought if I ate enough flies, consumed enough life . . ."

"You did what you could," Nomie whispered, and held him close as fresh gusts of weeping shook him like a storm-tossed oak. "You only did as you knew how. But it is done. You did your best, and your bravest, but they cannot be brought back."

"Then send me with them!" sobbed Renfield. "Let me go, too. They were my life!"

"And your life is over." At the sound of that deep cold contralto, Nomie and Renfield broke apart. The Countess and Sarike stood on the steps of the sub-cellar, the garnets in the Countess's hair twinkling darkly, like droplets of blood. "You are now one of us."

Revulsion seared through Renfield like a bitter poison. Shoving Nomie from him, he snatched up from its shelf the long, sharp chisel that the Cook had used to open crates, drove it with all his strength toward his chest . . .

And doubled over, paralyzed with shock, before the iron touched his body. Gasped as if his brain had been sliced apart with broken glass, as if his body were turned inside-out by icy claws, and in his mind as well as in his ears he heard the Countess's voice: "Don't."

Sobbing, he tried to press the chisel toward his flesh again and pain—and something worse and stronger than pain—closed around his body and his mind like a crushing vise.

She said, "Drop it."

He was back within her mind, where he had clung like a terrified child while his body died. He saw his hands open. Heard the iron clatter on the flagstone floor.

Sounds came out of his mouth that weren't words and were too suffocated to be cries. Still her grip tightened, her rage insupportable, slicing him as a grape is sliced by the sharpest of silver razors. At her will, he dropped to his knees—it was worse than dying, a thousand times worse—at her will, he sank to his belly on the wet stone floor. At her will, he crawled to her, where she stepped down to the bottom of the stairs—hating himself, hating her, fighting and sweating and hurting every inch of the way and not able to keep himself from doing exactly as she willed—and kissed her feet.

He wanted to bite them. To tear her Achilles' tendons with his teeth. She was aware of his want, knowing him as intimately as if they had been lifelong lovers, and laughed at him; laughed harder as she made him bring up his own arm and tear at the bare flesh of his hand, worrying it like a dog.

"Be glad it's your own flesh I'm making you eat," said her voice in his ears, "and not that of your wife and your daughter."

He knew she could do it. When she let him go, he lay on the floor in smears of his own blood and wept.

"Go on," jeered the Countess, "weep. Weep now until all the tears are out of you, once and for all. You are now our servant, Renfield. You were the one who clung to us, through the darkness of death. It was for this we kept you back from passing through the Gate. Do you understand?"

He could barely get the words out. "I understand, Lady."

"You will do as you are bid, for you will find that you cannot do otherwise."

He would have kept his silence but couldn't. The words were squished out of him as if he were a frog upon which she trod. "Yes, Lady." To the bottom of his soul he understood then how they hated Dracula, hated him with the hatred of intimacy, and why they had pursued him to this land. Why they would never, could never, leave him.

Then like an icy storm-blast the room grew cold above him. He raised his head in shock and terror even as the Countess turned, shrinking back from the column of darkness that loomed behind them, above them on the steps.

"And you, my beautiful ones," said a harsh, deep voice, "could do with a lesson yourselves, to do as you have been bid."

And like the fall of night, Dracula came down into the cellar.

Letter, R. M. Renfield to his wife
4 October

My most beloved Catherine,

My most beloved wife—

I will be leaving England soon. In my misguided efforts to somehow make right the terrible wrong that I did you, I have put myself into the thrall of monsters.

The Countess Elizabeth is fearsome, cold and deadly as a steel blade, yet she pales in comparison to her husband, Dracula the Impaler, Viovode of Transylvania in the cruelest time of its history. The meeting between them can only be compared to the clash of storm winds against raging tidal floods, elemental, violent, appalling. He flung her to the floor as if she were a rag-doll, struck the others and hurled them against the walls with such force as to destroy the shelves, cursed them in German and in Magyar. He made the three of them crawl, as the Countess had made me crawl. My soul—if I can still speak of myself as possessing such a thing—trembles for poor Mrs. Harker, if and when he should claim her as his own.

"I am pursued by human rats, by the yapping curs of this land," he stormed at the three women, who crouched bloody on the floor before his boots. "Jealous suitors all, swearing vengeance, as the impotent Turk and the beaten Slav threw stones at me when I rode in triumph through their towns! Dogs! I spit upon their vengeance!" There was a fading red scar across his forehead, where, Nomie had told me, Jonathan Harker had struck him with a shovel as he lay sleeping in his coffin, and the front of his vest and coat had been ripped open, as if by the stroke of a knife.

"Vengeance! It is they who shall learn the meaning of that word to their sorrow! I have taken the soul of this girl they loved, and I have in my hand the soul of the other. She is mine, whatever time it is that she die, if it be seventy years from now! They play against me with their tiny mortal lives, but it is I who bear as my weapon the sword of Time. Against that they can do naught."

His red eyes raked the three women and he stooped down, caught the Countess Elizabeth by the thick coils of her hair, dragged her head back so that her eyes met his. "And you, wilful sluts! You dared pursue? You dared leave the castle that is my fortress, to follow me to this place?"

"And you dared to leave us?" retorted the Countess, and Dracula struck her across the face, so that blood trickled from her lip.

"Silence, hag!" In their locked gazes there was a fearful understanding, the fermented knowledge of the very depths of one another's minds, as only hatred can be when it is rooted in the confidences once exchanged in love. Then he thrust her to the floor again.

"In one way and one way only is it well that you have come," he said. "The ant can be crushed beneath the boot, but still the bite of an ant can poison the limb, and so kill the man. I return now to my own country, to Transylvania—to the place that I left in your charge, faithless trulls! You will go before me, to make ready my fortress." The red gaze moved to Nomie, crouching with bowed head, "And you will travel behind me—with that cringing Judas who once called me Master!—and you will pick off any who straggle or lag. For they will follow." And he laughed, a hollow and dreadful sound. "They will follow to their deaths."

He reached into his coat and drew out a handful of banknotes and golden sovereigns, which he threw to the floor between the three women, the gold tingling musically on the stone.

His voice changed, and he drew the Countess to her feet, speaking to her in Hungarian rather than German as before, and I caught the words *haboru*—war—and *ver,* blood, spoken in the tones of tenderest love. He cupped her cheek in his hand, and swiftly turning her head, she bit the fleshy heel of his thumb, so that the blood spattered on his cuff.

At this he laughed, as if at some uproarious jest, and when I raised my head, he was gone.

* * *

Now they, too, are gone, my beloved, my treasure. I write this kneeling at your side. The Countess and Sarike have departed to find their little poet Gelhorn, who has all this time been meeting them for midnight suppers and walks along the Serpentine. They will make arrangements to cross the Channel under his care, since Van Helsing knows nothing of their presence in this country and will not be watching for them, and travel by rail back to Klausenberg, and so up the mountains to Dracula's castle once again.

Dracula himself will travel by ship, as he came to this country, packed in the single box of his native earth that Van Helsing and his cohorts have not found and sterilized with holy things.

After they had gone, I tried to comfort Nomie, whose face was cut and bruised by Dracula's violence. But she slipped away from me as mist. The night is deepening to morning's small hours. Soon I must return to Highgate, to the only earth that will give me rest.

A burning hunger rises in my flesh. I caught mice—nearly a dozen, fattened for months on the spoiled flour and rotting vegetables in this kitchen when the servants could not return to the locked house. I can now move with great speed and can, to some extent, dull their animal minds. As I have long suspected, their blood does indeed in part quench the ravening hunger of the vampire.

But only in part. I know not how long it will be before I, too, begin to kill the innocent, like the children that Lucy Westenra took in her state of revenant shock.

And so I must depart. I will return with fall of night, beloved. Mortality and the effects of time hold no horrors for me, and to me your face is as beautiful now as it was that first moment I saw you, at the lecture-hall in Leicester Square, in that gown of iris-colored silk. We depart for Transylvania, Nomie and I, probably next week. It depends on how long it takes Seward and young Lord Godalming to wind up their affairs in this country, and Van Helsing to make his preparations. With your permission I will come here to be with you every night until then. For six months I longed for nothing but to sit beside you and to look upon your lovely face, and now nothing can prevent me from doing so, for what time is left to me.

And if I can arrange it, that time will be short, please God.

Between enslavement to the Countess Elizabeth, and through her to the terrible Count, there is nothing whatsoever to choose. Hell itself cannot be as dreadful as that occupation for eternity.

Poor Lucy Westenra's suitors will be in pursuit of the Count, and in them lies my hope. They hunger for revenge as I do for blood. It will be no difficult matter to place myself in their path, to embrace the oblivion I seek, and the way through the Gate on whose other side you and Vixie wait.

My darling, I want nothing now but to be with you. When that is accomplished—when we do indeed meet on the Other Side—I can only beg that you understand, for I know that I cannot hope that you might forgive.

Still I remain, in spite of all, forever,

Your loving husband,
R.M.R.

Chapter Twenty-two

R.M.R.'s notes
5 October
17 mice, 6 rats, 3 moths
Flies scarce even in London with advancing cold.

Spider season. Although I have access now to the hot blood of rodents, I still find a special pleasure in the sharp sparkle of these predatory smaller fry. Though I do enjoy moths. Having only the night to hunt in, birds are no longer a possibility. Dogs I will not kill, though I have found that I can summon them with my thought, as Dracula summoned the wolf from the London Zoo to break through the shut windows of Hillingham and tear away Van Helsing's protective wreaths of garlic. Dogs are faithful, and it is ill to reward such innocent helpfulness with death. The cats with which Highgate abounds stare in disbelieving affront at my summons, then sneer at me and run away. A pity—Puss eats of many mice and sparrows in her life. Is that why she has nine of them?

6 October
22 mice, 4 rats, 18 spiders, 2 moths
In Regent's Park this evening a child of eleven or so accosted me, tawdrily clad in a grown woman's cast-offs. She fell into step with me, winked, and said, "Cold night, eh, guv?" and looking down into her calculating eyes I was filled with such blinding hunger, such overwhelming need, that I could literally smell the blood that coursed in her veins. I bared my teeth at her—like Dracula's, and the Countess's, and Nomie's now, long and sharp as a wolf's fangs—and widened my eyes like the horrors of a Kabuki mask, and snarled in a good imitation of Emily Strathmore when she was getting ready to slide into a fit, "Cold indeed, little posset." I lunged at her, giving her ample time to flee down the path, for indeed she needed a lesson, poor child, about better picking her clients.

But as I watched her go, I wondered how long it would be before I began simply to troll the streets of the East End in earnest, and take that poor child's older and more slatternly sisters as my victims. Though God knows, with the amount of alcohol and opiates I would imbibe with the blood I should undoubtedly stumble back to Highgate drunk as a muleteer. The blood of rats—the energy of their fierce little minds—lessens the desperate fire in my own veins, but it does not cure the scraping, searing need in me.

That need, Nomie tells me, is assuaged only by human blood, and the psychic inhalation of human death. It is from the death, as well as the blood, that we imbibe our strength. We need the one as greatly as we need the other. I do not know how long I can survive before I become even as Dracula is.

Was he different in his first century of Un-Life? His second?

Somehow I think not.

I pray that I will engineer my death—my true death—at the hands of Seward and Van Helsing before I become in my heart as he is now.

I was in Regent's Park to meet the Countess, Sarike, Nomie, and their human agent Gustav Gelhorn, whom I recognized at once, at one of the new cafés on the Circle near the Boating Lake. In the glowing jewel-box of lamps and passers-by that pasty-faced little man seemed more anaemic than ever, his pale blue eyes traveling with reverent adoration from the face of one woman to the face of the other, and barely glancing at my own. I am positive he made not the slightest association between the "Mr. Marshmire" who wrote him out a cheque for three hundred and fifty pounds on the Merchants' Bank to pay expenses for himself and his "beautiful spirits" to journey back to their native mountains, and the screaming wretch he had seen in the padded room at Rushbrook House.

He was a very unpleasant little man, a disciple of Gobineau and Marr and other writers of the Volkish Movement, and full of his own importance as a member of the "pure Aryan race." An astonishing combination of smug vanity and self-pity. At one point, in between endless ramblings about the "German race-soul" and the dire international plots of "degenerates" like Jews and homosexuals, he made reference to the "special circumstances" of the journey, with a covert glance at the Countess, who merely looked amused. Nomie said to him, "Our dear friend Marshmire is aware of our . . . limitations, Friend Gustav," at which he slid his gaze sidelong at me with wary disbelief not innocent of jealousy.

In my loftiest German, I said, "Because a man passes by an

English name, Herr Gelhorn, does not mean that he shares the soul of this island race of debased counter-jumpers. Did you think yourself the only man who has heard the Rhinemaidens sing, as they combed their hair upon the rocks in the moonlight? For the voices of the spirits of the German Race-Soul carry far, across rivers and mountains, and even the seas."

Gelhorn looked properly chastened, and for an instant I met Nomie's eyes and was hard put not to burst into laughter, at the shared mental picture of some fat American railroad baron waking in the night in his mail-order castle in Chicago crying, *The Rhinemaidens! The enchanted spirits of the German Race-Soul require my help!*

Gelhorn even mumbled, as we shook hands in parting, "Thank you, *mein Herr,* for your assistance to these spirits, these wandering elementals, in their quest across lands and seas. You and I are privileged beyond the part of most of the Mortal Race, to look upon their faces, to realize that the true spirits of the Fatherland still walk this earth and extend their friendship to men of pure blood."

His bespectacled gaze lingered reverently on the Countess, whom Sarike was helping into her very stylish sable pelisse— where Gelhorn thinks she acquired the two hundred guineas that such a garment costs, I cannot imagine. Rhine gold, perhaps?

"I swear to you," Gelhorn went on, "that I shall protect these spirits with my very life, on the cross-Channel boat, and on the train from Paris, until they are returned again to their sacred mountains."

I inclined my head, and let him pay the bill. I don't think he was aware that I—supposedly human—had sipped no more of the coffee than had the three representatives of the German Race-Soul he was helping. Nomie and I stood at the edge of the café's golden lights, and watched him escort the Countess and Sarike away into the thick mists that lay beneath the park's leafless trees.

"Fortunate for the Countess," I remarked, "that she found him," and Nomie regarded me with surprise.

"Fortune has little to do with the hunt, Ryland. To be vampire is to fascinate, men and women both. We lure by our beauty: it is how we hunt. We disarm the mind through the senses and the dreams. How else would we survive? Men see us, and follow, despite all they know, drawn by their need like your poor friend Jonathan. Else why would they go with us to lonely places in the dark, and yield to the kisses of a stranger? Will you hunt with me tonight?"

"The taking of lives has no savor for me, Nornchen," I answered—Little Norn, a jest between us: a sweet-faced sad little Valkyrie, riding with her sisters to choose who will be slain tonight. The protest was a complete lie and she saw it, glancing up into my face. When your soul has lain naked and helpless in the mind of another while you watch your body's death, there is no such thing as deceit. But she only smiled agreement at me, and said nothing. "I think I will return to Kensington, and sit for a time beside them whom I will never cease to love."

She touched my hand, and whispered, "Then give them greeting from me, and tell them I am glad, that they have found the path that leads to happiness."

And so saying she melted away into the lamplight and the fog. For a moment I heard a winnowing in the air, as if a bat was flying somewhere in the dark overhead. Then she was gone.

Letter, R. M. Renfield to his wife
7–8 October

My dearest one,

Please forgive my not coming to you tonight. I grudge the hours of my absence, the lost occasion stolen from our short time together, but now even more than when I hung chained in a strait-waistcoat to the wall of a padded room, I am not master of my own movements. Nomie begs your pardon for the necessity, a consideration which I find most sweet in her. She cannot, any more than can I, shirk what it is required of us both that we do.

Shortly after sunset we journeyed to Purfleet, where the marsh mists required only the very slightest effort on Nomie's part to thicken to the point where we could walk up to the windows of the house with absolute impunity. As the Count had suspected, preparations were clearly afoot to pursue him: Van Helsing at least knew the significance of the Count's exchange of blood with Mrs. Harker. By listening in a meditative state, akin to that of the yogis I met in India, Nomie and I could hear clearly all that passed in Seward's study, and pieced together their plan. They will take the boat-train to Paris on the morning of the 12th, and there board the Orient Express for Varna, to intercept the Russian freighter *Czarina Catherine* upon which Dracula's single remaining earth-box is being shipped.

For a man with a great deal of money—as I now have under the names of Marshmire and Bloem, complete with all identity papers, Catherine's accounts as well as my own—it is a simple matter, to make arrangements to have half a dozen of my own earth-boxes, as well as Nomie's, shipped under reliable guard to Paris, and put on the same train on the 12th. So now I know, my beloved, how many more nights I can pass at your side, before we depart!

Once when Mrs. Harker turned toward the windows of Seward's study, I was shocked to see a great burn, nearly the size of a penny-piece, glaring crimson on her forehead within the frame of her dark hair. I must have gasped, for Nomie looked up at me and said, "You did not know, then? Van Helsing burned her—pressed the consecrated Host into her flesh, which has already begun to assume some of the qualities of the vampire. Had the changes in her been further advanced, it would have been much worse."

"How do you know this?" I asked, shocked at the old man's carelessness, if carelessness it had been.

"I felt it," whispered Nomie. "In my dreaming I felt it, the afternoon that you were buried in Highgate. We all did. We are bound to her now, you see, as we are bound to the Count. In some sense, our dreams touch hers, as well as his. And in these dreams sometimes I see her, in the afternoons, alone in her room here. She will stare and stare at herself in the mirror, then throw herself upon the bed and weep like a beaten child." Her voice was calm and matter-of-fact as she said this. Yet I heard in my mind Vixie's despairing voice: *I would rather be dead, than turn into what they want me to be!*

And poor Mrs. Harker has not even that option!

Nomie went on, "When Jonathan, or any of the men comes in, she is all smiles and cheerful calm."

"Was Jonathan indeed the Count's solicitor?" I asked, observing that thin, alert man with haggard eyes and white streaks starting in his hair as he stood talking to Van Helsing, his wife's hand gently clasped in his. "I dreamed of him—I think I dreamed of him—at the castle in Transylvania."

"He was there," agreed Nomie. "The castle itself stands upon a very high shoulder of rock, overlooking the Borgo Pass into Bukovina. The only way out of the Castle is through the court-yard. Sometimes the peasants, or the village priest, will place holy things in the road, or on the gates, so that we cannot pass them. It is a nuisance, no more, of course, as it is just as easy for us to come and go down the wall and the cliff-face, or to fly in the form of bats. On the night that the Count left—left us there and fled to England—Harker climbed down the wall and the cliff-face, a very difficult thing for a mortal man."

She tilted her head on one side, watching from the darkness as Harker escorted his wife from the study. Nomie must, I realized, know this deceptively gentle-looking young man well. He came back in alone, and out of his wife's view his face looked as if he'd aged ten years. "There was nothing different this after-noon?" he asked.

"Nothing," said Van Helsing. "When Madame Mina is un-der the hypnosis, she only hears the lap of the water on the ship's hull, and the thud of feet upon the deck above. And so I think it shall be, until the *Czarina Catherine* come into Varna, and we shall be there waiting for him, eh?"

Nomie and I traded a glance. "They are using Mrs. Harker to trace him," I said.

"Be glad then that it is only him, whom she and they seek with her mind."

The remainder of the night, Nomie and I spent making ar-rangements for our own travel and the shipment of the boxes of the soil in which we were buried. Nomie, she told me, along with her sister-wives, had had to dig up her own from the chapel floor of Castle Dracula, the Count alone being able to command the gypsies who provide what service there is at the Castle.

We met with two gentlemen named Greengage and Bray, ex-soldiers and recommended to me by my old friend the publican at the Goat and Compasses as honest roughs, who for a price can be depended upon to make sure that the earth-boxes in which Nomie and I must be carried across the Channel will in fact be placed speedily and safely upon the Orient Express. We shall depart for Paris on the 11th, a day before Van Helsing and Company. Once in France, we shall of course be able to come and go through the chinks and holes in the boxes, as we do through the minute holes in the lids of coffins and the doors of tombs.

Will you, my dearest, forgive me if I make financial arrangements for Nomie to have access to our money, once Van Helsing or one of his myrmidons makes blessed quietus for me? Once that happens, neither you nor I, nor our dearest Vixie, will ever require a penny, ever again. My little Nornchen has been so great a help to me, instructing me in the ways of getting along in my new, strange, vampire state—something the Lady Elizabeth taught her, rather than the Count—that I feel I cannot simply abandon her on a train in the midst of Bavaria without making some provision for her to return safely to her home.

I beg for—and rely upon—your kindness toward one who has been most generous and helpful to me in a terribly difficult time.

Autumn nights fall quickly, and last long. My deepest regret, in this strange night-time life that now I lead, is that I will seldom see the flowers you so loved blooming in sunlight, and never see them again without pain. That I will never catch, through our windows, the burnish of sunset on your hair. Still every day brings me closer to joining you in fact, never to be parted again.

Your own forever,
R.M.R.

R.M.R.'s notes
8 October
18 mice, 10 rats, 20 spiders, 12 moths

9 October
22 mice, 11 rats, 9 spiders, 6 moths

10 October
16 mice, 13 rats, 4 spiders, 9 moths, & Georgina
Clayburne

Chapter Twenty-three

Renfield heard the key turn in the front-door lock upstairs.

Heard the click of shoe-heels—a woman's shoes—on the hall floor, and felt the infinitesimal creak of weight mounting the stairs. Sitting quietly beside the table in the sub-cellar—he'd brought down a chair from the kitchen, clean sheets to lay over the bodies, ribbons for Vixie's hair—he debated about locking the sub-cellar door, moving boxes in front of it and being gone before the visitor came downstairs. It was his last night in London—his last night with the physical entities that had been Catherine and Vixie—and he didn't want to destroy the nostalgic sweet savor of his thoughts with some stranger's conventional expressions of horror and distaste.

But it wasn't a stranger.

He heard her, as she mounted the stairs, say, "Tch!" and knew it was Georgina, Lady Clayburne.

Had she glimpsed him, when he stopped by the flower-sellers

in Leicester Square to get some late hothouse roses? He'd done so these past three nights, heaping the table with them. He'd walked as a man does. She could have followed.

Or had she somehow learned of the house, and had it watched?

The anger that swept him at this thought was so intense that he felt the hair on his nape prickle, like a savage dog's. His rage had nothing in it of the clouds of senseless crimson fury that had used to descend upon him in life: that was something that seemed to have been rinsed away by dying. But this bitterness, though colder, pierced deeper. He couldn't erase from his mind Vixie's frantic tears at the thought of having to go live with Georgina and her vain and distant husband, the thought of being pushed and moulded by loneliness and emotional blackmail into a "proper young lady" who wasn't permitted to read Freud or smoke and certainly wasn't permitted to paint nude models. He couldn't forget those horrible scenes between Catherine and her sister that would leave Catherine ill with anxiety for days.

He remained seated beside the table, holding the rotted and leathery fingers gently in his, and listened to the footfalls explore the upper regions of the house, then descend the stairs again.

Descend to the kitchen.

"Tch!"

That was unfair. Renfield had been very careful about clearing away the sucked-dry carcasses of his rats and mice.

The sub-cellar door opened. The light of the lamp she held streamed down into the chilly darkness that reeked of decay and roses.

She gasped, "You!" and almost dropped the lamp.

Renfield said, "Yes. Me."

She hesitated at the top of the steps. If she'd fled, he could have caught her, but she didn't. The temptation to have a scene with him was far too strong.

"I should have suspected you'd find a way to corrupt that fat clown Hennessey. I always did wonder if you were paying him more than Mother and I were."

The wave of anger recurred, prickling his hair again, but he remained sitting and said, "I take it you didn't bother to attend the funeral?"

"Good God, no!" She sounded startled at the idea that she might even have considered doing so. "With all Wormidge had to do, to get hold of your solicitor's papers, finally . . ." She had reached the bottom of the stair, and the lamplight widened into the room, illuminating the red hair coiled on the sheet, Vixie's dark curls among the roses. Georgina's eyes grew wide, and fairly blazed in the dim orange glow.

"You beast." She fairly spit the word at him. "You sneaking, greedy animal. That was your plan all along, wasn't it? To marry her and to make away with her, so that Father's money would come to you. Yes, and even to make away with your own daughter, so you could have it all!"

Renfield stood up at that, and Georgina fell back a step, her arm cocked a little, as if she'd throw the lamp at him next. Disbelievingly, Renfield said, "That is all that you can say? All that you can see, in the death of your lovely sister and your niece? The whereabouts of your father's money, that might go to me instead of to you? That is the only thing that Catherine's death means to you?"

"Of course not!" Georgina snapped quickly. "You should talk about what her death means! Murderer! Brute! Thief!"

"Thief?" Renfield took a step toward her. "I was married to Catherine for eighteen years, Georgina. Had I been the fortune-hunter you always claimed I was—as if I had not found my own fortune in India—would I not have made away with her earlier than that?"

"Don't you argue with me!" shrieked the woman. "I know of your life in India. I've had Wormidge on to that as well. Once we started asking, we learned about those girls who disappeared there! *And* what you used to do with animals and snakes! You were unfit to speak to Catherine, let alone marry her, and certainly the pair of you were unfit to raise a granddaughter of Lord Brough's to be the . . . the bohemian suffragist sensualist you were turning Vivienne into! That you turned Catherine into as well, with your theosophy and your heathan gods! Now I know that she is dead, whether you escape or not, we can put an end to all this legal shilly-shallying with the trust funds."

"Do not," said Renfield quietly, "name your sister to me. Certainly not in the same breath as complaints about trust-funds."

He stood only a yard from the enraged woman now, close enough to smell the musty lavender of her dusting-powder, close enough to see the broken veins in her cheeks, the caked rice-powder at the corners of her lips. He towered over her. With a sudden move she dropped the lamp to the flagstone floor and fled, dashing up the steps, Renfield following with a vampire's preternatural speed, leisurely as a shadow. He let her dash before him up the kitchen steps and through the pantry, hearing the rush and roaring of the spreading lamp-oil as it ignited the broken shelves, the trailing sheets, the roses and the table . . .

He caught her, easily, just inside the front door.

Deep in sleep, Mina Harker heard Dr. Van Helsing's gentle voice, coming to her from far off, as she had heard it now for nearly a week. "What can you hear, Madame Mina?"

Through lips that felt as if they belonged to someone else, she mumbled, "Water. Water lapping at the hull."

Darkness lay around her. She was aware of that dark mind, sleeping, hungry—wary as a wolf. Angry as a wolf, that flees back to its lair with a burned nose. The thoughts of revenge colored the black darkness like a blood-colored cloud. She was glad Van Helsing, when he hypnotized her like this, never asked her about what she felt.

"And what smell?"

She said, "Earth. Salt. Blood." A little blood, from the carcass of the dead rat, clutched still in the Count's hand. *Does he know I'm aware of him like this?* The thought that in the darkness his eyes might open, his mind might reach out to hers, filled her with terror. She knew that if he said to her, *Come,* she would move Earth and Heaven to go to him.

But he slept.

She heard Van Helsing say, "Sleep now, Madame Mina, and when you wake, you will wake refreshed." It was how he always left her, and she heard his voice and Jonathan's, quietly, as they left the bedroom: "All still seem as it was. This is good. When we leave tonight . . ."

The door closed. Mina knew they were leaving—for Transylvania, she assumed—but had made the five men swear never to speak to her of destinations or plans. If she could listen to Dracula's dreams, there was the chance that he could listen to hers.

Only in this way could she help them, she knew. Only in surrender, in making herself the object she had all her life struggled not to be. All her life she had been a doer, an organizer, memorizing train-schedules and typing notes and taking correspondence courses. Now it was as if a hand had been laid on her head, saying, *Learn stillness.* Only by quietness, stillness, absolute trust could she fight back to reclaim her own soul and her own life.

But the thought that she was linked to the Count—the thought of her flesh changing, as Seward had told her poor Lucy's flesh had changed as the result of drinking the vampire's blood—revolted her. She found herself filled with a loathing for her own body that she could not describe. In that dark dawn when they had driven the Count from her bedroom, after the Count had held her mouth to his bleeding chest and forced her to drink, she had screamed, "Unclean! Unclean!" She doubted whether any of the men even understood, or could begin to understand, her sense of horror at the thought of her own flesh, her own organs. Daily she felt herself sliding toward double change, alien from them in body and in every thought and perception of her mind.

Each day she looked in her mirror for signs of further change. Each day she tried to see the reflection of herself in Jonathan's eyes. He was—they all—were becoming strangers to her, and in some ways that was more terrible than all those surreptitious probings with her tongue at her gums and teeth.

Each day she tried to pretend that she didn't smell the blood in Jonathan's veins. That she didn't dream about waking beside him, hungry and changed; that she didn't dream of leaning over him, pressing the soft skin of his throat between her lips. His blood would be delicious. And more delicious still, his dying despair as he opened his eyes and knew himself utterly betrayed.

It was dreams like this that brought her sobbing from sleep

at night, to lie trembling, staring at the ceiling in the dark. Jonathan had enough to bear, without her waking him to share her horrors. She slipped so easily under Van Helsing's quiet-voiced commands, and slept so deeply afterward, because most nights she lay awake.

Poor Lucy, she thought, as she slid deeper into sleep. Poor, sweet Lucy, who had had to go through this alone, not knowing what was happening to her . . .

Or would it have been better not to know? Not to hope?

Had she dreamed of drinking Arthur's blood, before she died?

Her dream shifted, images sliding from what she knew to the tantalizingly half-familiar. She thought for a moment she was seeing Lucy in her dream, but the next instant knew it was not so. The chamber where the blonde girl knelt belonged to another place, another time, furnished with pieces of Louis XV or an imitation of it, delicate against the heavy stone of the walls. A great window opened into distant vistas of mountains and trees, to a sunset bleeding itself to death in streaks of cinnabar and gold. The girl who knelt beside the great bed was praying, but as Mina watched, she groped in her old-fashioned coiffure of wheat-gold curls and drew out a jeweled comb, whose golden interior was at the base smooth and flat enough to serve her for a mirror. There was no other mirror in the room.

The girl angled the comb to the branch of candles burning beside the bed, opened her mouth, and drew back her upper lip in the exact fashion that Mina did several times a day. On her throat Mina could see the white, mangled punctures of the vampire's bite. The comb slid from the girl's hands and she dropped across the bed again, hands clasped as in prayer, but what she whispered was, "Papa . . . Mama . . ."

"Papa? Mama?" Mina knew the sneering voice. Would recognize it, hear it, in her dreams, she thought, for the rest of her life. He stood in the shadows beside the bed, his eyes glinting red in the candle-light. Mina knew he had not been there before. "You vowed that you would forsake all others, little Goldfinch." His deep, harsh voice spoke in German. She wondered at it that she would be dreaming in that language, though she had spoken it a great deal, traveling to Buda-Pesth to bring Jonathan home. "How is this that you will be forsworn so quickly?" He advanced to put his hands on her shoulders, and she jerked away, sprang from him, sobbing, to the window. He only smiled, long teeth gleaming. "And will you forswear all those times that you said you loved me? Even in the presence of the priests of God?"

Her eyes were huge in her emaciated face. "I knew not to whom I spoke."

"You spoke to *me,* little Goldfinch." He pressed a mocking hand to his breast, where his long old-fashioned waistcoat of black silk was embroidered with crimson flowers like a spattering of blood. "I have not changed." His voice was soft, his eyes mockingly amused, as he had been amused at Mina's struggles to turn her head aside from the bleeding gash in his chest.

With a sudden motion the girl jerked open the casement of the window, making all the candleflames bend and her blonde hair stir around her face. She stood on the window-seat, framed in the darkening abyss.

"What, do you seek to part already?" Dracula did not move, and at his voice the girl looked back into the room. "*'Til death do us part,* you said, before that God by whom you set such store. But you will find, I think, if you do jump, that death will not part us. That we will never be parted." He walked slowly toward her, holding out his hand. "That is what you wanted, is it not? It is what you said you wanted, upon all those occasions when you were in my arms."

The girl clung to the side of the open casement, trembling, tears running down her face now as she watched him advance; Mina guessed from her quick glance, quickly averted, how deep and terrible was the drop beyond. Dracula reached her, his hand still held out; the girl cried, "I hate you!"

"Ah, but you will love me, my sweet bride, my treasure, my winepress. You will have no choice."

She wavered, irresolute, and in that instant he moved, with the panther-like speed Mina had seen. In an eyeblink he was beside her in the window, his dark velvet arm circling her waist, bending her backward over it, out the window and over the abyss. Her feet groped for purchase, toes scrabbling frantically as they were lifted from the window-seat, so that she was forced to cling to his arms. He bent down, as she hung above the empty fall, fastened his lips to her throat.

The girl was still breathing, though gasping for air, when he drew her back inside. He released her, and faded away into the shadows, leaving her lying on the window-seat with her golden hair streaked with blood.

Chapter Twenty-four

Strasbourg. Munich. Vienna with its pink-and-gold buildings looking as if some mad cake-decorator had assaulted them with frills of buttercreme.

Sunset. Darkness. Intolerable thoughts. A day of watching trees and villages and distant mountains flash past, of listening to Art and Quincey play endless games of cribbage. Night again.

John Seward closed his eyes and wished with everything in him that he could just give himself an injection of chloral hydrate and sleep for days. Months, if possible.

Sleep without seeing Lucy's face as he'd seen it in Hampstead Cemetery, with blood dripping down her chin and fervid lust in her eyes. Sleep without hearing her scream when Art hammered the stake into her breast, without seeing her hands scratch and claw at the hammer, the wood, Art's wrists. Sleep without seeing Van Helsing gently lift up her severed head to make sure of its disattachment, then lay it down again and stuff the mouth with the blossoms of the garlic plant, whose scent Seward had come to so profoundly hate.

Oh, my dearest one, he thought, his heart wrung with emotions he could not even name, much less let himself actually feel. *Thank God your mother was dead before that came to pass. She might have pulled you out of my arms, but she did not deserve that.*

And I could not have saved you.

He opened his eyes again. More little fairy-tale villages against the dark slopes of pine-woods. He'd asked Jonathan Harker about them yesterday, and to his surprise the younger man had kept them all in a ripple of laughter about strange old beliefs and curious customs he'd encountered on his journey here last April. "Of course, I didn't travel in such luxury as this," Harker had added, gesturing around him at the little compartment with its small sofa and table, its Turkey carpet and wood paneling, and had gone on to recount tales of the other occupants of the second-class coach cars at night—blessed, blessed relief of laughter.

The compartment door opened and Seward thought it must be a porter, come to light the lamps that tinkled with their continuous silvery music in time to the rattle of the train. He realized the compartment was almost pitch dark. Time and past time, he reflected, to go next door to Art and Quincey's compartment, to play cards while Van Helsing pored over those arcane books he'd brought and the Harkers chatted as gently as any married couple might . . .

"Dr. Seward?" said the shadow that loomed over him in the dark.

Whose voice is that?

"Yes?" He sat up on the little sofa, felt for a match, but his visitor closed the door and struck a light, held the springing little flame to the lamp-wick as Seward apologized. "I'm sorry, I'm half asleep. Travel in this part of the world . . ."

His voice trailed off.

"Yes," said Renfield. "It's me." He replaced the lamp-globe. And all Seward could think was, *Dear God. Dear God . . .*

"It never occurred to you, did it," said Renfield, "that the Count would make anyone his victim—and his slave—in that house but Mrs. Harker? You never thought to check the state of my teeth and gums before you turned my body over to Lady Brough's solicitor for burial?"

Dear God . . . Seward felt exactly as if someone had rammed him in the chest full-force with the end of a barge-pole. Unable to breathe, and for a moment unable to think. Then another inference lept to his mind, another shock . . .

"No," smiled Renfield, as if in his widening eyes he read Seward's horrified thought. "To the best of my knowledge the Count—now my Master—limited his depredations to two. I doubt that even *he* could cope with Emily Strathmore. How is Mrs. Harker?"

Seward collected himself, his mind racing now. He settled back a little on the sofa, gestured to the single chair. "She is not well," he said, "as you must know. Will you sit? Are you a passenger on this train yourself, then?"

"Good Heavens, no!"

"Then how . . ."

"That is my own affair." Renfield smiled again, and this time Seward could see the length and whiteness of his canine teeth. Seward noticed also that his former patient had lost the unhealthy flabbiness that had begun to blur his burly frame in the months at Rushbrook House. He looked, in fact, younger than the sixty-three years Georgina Clayburne had given as his age, as if even in the short time since his death he were slipping back into the prime of his strength.

"I'm not an apparition, if that's what you're thinking," added Renfield, and held out one powerful hand. *"Put your finger here, and see my hands,"* he quoted Jesus' words to Thomas the Doubter in the Bible, *"and put out your hand, and place it in my side; do not be faithless, but believing."*

Quietly, Seward said, "I believe. If the Count is, indeed, your Master, what do you want? Why are you here?" Renfield wore a dark suit and good linen, well-fitting and very different from the clothes he'd been brought in and the clothes he had worn to be buried. Where had he gotten them? He was also able to observe, watching Renfield carefully, that he was not breathing.

"Because the Count is my Master, I was ordered to pursue you, to come upon you singly in the dark—as you observe that I have—and to pick you off, one by one, as the Count's irregular cavalry and his gypsy servitors picked off so many of his enemies in centuries gone by. As to what I want . . . Because the Count is my Master, I should think that would be obvious." All the sly humor, the ironic amusement that had convinced Seward that this was in fact no apparition, but Renfield indeed, faded from his square-jawed face. "I want you to kill me."

Seward drew in his breath to speak, then let it out.

Dying, Lucy had kissed Van Helsing's hand, whispering her thanks that he had thrust Art from her in her trance-bound demon state.

On the night before their departure, Mina had made each of them swear to kill her—with stake and garlic and decapitation—before they would let her fall into Count Dracula's hands or service.

Renfield's eyes, though they had the curious reflective brightness of a vampire's, were entirely sane, and deeply sad as they looked down into his.

"Can you tell us . . ." Seward began, and Renfield shook his head.

"I am not offering to betray my Master," he said. "I cannot, for one thing, and for another, there is little I can tell you beyond what you have learned from poor Mrs. Harker. I am free to act only for a little time. While he is on the water, his power is limited, but if he becomes aware of what I've done, he can exercise it, at the moments of sunrise and sunset, at noon and at the slack and turn of the tide. Dr. Seward," he went on, holding out his big hands, "I was your patient for six months, and never during that time were you anything but humane, professional, and well-intentioned in the face of my admittedly erratic behavior. In my saner moments I never had a doubt that you would do all within your power to help me, not because you knew me or loved me, but because it is in your nature, as well as your profession, to help those who come to you for help.

"I am asking you," he went on earnestly, "I am begging you: call your friends in. Grant me peace, as you granted your poor beautiful Lucy peace. I would not serve Dracula, but while I exist, I cannot now do other than serve him. And I cannot do this thing myself."

"You are sure, then?" said Seward, deeply moved and at the same time profoundly curious. He had observed how with Lucy's death, and her transition to the vampire state, her body had become perfect, inhumanly beautiful and shed of its moral flaws.

Had this process extended to whatever flaws existed in Renfield's nervous system?

Which was more perilous, a mad vampire or a sane one?

His mind chased this thought even as Renfield said, "I am certain," his voice sounding suddenly tremendously far off. Seward yawned hugely, his awareness drifting in spite of all he could do.

"Van Helsing," he said, making ready to rise and then sinking back onto the couch. "Van Helsing will know . . . how to go about this . . ."

Then the next moment the gentle jostling of the train-cars transmuted itself to the jogging of those ridiculous shaggy ponies they'd bought from the villagers in Tobolsk, and he was gazing with Art and Quincey out across the endless barren brownness of the Russian steppe, looking for the slightest sign of the vanished Uncle Harry.

"And I swear if he's gone back to marry that Cossack woman, he can blame well *stay* in Siberia, for all of me," Quincey said, and handed the binoculars disgustedly to Art. "We can tell your pa he got himself killed by them headhunters in Singapore and I'll trim up the mustaches on that shrunken head the doc here bought so it'll look enough like him to pass muster with your aunts."

Art turned to Seward. "What do you think, Jack? You're Uncle's nanny, after all."

Seward, whose shoulder still smarted from a Cossack bullet collected two days before, said, "I think we should leave him."

"What?" said Art. "Who?"

"What?" Seward opened his eyes. He was in the wood-paneled compartment of a wagon-lit. Arthur was bending over him, holding up a lamp. In that first instant he thought, *We must have tracked Uncle Harry back to the Cossacks* . . . Then he saw that Art wore the black of mourning—saw Van Helsing in the doorway behind him, and gray-haired Jonathan Harker—and memory fell into place.

He blinked, grasping at fading images. "I had—I had the most *extraordinary* dream . . ."

CHAPTER TWENTY-FIVE

"Don't leave me, Ryland!" As Nomie tugged him from the corridor into their lamp-lit compartment in the next car, her hands were shaking, her blue eyes pleading.

He put his hands on either side of her face, trying to quiet the desperation from her eyes. "My little Norn, I've made every provision for you! You'll be in no danger, all arrangements are made to get you across the Danube at Giurgiu, to get you onto the next train to Varna . . ."

"I don't want arrangements!" She pulled from him, shook her head, caught his wrists in her small white hands that were so strong and so cold. "I want a friend!"

Renfield said nothing, and she pressed her face to his hands.

"Do you know how long it has been," she whispered, "since I have had a friend to talk to, as I talk to you?"

The compartment had been set up for night, the small bunks unhooked from the walls. The bedding was all made up, for "Mr. and Mrs. Marshmire" to disarray before they slipped through cracks and knotholes into the baggage-wagon shortly before morning. They had made arrangements to travel with a dozen rabbits in cages: Renfield knew well how meticulously the Orient Express kept track of its passengers and personnel. He had been careful to tip the porters heavily and had explained to them that since his wife disliked being cooped up, they might be anywhere on the train, day or night.

He guided her to the little sofa, took her gently into the circle of his arm. She rested her head on his shoulder: more beautiful than the most beautiful of living women he had ever seen, with the exception of Catherine and Vixie. Yet he felt for her none of the physical need that at times during his incarceration seemed almost on the point of setting his flesh on fire. That, too, it appeared, was a thing of the body.

And the deep affection he felt for her, evidently, was not.

"Days are no less long for the Un-Dead than for the Living," she murmured after a time. "I married the Count—God help me!—in 1782, and for over a hundred years now have had no one but him, and the Lady Elizabeth, and Sarike for companionship. I read . . . except that I dare not be seen to favor anything too much, for when we disagree, or are angry with one another, the others are spiteful and destructive. For them, there is nothing but the hunt. They laugh at the idea that one might be interested in the lives of people long dead, like Heloise and Abelard, or who never existed, like Beatrice and Benedict."

He was silent, remembering Vixie's tears the first time she read *Notre Dame de Paris*. Georgina Clayburne had called all novels "rubbish" and had urged him and Catherine to burn Vixie's.

For Georgina, as for the Countess, there was only the hunt.

"I used to be a good Catholic girl." Nomie's sob might have been the softest of rueful chuckles, and she sat up a little, and wiped a tear like cold crystal from her eye. "Our priest back in Augsburg used to tell us, as a threat, that those things that we loved above God, we would find ourselves shackled to in Hell, for all of Eternity. As a little girl I would have terrible visions of myself dragging a long chain of dolls and pretty dresses and story-books through a wasteland of flaming mud and devils. But at least, I told myself, I'd still *have* them. But he was right," she finished sadly. "He was right."

"What a ghastly thing to tell a child." Renfield recalled some of the things his own parish priest had told him about what became of little boys who couldn't control their tempers.

Nomie sighed. "But you see, I did love the Count above God, above all mortal things. When he held me in his arms, I remember saying to him, *I would count myself blessed to dwell forever in Hell, if I could dwell there at your side.* I was very young." A tiny fold touched the corner of her lips. "Not twenty." She closed her eyes, and her long lashes dislodged another tear.

Renfield caught it on his fingertip. It was cold as winter rain.

Yet he put it to his lips, tasting it as in dying he'd tasted her blood.

The blood is the life, he thought. *But the tears are something more.*

Outside the windows, the Italian Alps flashed past in the darkness, moonlight cold upon their snows.

"And now here I am," Nomie said softly. "Exactly where I wanted to be, dwelling forever in Hell at his side. With no one but Elizabeth for company, and Sarike, who has the heart of an animal. No, that's unjust. Animals show kindness to their own, and even a wolfhound bitch will nurse an orphaned kitten. Sometimes still the Count will talk to me of Goethe, and Shake-speare, and Montaigne—he's very widely read, and I think he valued me because I read, and he wanted someone to converse with. But for him, all of literature comes back to power, and to contempt for those who have none. To talk with him is sometimes like being beaten. To travel with you, to speak with you, heart to heart and not afraid, is like a chilled cloth upon my face after a long fever. Don't take that away. At least . . ."

She opened her eyes, sat up straighter, as if ashamed of her weakness. "At least not for a little while yet."

Letter, R. M. Renfield to his wife
13 October
My beloved,

How could I turn my back upon that poor child?

The cynical will doubtless cry, *Coward, to hide his own craving for a life eternal, stolen from the lives of others, behind a farce of pity! Child forsooth! This woman is an Un-Dead murderess who seeks to keep a servant with no more expenditure than a tugged heartstring or two.*

Perhaps I would have said so myself, before I knew what Hell is. Before I had seen, close-to, the naked essences of those monsters that go by the names of Dracula, of Elizabeth, of Sarike the Turk.

The cynic might also point out that, as Nomie said, *To be vampire is to fascinate* . . . And accuse Nomie of setting out to fascinate me, as the Count fascinated her.

But I know you, Catherine, as I know my own heart, clearer now that the vampire state has healed me of madness. You were no cynic in life. Death, Dante and others tell us, clarifies the awareness even of the damned, and how much more so of the blessed! I know you will understand.

Nomie is what she is, no saint, but no demon either, and

lonely as for half a year I was lonely in the terrible walls of Rushbrook Asylum.

I long to be with you as a child longs for his mother's breast. I would count the days until I see you again, face to face in the light, save that I do not know how many they shall be.

They shall be as few as possible, my truest love. I am torn between the duties of friendship, my love for you and Vixie, and the cruel constraints of Time. I will do what I can for my pretty little Norn, to make easier the slavery into which she was tricked by her love, all those years ago.

But that being done—if it can be done—I shall come to you, in whatever fashion I can contrive. If God is kind, He will allow me to tell you, face to face, on the threshold of the Heaven you now inhabit, how sorry I am, before consigning me to eternal sleep. This is the best that I can hope for, and to this I look forward as to light in blackness.

My love, until that day, I am,

Forever, your husband,
R.M.R.

R.M.R.'s notes
13 October
3 rabbits, 4 spiders

14 October
3 rabbits, 2 rats

15 October
Baggage-thief in luggage shed at Varna
My self-disgust is no less intense than my horror at the degree to which the drinking of human blood—the taking of human life—

exhilarates me, sharpens my mind and my senses and, more frighteningly, increases the speed with which I can move and with which I can dislimn myself to pass through knotholes and cracks. I find that Nomie's superiority in the so-called supernatural aspects of the vampire state is only in part a function of her greater age and experience. In part these abilities depend upon her greater readiness to consume the psychic energies of the human brain at death.

What am I to make of this?

"What a pity," sighed Nomie, as we stowed the body of the dead robber beneath the wheels of one of the coal-cars in the maze of sidings in the railway yard, "that we cannot find a village of robbers, upon whom we could feast nightly without concern about whether their wives or their mothers will find themselves in want at their deaths, or whether their children will weep. I used to pick and choose, to kill only the bandits and horse-thieves who inhabit the wild countryside: men whom I could not pity. But such men are wary, unless they're in drink, and walk in bands. And sometimes the craving becomes too much."

"Ah, my Nornchen, I have seen such villages," I replied, a trifle flown, I admit, on the alcohol-content of our victim's blood. "Up the country, as they say of the Indian hills, there are places where the Thugee make a habit of murdering travelers, and families hand the profession down for generations, as surely as the butchers of cattle and pigs do in other lands. The Governor-General would give us a medal for our conduct, rather than sending pompous Dutchmen and crazed solicitors' clerks after us with Ghurka knives."

From somewhere—I suspect from young Lord Godalming—Jonathan Harker has acquired a curve-bladed Ghurka *kukri* even longer and more savage-looking than the bowie-knife Quincey Morris habitually wears sticking out of his boot-top. He spent a great deal of our three days on the Orient Express sharpening it, as he sat at the bedside of his poor lovely wife, who slept most of the journey.

It is clear to me that knowledge of Dracula's assault upon his wife has driven Harker a little insane. This is not to be wondered at. What man, knowing Mina Harker's kind spirit and lively intelligence, could not love her to distraction? What husband, seeing the woman he adored infected with the terrible poison that slowly transforms the human flesh into vampire flesh and brings the human soul into thrall of the demon, could remain wholly sane?

Kind is the God who denies him knowledge of the depths to which the Count's domination will bring her, after death! Such knowledge would induce madness indeed.

And as if mere knowledge of his beloved's peril were insufficient, Harker had the daily reminder, upon the journey, of the chain that binds his beautiful one to her supernatural rapist. Daily, at dawn and sunset, Van Helsing would hypnotize Mrs. Harker, searching through her mind to touch her master's. In so doing he would touch my own, and Nomie's, where we lay in our coffins in the baggage-car.

I would be aware of such times, as I drifted off to sleep or back into waking, of Dracula's thought and sensation as he lay in his own single earth-box in the hold of the Romanian freighter the *Czarina Catherine*. I would hear, as Mrs. Harker heard, the lap of waves upon the hold, the thud of sailors' feet on the deck, and the creak of ropes; would hear, also, Van Helsing's voice gently probing with questions, and now and then one of the men mutter to another.

How could Harker be witness to all that taking place around the woman he loves, and not go a little mad?

But having been a madman myself, I do not look forward to having to deal with one at my Master's behest.

And though nothing will please me more than the sensation of that Ghurka knife in my own heart, and the severing of my own head that will bring me peace, I wonder how I can protect Nomie from a like fate without resorting to more human blood, more human deaths, to strengthen me.

CHAPTER TWENTY-SIX

R.M.R.'s notes
17 October
12 rats, 27 spiders

Coming from Paris on the Orient Express, Nomie told me of Count Dracula's intention: to divert the *Czarina Catherine* from its registered destination here in Varna to Galatz on the Danube mouth, leaving Van Helsing and his allies to await it here while we, Nomie and I, pick them off one by one.

Sleeping in my coffin during the day, in the small lodgings we rented, I feel the Count's impatient anger press upon me like a fever. Anger at those who would dare to pursue and defy him. Anger at us, who cannot or will not guard his flanks. Through the boards of my coffin I hear Nomie cry out in terror, like a child in the grip of a nightmare she cannot wake from. And though I strive to break my own thick day-sleep to go to her, to comfort her, I can only lie in the clayey soil dug from Highgate Cemetery, and listen to her weep.

Jonathan Harker's Journal*
17 October

Everything is pretty well fixed now, I think, to welcome the Count on his return from his tour . . . Van Helsing and Seward will cut off his head at once and drive a stake through his heart. Morris and Godalming and I shall prevent interference, even if we have to use the arms which we shall have ready. The Professor says that if we can so treat the Count's body, it will soon after fall into dust . . .

Letter, Quincey Morris to Galileo Jones
Foreman, Caballo Loco Ranch
San Antonio, Texas
17 October

Pard,

It's been too long, a thousand years it feels like, and stranger portents have come to pass than ever I wrote of in all those foot-loose traipses riding herd on that crazy English lord around the world. Doc Seward, and Art Holmwood, and I thought we saw the elephant then, and maybe we did.

This is something different, dark as the snake-caves along the dry washes in the hills and twice as deadly. I write because I could use the sight of your ugly face just now, and use even more you and six or seven of the boys from the bunkhouse.

When last I wrote, I said I'd been shot bad by Dan Cupid, shot in the heart with his little gold arrow: I said a lot of hopeful fal-lal and I hope to God you burned that damn stupid poem. She turned me down for a man just as good as me and better in her mama's eyes, though straight and true as she was, I know that didn't weigh with her, and I knew even then I wouldn't get over it. May through to September, I kept telling myself I'd write and let you know how I was, when the pain let up some. But it never did.

I thought that was the worst wound I'd take in my life. I wish it had been.

I say of Miss Westenra, "was," because she died, not many days before her marriage to Art. And not many days after, we—Art and I and Doc—learned that she'd been killed, by the kind of man-monster the Commanche sometimes speak of, and the villagers deep back in the Mexican hills where modern times and modern blindness haven't yet touched.

And this is what I'm doing here, footloose again and heading East in country as wild as any we crossed coming west from Vladivastok. The place I'm at is called Varna (Wasn't "Varna" the name of that red-haired madam in Dodge? The one with the fingernails?), and it's a good-sized burg and pretty, near as warm as Texas for this late in the year. It's a port on the Black Sea and the crowds you see in the streets remind me of San Francisco, French and Greeks and English and Russians and Germans: same ships in the harbor, with coal and timber and iron and German steel. The only difference is there's Arabs everywhere instead of Chinese, and the hills aren't as steep.

We've taken rooms—Art and the Doc and I, and other friends of Miss Westenra's who are helping us with the chase—and all we can do now is wait. Our bird is coming in on a freighter from London; he'll find us waiting for him on the dock. Between us we have five Winchesters and seven pistols, plus my Henry, which is the best rifle man ever made, as well as my bowie and assorted other cutlery. More than any weapon, we have minds that are made up and hearts bound in brotherhood.

What he—It—did lies beyond the proof of any law but God's.

But you and I have both dealt with justice on those terms, out where the law doesn't run.

And so we wait. One of our number, Mrs. Harker, as smart and sweet and good-hearted a woman as ever wore shoe-leather, has suffered a terrible wound that may yet turn into her death because we underestimated our friend, and it is like a knife in my heart every time I see the mark she bears of it. The night she took that mark, I should have known better, and set a guard, even though there was no danger in sight. There isn't a night I don't dream about doing it differently.

For that reason I've gone back to my trail-driving days, and have insisted that while we're here we stick together, and stay within-doors from sundown til sunup, which is when our friend likes to mosey around. Most nights I take the graveyard watch, like I did on the trail, that dark pit from three 'til the first birds start to wake, when even the whores sleep and the streets are so still you can hear the clink of the tackle down in the harbor.

This is the hour in which I write to you. The others sleep, bedrolls on the parlor carpet around Mrs. Harker's couch, comical unless you knew the reason for it. Like on the trail, what name each man mutters in his sleep the others forget come morning. I've been to the window, and through the other rooms of our suite, three times since I came on watch, knowing our friend is still on the high seas someplace: I've seen nothing and yet the air prickles and whispers. There's danger here, closer than the Doc or *his* Doc—old Doc Van Helsing—think or know. I smell it, like a longhorn smells thunder. Nobody who hasn't taken a herd through Indian country can know what that's like.

Whatever it was, it's gone now. And so I write to you, and think of you, old friend, who *does* know what that feels like, that invisible danger, waiting to strike.

Enclosed with this letter you'll find my will. Once I thought to bring a gold-haired bride home to Caballo Loco, to make a whole lot of little Quinceys and 'Laios and Jacks and Lucys to take the place over; I know that won't happen, now. Pa told me I had cousins back in Virginia, though I don't know if any survived the War any more than my aunts and uncles of Pa's family did. Do what you can to find them, and if any come out to take up their share of the land, please do what you can to knock some sense into their heads, seeing as how you'll be their neighbor, on what'll be your half of the ranch.

You think dark thoughts in the dark of the graveyard watch, out here on the eastern edge of the world. One day I pray I'll take this letter out of your hands, and laugh, and tear it up. But that day seems far from me now, like a dream that I know damn well isn't going to come true. By the time this gets to you, it'll be over, one way or the other.

Til that time it's Hooray for Texas! And tell those lazy sons-of-bitches in the bunkhouse that their boss says Hi from the edge of the world.

Your pal,
Quincey Morris

R.M.R.'s notes
18 October
13 rats, 20 spiders, owl, 2 mice
I keep these records from habit, and as a means of reassuring myself that though I choose not to kill human beings, I am in no danger of starvation. My cravings spring from my mind and my blood, not my flesh.

My mind is still linked, in the hours of my sleep, to the Count's. When his red eyes glare into my dreams and his deep hoarse voice demands why I have not yet slain Van Helsing or Godalming, I hear also the sighing lap of waves against the *Czarina Catherine*'s hull, and sometimes snatches of men's voices from the deck. "It is the devil's wind, and the devil's fog, that drive us!" I heard a man cry in anguish, and a thick Scots voice replied, "I' the de'il wants us to make Varna so quick, then Dickie Donelson's na the one to say him nay!"

"Cast it overside, Captain! Cast that accursed box into the sea! Grief only will come of keeping it aboard!"

And there was a confusion of voices, and the meaty slap of a belaying-pin striking flesh as the sounds faded into the sea-rush of my dreams.

"He paid Captain Donelson well," whispered Nomie to me later, as we stood in the balmy darkness across from the Hotel Odessus's front doors, our shoulders touching slightly, watching the windows of Van Helsing's suite. "As he has the men at Galatz, who will take the earth-box ashore and put it on a barge upriver, to where the Bistritza River curves below the Borgo Pass where the Castle stands. And he learned well his own lesson, to travel on a ship crewed with Scots and Frenchmen as well as Romanians and Greeks, and to let the crew alone. Coming to England on the *Demeter* in July, he would drink the blood of the crew. When it arrived, the ship was a ghost-ship, the captain chained dead to the wheel with a crucifix wound round his hands."

"He was lucky his entire cargo of earth-boxes wasn't confiscated by the customs authorities," I remarked. "Or sunk in Whitby Harbor, for that matter."

"He had long been fasting in Transylvania, with the impoverishment of the countryside. Now he has had three months, almost, of hunting in London's dockside slums."

"Do you still defend him, little Norn?" I asked her, smiling, and had she not been pale as bridal satin, she might have blushed. More gravely, I went on, "He killed the crew of the *Demeter* because he was greedy. He would kill that of the *Czarina Catherine,* and its Captain, too, if he thought he could do so and still make port safely in Galatz. You know that is so."

She said with a trace of bitterness in her voice, "I know."

We returned our attention to the warm rectangle of gas-light on the upper floor of the Hotel Odessus, crossed now and then by shadows. When one came near enough to its curtain, I pointed them out to her: "The tall one is Quincy Morris; that will be Lord Godalming, who is only a little shorter—"

"The handsome one with the golden hair?" She cocked a co-quettish eye at me, the white lace of her jabot like flowers against the embroidered pink-and-blue of her jacket.

"Minx. The slighter one is either my own friend Dr. Seward, or *your* friend Jonathan Harker—and don't tell me you didn't find him attractive, my girl . . ."

She laughed like the cold tinkling of silver chimes. "He was very sweet, really. I used to watch him at the Castle, from the shadows when he couldn't see. He would sit at his desk, writing love-letters to his fiancée, or scribbling in his journal, as if his very life depended upon it. I would sometimes slip in just at dawn, when he slept, and try to read what he'd written to his Mina. Sometimes he wrote in English, sometimes in a code I could not understand, but while he wrote, he would sigh and speak her name. The others would laugh at me for it, and talk about how they would make him forget her, once they could have their way with him, and about how long they could make him last before he died. That is a game that vampires play."

She returned her eyes to the window, where Van Helsing's stocky form stood briefly, illuminated from within as he parted the curtain and looked out to the dark, cobbled street.

For the second night none of them emerged. When, in the small cold hours, Nomie and I drifted like wraiths into the hotel's kitchen quarters at the welcoming behest of a venal servant-boy to whom we threw a coin, we found all the lights still burning in the avengers' suite, and heard the muffled mutter of Godalming's voice and Seward's as they played pinochle, and the mingled breathing of sleepers.

Nomie left me to hunt. I remained in the corridor, or drifted into one bedroom after the other of the suite in the form of mist beneath the doors. All the bedrooms were empty, though the beds bore the scent and impress of those who slept in them at odd hours of daylight.

Our friends were taking no chances. While I was still there, I heard Seward wake Harker, and after that, there was only the soft scrape of whetstone on knife-blade, until the approach of dawn drove me from the building and back to my own earth-home.

19 October

When I returned to our hotel at dawn yesterday, I found to my great disquiet that Nomie was still out. She was going hunting, she said, on the docks, not a part of the city where any woman should be afoot.

Though vampires do not crumble into dust with the first touch of the sun's rays, or spontaneously combust in daylight, as some penny dreadfuls would have it, once the sun is in the sky and until it vanishes behind the earth's curve, we are as mortals.

Worse off than mortals, in fact, for mortals may cross running water at their will, or touch such things as the garlic plant, the wild rose, and the emblems of their faith. Moreover, with the sun's rising I was crushed by a wave of almost overwhelming sleepiness, and when I emerged from our little *pensione* in Balchik Street, I found that the morning sunlight made me giddy, and that I could barely see.

Nevertheless I stumbled in the direction of the dark blue sea, visible between the white buildings of the upper town.

Coming down Nessebur Street, I was passed by a gang of seven or eight Slovak boatmen, rough arrogant brigands with their baggy white trousers tucked into high boot-tops, who bring loads of timber down from the Carpathians. They glanced sidelong at me from under long, greasy black hair, and muttered to one another in their own tongue. Yet as they passed, I smelled blood upon them, and the ground-in whiff of Nomie's perfume.

I saw where they'd come from, through a little gate into the yard behind a shut-up tavern. I ran in, and looked around: a narrow space between a warehouse and a chandler's yard, filled with debris and stinking of privies years untended. For a moment, dazzled by the sunlight, I could see nothing but the shabby fence, the straggling waist-high stands of broomsedge.

Then something moved beside the dilapidated privy sheds. A woman, her gold hair hanging tangled over the muddied remains of her pink jacket, blood dripping from the white hand that she held to her bruised and swollen face.

*   *   *

"I'll be all right," she whispered, as we staggered like two swaying drunkards back toward the safety of our *pensione*. Searching for her, I had been plagued by the recurring fear that I'd encounter Dr. Seward in the streets—though what the man would have been doing down by the shipyards I have no idea. Now the only thing that burned in my heart was rage. Rage and the desire to kill.

"The men surrounded me, I thought I could get away." Her voice came thick through lips puffed and discolored. Her hand trembled as she tried to put up her hair again, so that people would not stare so at us as we made our way back through the town. "Two of them wore crucifixes, and I could not slip past them. They called me witch, and Austrian whore. It's all they thought I was."

I said nothing. I was shaking with fury.

"And then the sun came up . . ."

We came into the *pensione* by the back door, unseen by the servants who had been well paid to leave our room strictly alone during the day. They'd left water in the ewer, however, and with it I bathed Nomie's cut face and bruised wrists. She fell asleep the instant I lifted her into her coffin. I dragged myself over to my own. Opium is not so black as the oblivion into which I plunged.

*   *   *

Ryland, she whispered into my dreams. *Ryland, thank you. Thank you.*

In my dream I reached out and gathered her into my arms. In my dream her face had already healed, beautiful and perfect as the young bride the Count had brought to his Castle, over a century ago.

Somewhere far off I could hear the Count shout at her, *Fool!*

Bitch! You will undo us all! I only held her tighter, and felt her shake in my grip. Through the sickened dread that radiated from her I could feel, also, the bitter grief of disillusion. *I would count myself blessed to dwell forever in Hell,* she had said to him once, *if I could dwell there at your side.* When Dracula, in his coffin on-board the *Czarina Catherine,* finally released her mind from his grip, her soul clung to mine in the darkness of our mutual dreams and wept.

With shame that she had loved him once? I wondered. Or with sorrow that the love that once had upheld her in Un-Death was gone?

Catherine, Catherine, thank God that God spared you the deeper Hells of pain such as this!

To cheer her through the day, I told her tales of India as we slept, conjuring for her, like a wizard of dreams, temples domed with peeling gilt and muddy streets aswarm with dusky-skinned men and women, white cows and coiled pythons as big as fire-hoses, insects bigger than English birds, and the teeming hot electricity of life that seems to radiate from the very ground.

That is where we need to live, my Nornchen, you and I, I told her. *We could sup like kings every night upon men who force their brothers' widows into suttee in order to get their property, or who murder childless brides because they don't want to return the dowries to their families! A thousand wolves of the Deccan hills would do our bidding, and we would sleep through the days in the crypts of demolished temples deep in the jungles, with cobras as our guards.*

And would I weave you crowns of flowers, as they do for the gods of that country? she returned, and I could smell those flowers, like good German roses though the image I saw in her dream—my dream—was of fantastic blossoms whose like the waking earth has never seen. *Would I play the flute for you in the jungle twilight, like the White Goddess of some blood-and-thunder romance?*

A little later I became aware of Mina Harker's mind, questing to touch that of the Count, in the hold of that ship that was being driven by the winds he commanded, cloaked in the fogs he had summoned to blindfold its captain and crew. "What is it that you hear?" asked Van Helsing's deep voice. "What is it that you smell?"

And then, more softly, "Friend John, what do you think? Do her teeth remain as they were, no longer nor no sharper than they were before?"

And Seward's voice, toneless and careful, "I can see no change in them, nor in her."

Far off it seemed to me that I could see them, like images I'd formed up in my mind to cheer my little Norn: Mrs. Harker lying on the rose plush sofa of the suite's overdecorated parlor, Van Helsing and Seward on chairs by her head. The others were gone, presumably attending, during the hours of day, to all those necessary tasks so that they could remain all together through the hours of darkness.

"Nor I, Friend John," Van Helsing replied. "But you must watch her, watch her as a doctor stands guard upon an ailing child, for the first sign of change. For if this change commence in her, it is not only her soul that is in peril, but she become a weapon in his hand against us all."

From there I slipped back into waking, with the soft warm winds of the Black Sea stirring the curtains of the window. And when Nomie sat up in her coffin, and shook back her golden hair, the bruises left by the Slovak brutes at the harbor were fading, and every cut nearly healed. Every hurt, that is, save the wound of fear that lay like a shadow deep within her eyes.

20 October
5 mice, 2 Slovaks

21 October
Owl, 3 mice, 1 Slovak
Nomie is teaching me the finer points of the vampire way.

22 October
12 rats, 27 spiders
Searched for the other Slovaks who assaulted Nomie. They seem to be lying low.

Transformation into a bat! What an astonishing sensation!

23 October
10 rats, 13 spiders, an enormous cockroach that crawled dazed and stupid from a bale of rugs from Samarkand. The taste of Oriental spices!
In bat-form flittered at the window of the Odessus Hotel. Godalming pacing, Dr. Seward reading or pretending to read a medical journal, though he did not turn the pages, Morris playing patience, and Harker sharpening his knife. Mrs. Harker asleep on the sofa, dark hair braided like a schoolgirl's. Van Helsing rose from his seat beside her and crossed to the window. I flew away at once, knowing that above all none of them must suspect that the Count has harrying forces in Varna. I do not think he saw me, yet he stood for a long time at the opening of the curtains, gazing with those sharp blue eyes into the dark.

I worry about Nomie, about the way the landlord of the *pensione* and his wife draw aside from her and whisper when she and I go up and down the stairs. In my sleep I sometimes hear the tread of heavy boots in the street below our window, pausing for too long, then going on its way.

Telegram, Rufus Smith, Lloyd's, London, to Lord Godalming, care of H.B.M. Vice-Consul, Varna.*
24 October
Czarina Catherine reported this morning from Dardanelles.

CHAPTER TWENTY-SEVEN

"What could go wrong?" Young Godalming had a voice like an operatic hero's, a Heldentenor, a Siegfried, a Radhames. Drifting as half-dematerialized mist in the darkness of the bedroom that was Mina Harker's by day, Renfield pictured the Viscount in his mind. Pacing, by the creak of the floor and the infinitesimal rise and fall of his voice. Golden hair tumbled on his forehead in the lamplight. Black-clothed as Hamlet, holding to the uniform of grief, keeping faith with the girl who had been his wife in his heart. "Rostov—the *Catherine*'s owner—never questioned my story that the box may contain something stolen from me. This should be enough to convince the Captain to let us open it."

Paper rattled softly, audible only to Renfield's hypernatural senses.

A letter? Money? Did it matter?

He remembered his dreaming visions of laudanum and madness in Rushbrook House, seeing those two goldenly beautiful young people on the sunlit deck of Godalming's little steam-launch one afternoon on the Thames. Remembered how he had envied them their joy as much as their freedom. Recalled the agony of knowing that Dracula even then had put his mark upon the girl; that their delight in the afternoon lay under shadow of horror.

Without doubt, that magic afternoon on the river was in Godalming's mind as well.

"What could go wrong?" he demanded again, louder, and Renfield could almost see Van Helsing's shushing gesture as well as hear the hiss of his breath.

"A thousand thousand things, my friend." Van Helsing's whisper re-enforced Renfield's awareness of Mina Harker's deep, sleeping breath. From her hypnotic sleep at sunset she often drifted so into true slumber, like the Sleeping Beauty awaiting her ultimate fate. "It is why we watch, and wait."

Did Sleeping Beauty dream?

"Can't be much longer now." Quincey Morris's flat American drawl was calmly matter-of-fact. "Wind's from the south. Queer, how it swung around that way so sudden from the east. But it'll drive the ship into our arms neat as a grand-right-and-left. Should arrive sometime tomorrow, strong as it's blowin'."

"And we will be there," said Godalming, almost gloating, "to greet him."

In his sleep that afternoon, Renfield, too, had felt the wind shift. At sunset, in the bat-form that still filled him with delight, he had flittered high in the lemon-hued sky to look south toward the forty-mile strait. Though he saw with a vampire's keen sight rather than with a bat's weak little eyes, the hills of Turkey had been veiled in mists whose white curtains had stretched far out over the sea.

But when Godalming and Morris left the suite to go down to

the hotel's smoking-room, Van Helsing murmured, "I do not like this, friend John. There is a feel in the air, as they say. A feel in my bones. Like the old wound who smart when the weather turns, my skeleton say to me, *Beware*."

They're armed, thought Renfield, as he'd thought whenever any of the men departed the suite for the smoking-room or the lavatories; and as they went out, he heard the minute clink of silver on porcelain as each man took from a bowl beside the door the rosaries Van Helsing insisted they carry when not in Mina's presence. An agnostic himself, Renfield had been both appalled and fascinated, four nights ago, when he'd killed the first of the Slovak boatmen who'd assaulted Nomie. The man's companion had had a crucifix around his neck and the energy from it, like a searing white heat, had driven Renfield back from killing him as well. When the bodies of two others of the band had been discovered a day or so later, all the rest of them had taken to wearing crucifixes, to Renfield's disgust.

Does God indeed protect men who'd beat a young woman for being blonde and German, if only they wear His sign?

Or is there something else operating here, something I don't understand?

But through the hotel's thick walls he heard other men's voices from the street, hoarse and jeering: *"Vrolok,"* one of them cried, and another, *"Stregoica!"* And he heard the quick retreating tap of Nomie's heels.

Heart cold within him, Renfield dissolved himself more completely into mists, flowed like water along the dim-lit hotel corridor and down the stair. He passed Godalming and tall Quincey Morris outside the smoking-room door—Morris looked around sharply, as if at a sound—and gaining the outer door, Renfield melted into the shape of a bat, flew toward the alley where the white blur of boatmen's clothing swam in the shadows.

They were following Nomie, not very closely, shouting obscenities and calling names. She could not, Renfield knew, slip away from them into another form without revealing that she was, indeed, what they labeled her, vampire and witch. So she only walked, very sensibly, down the center of the widest street she could toward the largest hotel immediately available that wasn't the Odessus, where there was the chance that Jonathan Harker might see her in the lobby. This was the Metropole, some three streets away. At this hour, close to one in the morning, the streets were nearly deserted, the fog that had all evening wreathed the southern hills creeping in thick over the town. There was no one to stop the mob from trailing only a few steps behind her, gaining courage as they gained numbers from the workingmen's taverns they passed. When she reached the Metropole's front steps, they fell back, and Renfield melted into mists again as the doorman opened the doors for her.

"Come in, come in, Madame! Ah, truly they are savages in this place!"

By his speech the doorman was French. Nomie turned, to look back at the some thirty men gathered before the hotel, who spat at her and made the two-fingered sign against the evil eye. Renfield let himself be seen for a moment, swirling as mist across the steps behind her, to let her know he was near. The mob didn't notice him, because of the general fog of the night: the lights of the hotel's door were blurred by it, and the sound of the sea at the foot of the esplanade muffled.

"Oh, M'sieu," he heard Nomie gasp as she went in, "it is only because I am a German, not even an Austrian as they say—"

She was still shaking when she joined Renfield outside fifteen minutes later, and in the form of bats they made their way back toward the *pensione* in Blachik Street. "You have to go back to the Castle," he said, when they'd seeped into their own room again in the form of mist. "It will be only a matter of time before the men from the taverns and the docks find out where you sleep, or before our landlady's husband hears one too many things in the tavern and decides we aren't paying him enough to mind his own business."

"We can't do that," whispered Nomie. "You know we can't."

Renfield knew. Yesterday, and the day before, the Count had risen like a cloud of darkness into his dreams, demanding why Van Helsing and the others still lived. *They twist that woman, that traitorous whore, to their wills, with their puny hypnotism and their canting piety! Fools! Fools and hypocrites, who whine that I have made her my tool, and all the while use her as theirs! But they will pay.*

And that morning, too, in the dark of his coffin, Renfield dreamed again of the dark gloating, the burning stench of the Count's delight in the anticipation of his vengeance.

When they see what I shall make of her, my bride, my slave, and my winepress, then shall their hearts weep beneath my heel. Even death will to them bring no comfort.

Destroy them! Destroy them all, except for Van Helsing— Him you let live, to see their deaths.

His words, his thoughts, crushed Renfield with terror, and it seemed to him that he knelt again in the hold of the doomed ship *Demeter,* confronting that column of shadow, those red, burning eyes.

But in his dream, this time, Nomie was with him. Nomie slim and beautiful, standing at his side.

Lord, we cannot, she said, and Dracula struck her, with casual violence that threw her back against the slimy dark wall of the ship's bulkhead.

Cannot? You say "cannot" to me?

They never go out alone! protested Renfield, springing to his feet. *They are armed, they cannot be finished off all together—*

He broke off with a gasp, the grip of Dracula's mind on his like a band of heated iron crushing his skull. Renfield sank to the deck-boards, the pain of his own death at Dracula's hands—bones breaking, flesh battered—returning to the reality of the dream.

You will find a way, said the Count, the voice in Renfield's mind deadly soft. *You will find a way, or it will go the worse with you.*

Then he was gone, and far off, deep in shattered sleep, Renfield heard Nomie weep. The morning sun climbed over the blue-black sparkle of the Black Sea, the strange southerly wind flicked foam from its waves. Far out over the water, Renfield was conscious of unseasonal banks of drifting fog, and in the dark of his dream, of Mina Harker dreaming about chasing Lucy as she sleep-walked down the halls of the school where they'd met.

Letter, R.M. Renfield to his wife
25 October

My beloved, my beloved, he is gone!

At noon I felt it, noon being the single period of the daylight hours when we of the vampire kind have the powers that the darkness gives us: to change our form, to utilize the strength of our Un-Dead state.

He has closed his mind against Mina Harker's probing, but in so doing, also against us!

Once when he turned away from me I wept, and ranted, and fought like the madman I then was. Today in my coffined sleep I could almost have cried like a child with relief. When sunset freed me of the daylight's thick thrall, I sat up shivering with dread that it was only a dream, but no! For Nomie sat up in the same moment, her golden hair hanging thick about her shoulders, and stared at me with huge eyes.

"Is it true?" she whispered. And scrambling from our coffins, we clung to each other in the narrow space between them, not daring to believe.

"I'm taking you back to the Castle," I said, and she shook her head.

"Ryland, you cannot. *I* cannot. He will know. When he comes there, he will know. And he will punish."

"I will return here and deal with the pursuit," I said firmly. "I will tell him that because of the Slovaks you had become a liability, and it is only a matter of time before Van Helsing—who speaks Slovak, and like all men of science is a natural-born snoop whose inquisitiveness rivals the worst grandmother in the world—hears of a fair-haired German girl whom the boatmen call *vrolak,* and puts two and two together. You must go back, little Norn. I will come to you when I can."

It was a lie, Catherine, and I knew it was a lie as the words came out of my mouth. She flung her arms around me and kissed me like a schoolgirl, and the lie burned me as if she had pressed a crucifix, or Van Helsing's Host, into the living flesh of my heart.

All this evening I have made preparations, visiting the shipping offices of Hapgood Company, in which as you recall I own considerable stock, and under my own name hiring a reliable agent, an expatriate Virginian named Ross who has spent over two decades in this part of the world. For his assistants I hired two Germans, Berliners who don't believe in anything. In this far corner of Europe, no one had yet heard of the incarceration or death of one of Hapgood's leading shareholders, and one of the office clerks, who had formerly worked in Calcutta, knew me well by sight. Tomorrow morning we take the 6:30 train to Veresti, where it will be possible to hire wagons to deliver Nomie, boxed within the coffin of her native earth, to the Castle Dracula above the Borgo Pass.

For my own coffin the instructions were more complex. Having brought five boxes of earth from Highgate Cemetery on the Orient Express, I rented space in Hapgood's Varna warehouse to store three of them until sent for by either myself or by the fictitious Mr. Marshmire. One earth-box I emptied, dividing the earth therein into four parts. Three of these I used to line, much more shallowly, boxes large enough to shelter me, which were to be stored until sent for in Veresti and in Bistritz, guaranteeing me a place of shelter near-by the Castle, should I require one. The fourth portion of my native earth I loosely stored in a fine cotton casing three layers thick, in fact, the emptied bags of three child-sized eiderdowns, which may be spread out in case of emergency and give me some semblence of rest, at least for the time that remains to me.

The remainder of the night, my dearest Catherine, I have spent in drawing up the various legal documents that will serve to transfer our money, and ownership of our secret accounts, into Nomie's hands. At some time in the future she may succeed in breaking free of Dracula's hold; the greatest gift I can offer her, who has been my friend in this terrible halfway house of Un-Death, is the freedom that money can bring.

For I do not mean to return to her, after I send her on her way from Veresti. Before I can return to Varna, the *Czarina Catherine* will make port in Galatz, where the shipping agents will duly wire news of her arrival to Lord Godalming, and thither Van Helsing and the others shall go. I will do what I can to delay pursuit, lest Nomie suffer punishment for my negligence. Yet I shall make sure that in so doing, I meet at last the joy of my own end, to be with you, however briefly, before a merciful God releases me to whatever Eternity He shall in His wisdom choose.

Yet just as poor little Nomie once said she would happily share eternity in Hell with the man she loved, so will I accept it with equanamity, if before I enter its gates I may see you and our lovely Vixie one last time.

Until then, I am,

Forever, your husband,
R.M.R.

CHAPTER TWENTY-EIGHT

"What is it that you hear, Madame Mina?"

Under the closed lids, Van Helsing saw the young woman's eyes move, as subjects' often did under hypnosis. As if they looked around them, seeing who knew what? The soft flesh beneath the eyes drew up a little, the dark brows, fine as the strokes of Japanese penmanship, drew down.

In a more commanding voice, he repeated, "What is it that you hear? Tell me."

She turned her head, like a fretful child avoiding the medicine-spoon. Harker, kneeling at the head of the sofa in the suite's pink-and-gold parlor, gave his wife's hand a gentle pressure, and glanced up into Van Helsing's eyes.

"Tell me what you hear, Madame Mina. This I command."

She brought in her breath, let it go in a sigh. Van Helsing leaned forward a little, to study, without seeming to—without letting Harker guess the direction of his eyes—the teeth set in those colorless gums.

When she lay dying, struggling against the changes that Dracula's contaminating blood wrought in her flesh, Lucy Westenra's teeth had lengthened to the sharp canines of the vampire, even before death had fully claimed her. Remembering that flaxen girl's struggle, Van Helsing could not repress a shiver, nor could he put aside, or pretend to himself that he did not feel, the traitorous stir in his loins.

Vile, he thought, *shameful and vile*. Yet how beautiful Lucy Westenra had been, how exquisite, the beauty of life mingling with the cold wonder of death's threshold.

And though her teeth had not yet begun to grow, nor her gums to shrink back, he thought he saw that unearthly vampire loveliness reflected now in Mina Harker's too-thin face.

"Water," she whispered. "Rushing waves . . . masts creaking." She moved her head again, her hair like sable velvet against the pale linen of the sheets and pillows they'd brought in, every night, from her bedroom. Against the dark of her hair, the wax-white of her skin, the round scar left by the consecrated Host on her forehead seemed lividly red, almost like raw flesh. Yet even that, to his own disgust, the old man found deeply erotic.

Dear God, what kind of man am I to look upon her who fights so bravely for her own soul—and she the wife of a man who loves her like the breath of his lungs!—and to think such thoughts as this? It had been twenty-five years since his own wife, his own beautiful Elaine, had disappeared into the terrible labyrinths of madness, leaving only a frightened, raving creature who bore little resemblance to the girl he had loved. In the first few years he had been driven to the prostitutes of Amsterdam, but shame had blunted his manhood without in the tiniest degree decreasing his aching need.

For two decades the life of the mind—and certain disciplines of the flesh—had proved a distraction. But like the physician of the Bible, he had never been able to heal himself. Nor could he now.

"Sleep now," he said gently, and passed his hand above her face. "Sleep now and dream, and when you wake, you shall be refresh, and full of hope."

The morning sunlight that filled the room, as Quincey Morris parted its curtains, had a chilly cast to it, grayed with the fogs that had for two days drifted over Varna's harbor. Jonathan Harker, haggard still but curiously ebullient since word had come, the day before yesterday, that the *Czarina Catherine* had been sighted in the Dardanelles, lifted his wife in his arms and bore her into their bedroom. Despite the morning's coolness Morris opened the window, for the parlor smelled of lamp-oil and too many people sleeping on its chairs and floor. John Seward, rumpled and reminding Van Helsing very much of the thin, earnest young student he'd known in Leyden thirteen years ago, began rolling up the blankets on which he and the other three men had slept, turn and turn about, for eleven nights now.

In those eleven days, no sign, no whisper of any paid agent of the vampire Count had so much as cast a shadow on their tracks. But Morris was right. Van Helsing knew this in his bones. It was not the time to take the slightest chance. Seward, Harker, and young Lord Godalming would all cat-nap during the day, as Van Helsing did himself, but for them all the main business of the day would be waiting.

Waiting for a telegram from the shipping agent, that would tell them that the *Czarina Catherine* was in port.

"It has to be today." Godalming emerged from his room in a fresh jacket and tie, on his way downstairs to the barber's and the baths. Morris, who'd proceeded laconically to his own morning routine of checking, cleaning, and loading every piece of the considerable arsenal they'd brought from London, only glanced up at his friend and scratched a corner of his long mustache.

Seward remarked, "I'm a little surprised it's taking this long. They may have had to lay by because of the fog. You go on ahead, Art. I shall join you in a moment." His brown glance touched Van Helsing's as he gathered up the bedding. Van Helsing rose, and followed him to the door of Mina's room, as Harker came out.

"She's sleeping well," the young solicitor said. "Better I think than she has in some time. Her color's better, too, don't you think?"

Van Helsing replied softly, "Even so." The curtains of the bedroom were drawn; he could see the young schoolmistress sleeping in the gloom, dark braids laid gently on either side of her face.

Was she more beautiful than she had been yesterday? Pinker and healthier-looking, as Lucy had become when the vampire death stole over her? Harker hadn't seen his wife's dear friend succumb to Dracula's curse: he would not know what her livelier demeanor, her brighter spirits yesterday might mean. Van Helsing was conscious of the young man's dark gaze resting on his face, questioning, before Harker turned away.

But Seward knew. And Seward was watching him, too, as he looked at Mrs. Harker in the bedroom's dusk.

How can you think such thought as this? he asked himself again, hating what he felt. Hating the image that seemed to burn itself into his brain, of kissing those vampire lips, of holding that coldly perfect flesh in crushing embrace against his own. *This* woman, so clever and so logical and so good in her heart, she is fighting for her own soul, and for her husband's happiness and perhaps his very life as well, for it is certain that if she die, he will not leave her long alone in her grave.

Yet the flesh, like the heart, has reasons of its own, of which the reason knows nothing and cares less.

And as he saw the unearthly beauty of the vampire make its first inroads on that lively, lovely woman, that kind-hearted person whom he had come to love as a daughter, he felt the insane whisper of lust chew at the inner corners of his brain.

Before they had left London, Mina Harker had made them read over her the Service for the Dead. Had made each man swear that before they would let her become vampire, they would stake her through the heart and cut off her head, as they had done with Lucy, and this oath Van Helsing knew he would force himself to honor, out of the love he bore her. The most he could do for her was that, and to dissemble his private madness so that she would continue to trust him as a friend. They were like a band of brothers to her, among whom she could sleep without a second thought; her only comfort, Van Helsing knew, in a time when she must have been living in a nightmare of hard-hidden terror.

He would die himself rather than take that comfort, that trust, away.

Yet when he lay down to sleep later that morning, it was of the vampire-Mina, the voluptuous smiling demon-Mina, that he dreamed.

*Dr. Seward's Diary**
27 October
No news yet of the ship we wait for . . .

"Mrs. Marshmire will meet you at Bistritz," explained Renfield, as in the pre-dawn cold he, the shipping-agent Ross, and the hired drivers checked the harness and wagon for its journey up to the Borgo Pass. "She has made her own arrangements to get there, and you will find rooms for you and your men at the Golden Krone Hotel. She is going home to her family there to rest, and to recover a little of the tenor of her mind. Please bear with her fancies, and indulge them so far as you're able. I assure you, they are only fancies, and nothing of a serious nature. But it will disturb her very much if her will is crossed."

The slender, graying Virginian smiled reminiscently. "I did have an aunt that took it in her head that my daddy's roses were the re-born souls of the knights and ladies of Camelot," he remarked. "When I was about five, she took me out and introduced me to Sir Galahad and Sir Bors and Morgan le Fay, and told me all kinds of tales about their deeds on Earth before they became rose-bushes. It was kind of sweet, really."

Renfield smiled. Such conduct would hardly have raised an eyebrow at Rushbrook. "Exactly," he said. "I am glad and grateful that you understand." He gave the man fifty pounds for expenses, having the head shipping-agent's assurance that in more than twenty years Ross's accounts had never showed so much as a penny's discrepancy; he had learned, in nearly twenty years in the India trade, to read men well.

"Please bear in mind," he added, "that this is a strange country, and Mrs. Marshmire comes from a very old family that is both eccentric and a little dangerous. In particular watch out for her sisters, should you encounter them. My wife will do all she

can to assure your safety, once you get among the Szgany gypsies that owe them alliegence, but I need hardly tell you to watch
your backs and not take any foolish risks."

"Won't be the first time I've been up the country in these
parts," replied the Virginian, unperturbed. He pulled closer
about him the sheepskin coat he wore, for once away from the
warmth of the Black Sea the air had grown steadily colder, and
the mountains before them were thick with clouds that smelled
of snow. "And I'll do my possible to make sure it won't be the
last. Thanks for your honesty with me, sir."

Not precisely honesty, reflected Renfield, watching the lights
of the wagon dwindle into the icy iron twilight of the road out
of town. *But how many battles would you have ridden into,
during your State's rebellion against the Federals, had your General Lee been completely honest with you about the politics,
bribery, and power-struggles that led up to the war?*

He turned his steps, not back into the yard of the modest inn
where they'd spent the night, but toward the railway station,
from which the train would leave for Galatz sometime before
noon if he were lucky. He ached all over, from days without
rest, pretending to be mortal and human for Ross's benefit and
living only for the time when he could seep as mist through
the holes in his coffin in the baggage-car, and rest in his native
earth.

The thought that he was helpless, through the two days' rattling journey from Varna, had filled him with dread and had in-
creased his hunger five-fold. A dozen times he'd had to leave the
compartment lest the craving for blood overcome him and he attack Ross or the two hired drivers. Through the night, lying in
his earth-box, he had whispered to Nomie as she lay awake in

hers, reassuring her and being reassured. It was good beyond measure not to be alone.

A look at the roads in this part of the world, glimpsed through the train windows during those two endless days playing cards with his hirelings, had demonstrated to Renfield at least why the Count had chosen to be conveyed back to his Castle by water instead of by land. Once past Bucharest and into the rising hinterlands, the roads deteriorated sharply, sometimes to little more than muddy tracks, and as the land rose toward the Carpathians, the trackless forest crowded in many places down to the road's edge.

On running water, the Count might be helpless, reflected Renfield, as he slipped into the open baggage-shed past the dozing guard, but there were fewer robbers on the water, and the direction of their attack was perforce more controlled. Having journeyed now so far from his native earth, he felt a deep and intense sympathy for the Count's obsessive precautions. Only the knowledge that his henchmen were skeptics—American and German—had given him the confidence to travel with them. Slovaks who'd grown up believing in vampires, or Englishmen who'd had their existence unarguably demonstrated to them, might have spotted him for one at once. And in daylight he was helpless.

As it was, he found it difficult to melt into mists, to flow into the earth-box labeled, R.M. RENFIELD—HAPGOOD'S—VARNA. Exhaustion seemed to have turned his Un-Dead flesh to lead. He cast a longing eye at the snoring guard, but knew it was too dangerous. Veresti was a small enough town that those who found an exsanguinated corpse would have no doubt in which direction to look for the killer. A box full of earth with small holes in its lid would be the first they'd open.

Nomie, thought Renfield, as he seeped finally through into the comforting darkness, *Nomie be safe!*

For a moment their minds touched, like hands questing for comfort in darkness. He saw her before him, in dreaming as she had looked in life, a sweet slender golden child in the flowing gauzes and striped satin jacket of that most graceful of eras in which she'd lived.

And in the distance, as if through her eyes, he saw the Castle Dracula, brooding half-ruined on the shoulder of cliff above the Borgo Pass. But it was shelter and safety to her, no matter what memories it held or what future; and there she could rest. In his mind he sang to her Wotan's song from *Das Rheingold,* the most beautiful piece of music Wagner ever wrote. The most beautiful, in its soul-deep soaring peace, of all the music of the earth:

> *"The evening beams*
> *Of the sun's eye*
> *Sumptuously gild*
> *Those walls! . . .*
> *Near is night;*
> *From envy and grudge*
> *It shelters us now.*
> *I greet this place!*
> *Secure against horror and fear.*
> *Come with me, Lady:*
> *In Valhalla dwell with me."*

Be safe, my child, my friend, he thought. *I have done for you what I can.*

R.M.R.'s notes
Train, Veresti to Galatz
28 October
4 chickens

What a thing it is to travel on a country train!

There remain only two things left for me to do.

With luck, Van Helsing and his companions will still be in Galatz when I arrive, depending on how well the Count has covered his tracks. Money can buy silence, if one knows where to shop. But I suspect that Dracula does not.

The Count is a *boyar,* a nobleman, like the great princes of India whom for twenty years I watched quite ordinary British middlemen bilk daily. His approach is, like theirs, a simple one: sword in one hand, a large pile of gold in the other. And no idea about how to finesse a believable story or which strings of influence to pull.

Godalming is rich. Quincey Morris is rich. Any silence the Count can buy, they can undoubtedly purchase retail at a very small mark-up. Van Helsing speaks enough Russian and Romanian that they can probably hire whatever vehicles they need for pursuit. If they guess, or are informed, this will probably be a vessel of some kind to pursue up-river with possibly outriders following along the shore. At a guess, they shall leave one of their number in Galatz with Mrs. Harker, and that one probably Seward, who is less accustomed to rough-and-tumble work than Morris. Harker has at least been to Castle Dracula, and his experience might be of value if they get that close to the Borgo Pass; besides, I cannot see him letting himself be done out of the kill.

A pity, for I like Seward and trust him. Nevertheless, Go-

dalming, Morris, and Van Helsing all met me at the asylum—
what a long time ago that seems! They will recognize me, and
Van Helsing will certainly understand my request.

But I smile at my own foolishness even as I write these words.
With Godalming and Harker of the party, I won't even be put to
the momentary embarassment of explaining myself. They will
slaughter me at sight.

What a deep sense of happiness that anticipation brings me,
as I settle for sleep, a stranger in a strange land, in the comfort
of my native earth!

CHAPTER TWENTY-NINE

*Jonathan Harker's Journal**
30 October—night

I am writing this in the light from the furnace door of the steam-launch: Lord Godalming is firing up. His is an experienced hand at the work, as he has had for years a launch of his own on the Thames . . . Regarding our plans, we finally decided that Mina's guess was correct, and that if any waterway was chosen for the Count's escape back to his castle, the Sereth, and then the Bistrizia at its junction, would be the one . . .

Lord Godalming tells me to sleep for a while, as it is enough for the present for one to be on watch. But I cannot sleep—how can I with the terrible danger hanging over my darling . . . My only comfort is that we are in the hands of God . . .

We seem to be drifting into unknown places and unknown ways; into a whole world of dark and dreadful things. Godalming is shutting the furnace door.

"Not what you'd call a promising lot." Seward surveyed the six horses assembled in the livery stable yard. The best the town has to offer, the stableman had assured Quincey, and if that were indeed the case, Seward reflected, his heart bled for anyone in Varna who wanted to get anywhere in a hurry or in any kind of style.

"You by any chance referrin' to them banditos we just enlisted?" Quincey gestured with an eyebrow—he was the only man Seward had ever seen who could do such a thing—to the two Romanian grooms the Vice Consul's chief clerk had recommended to Godalming on the strength of the fact that one of them, Chernak, allegedly spoke English and the other, Nagy, allegedly spoke what was alleged to be French, though you couldn't prove it by Seward.

And Seward had to admit that the scrubby, shaggy, under-sized horses did have a slightly more wholesome aspect than the men.

The thought of trusting his life to either group made him queasy.

Still, he went over to the two grooms and explained—with the stableman's questionable help—what he wanted of them: ride fast, rest seldom, change saddles when necessary to the remounts who'd carry the provisions. The expressions on their faces were hugely reminiscent of that worn by Mary the parlormaid at Rushbrook House when she was in the process of hopelessly misunderstanding his instructions about rotating household linens or setting the table when Sir Ambrose Poole came for Sunday tea. The recollection filled Seward with a curious sense of deep isolation, as if the Superintendant of Rushbrook House, who'd conscientiously recorded entries concerning every patient in his daily phonographic log and who'd dealt patiently with the Hennesseys and Lady Broughs and Ambrose Pooles of the world, were someone else entirely from the man who stood here now in the stable yard of a Black Sea town, trying to hire servitors in grammar-school French for—

For what?

For the pursuit of a monstrosity that the Superintendant of Rushbrook House, back in August, would never have believed in.

For the vengeance he would wreak, on the thing that had first dishonored poor beautiful Lucy, and then had taken her life.

And after that vengeance, what?

"Vous comprenez?" he asked, and Chernak and Nagy regarded him with blank and total incomprehension before they both nodded vigorously.

I've come four and a half months and over a thousand miles and I feel like I'm back where I was explaining about getting supper on the table on time.

Which it wasn't, of course.

Renfield, he thought, as the two grooms turned away and went to gather their own bedrolls from the corner of the courtyard. *Supper didn't get on the table because Renfield escaped.*

As if the name were a trigger to some obscure irritation of his nerves, for an instant a sense of horrified enlightenment flooded into his heart—*Dear God, Renfield!*—and then blurred away almost immediately into the cloudy sensation of a dream.

I dreamed about Renfield, he thought, his mind groping at

what felt like an almost palpable barrier of oblivion. *Dreamed about him on the train. Well-dressed, well-groomed, soft-spoken, sane.*

He said . . .

He said . . .

"They understand?" Quincey loomed up out of dark and torchlight beside him. The light of the wasting moon wickered through the breaking clouds, and though it was only a little after suppertime, it felt later.

Seward sighed. "Not a solitary thing."

The Texan spit a stream of tobacco-juice into the moist muck of gravel and hay underfoot. "Can't be worse than the Hakkas we hired in Singapore, and that worked out all right."

Looking up into his tall friend's face, Seward felt again that great sense of distance, not from Quincey himself—that friend with whom he'd traveled three-quarters of the way around the world—but from Quincey's thoughts and heart. It occurred to him that since the horrible afternoon in Hampstead Cemetery, when they'd driven a stake through Lucy's heart, when they'd cut off her head and stuffed her mouth with garlic as if they were superstitious savages and she some ritual beast, neither he, nor Art, nor Quincey had spoken one word to one another of what they'd done, or what they'd felt. All the way across the Channel and across the continent of Europe, Art had lapsed again and again into terrible silences, staring out the windows of trains or hotels struggling against tears, hand over his mouth and the muscles standing out on his temples with the tension of his jaws. At such times Seward, or Quincey, would sometimes drop a hand to his shoulder, or grip his arm in passing.

Quincey's silence was something different.

"Do you ever wonder," Seward asked him now, as they walked to the corner where the saddles and bedrolls were heaped, "if it could have been different? If Lucy had accepted my offer, or yours, instead of Art's? If she'd stayed in London last summer . . ."

"Or gone to America with me?" Quincey's gray eyes seemed dark in the torchlight, shadowed under the long sun-bleached brows, empty and infinitely tired. "Jack, there is not a day that it doesn't occupy the whole of my thought, from my waking until the moment sleep takes me. Had I known what was coming for her, I think I'd have carried her off like the villain in a play, and risked her mother shooting me dead. But I didn't. And you didn't. And maybe if she'd married you or married me or stayed in London or gone to the Moon, it would have been the same anyhow, like the philosophers say. And if it wasn't you and me standing here on the back-doorstep of the civilized world, it'd be two other guys avenging the death of some other gal, with just as much pain involved all around. And in any case it makes no difference."

He spit another line of tobacco, and picked up a saddle—a horrible Russian cavalry cast-off, stiff as a plank and entangled in a granny-knot of snarled straps. "From the time Miss Westenra said she would not have me, there was nothing for me, except her friendship, and yours, and Art's. It was that friendship that kept me in England, and that friendship that's drawn me here. Live or die, it does not matter to me anymore, for those two states are now to me exactly the same. Now let's get these fucken crow-baits saddled, and get on the road while there's still a Moon in the sky."

R.M.R.'s notes
31 October
2 chickens, 3 rats, Romanian pimp, 17 spiders
Still no contact of the Count's mind upon my own. Nor can I
sense him reaching out to Nomie. At sunset last night I was
aware of Van Helsing speaking to Mrs. Harker in hypnotic
trance, but with the Count's self-imposed isolation these impres-
sions have become so attenuated that it is only by deep medita-
tion that I can detect them at all, and at sunrise I was able to
sense nothing. I do not know whether this is because of Dracula's defense against this probing, or because Van Helsing and
his friends have guessed the direction of his flight and have set
off in pursuit, leaving Mrs. Harker guarded in Galatz.

Letter, R. M. Renfield to his wife
Galatz, Romania
At the mouths of the Danube
31 October
My beloved Catherine,

Please forgive my negligence in writing lately; I blame the difficult conditions under which I have traveled. Nor do they appear likely to become easier, but I shall write when I can. I count,
as ever, on your always-warm understanding.

The train from Veresti reached Galatz shortly after noon, after the usual maddening delays typical of this part of the world.
I waked after an admittedly uneasy sleep in the hushed stillness
of the goods shed, just at sunset. I went at once to the offices of
Hapgood's and found the agents there still talking about the brutal murder of one of the contractors who hire crews of Slovak

boatmen, an event which has thrown the whole riverfront community into superstitious panic, though the man himself was apparently no social loss.

With only minimal inquiries I was able to ascertain that the Count had come ashore on the 28th, hired a large, open barge with a double crew through this contractor, Skinsky, and departed before dawn yesterday. That same day Van Helsing and his friends arrived, and by sunset had hired a steam-launch, purchased six horses and appropriate gear (for the roads become extremely problematical as little as thirty miles upriver), and hired two grooms, evidently meaning to travel fast.

This brought me, unfortunately, face-to-face with some of the more practical drawbacks of the vampire state. Now in my heart I can see you and Vixie smile, for you have surely been waiting for me to realize that this very complication would arise.

I understand from Nomie that the Count, with his vast abilities to dominate the minds of beasts as well as of madmen like myself, is able to exert mastery over horses to the extent that he is able—for short distances, and during the hours of darkness when his powers are acute—to actually ride them. He long ago fell out of the habit of doing so, however, for the poor beasts did not bear him willingly, and would tremble and sweat so terribly as to cause comment among every man who saw them, and him. For myself, however, it is as much as I can do to harness them, and their fear at the scent of a predator is such that they are difficult to manage, and, I fear, are like to exhaust themselves in a very few miles.

I purchased a small calèche and team of those scrubby little horses one finds in this part of the world, barely larger than ponies, and a spare team in case I should not find a posting-house farther up the river. At the recommendation of the Hapgood shipping agents, I hired a French-speaking Negro named Salaman as a driver, and frequenting the riverfront taverns during the early portion of the evening, I found a suitably brutish and violent Romanian whose murder would cause me no qualms and whose disappearance would not result in questions or pursuit. I sensed then—and feel still more strongly now—that I will need all the strength and power that I can achieve.

When I was a child, I spake as a child, I reasoned as a child, says the Apostle, *but when I became a man I put away childish things.* In my madness I consumed all life in the illusory pursuit of exactly those things that, in the vampire state, the blood and the life give unto me; but now I am not mad. I would like to say that I derive no pleasure from the drinking of human life, but oh, Catherine, oh my beloved, that would be a lie. It is a pleasure I will be glad to put by in the eternal sleep of death, but it is one that I can no more deny than I could deny the rages of my madness.

I am writing this in the back room of a little tavern near the waterfront, where Salaman is to meet me as soon as there is enough dawnlight to drive. I have my roll of earth-imbued bedding, and hope that I will be able to get at least a little rest during the daylight hours. Yet sleep is not for me, for I must watch the river, and the road, for my master's enemies—and my own deliverers. Moreover, I must watch for the robbers who hear everything that goes on in the rough world of the river-traffic with the hinterlands, who will know that an Englishman is traveling with money and horses and only a single servant. In the hours of daylight I will be only as a man, and less strong than a living man in my own defense.

No wonder the Countess Elizabeth wanted a better servant

than that incompetent poet Gelhorn, to defend her and her sister-wives in their journey to London! I can only assume that he lasted no longer than their arrival at Castle Dracula; I cannot imagine she would have found in him the material to create another vampire servant.

And there, but for my little Nomie's friendship, go I.

Here is Salaman, framed in the doorway in a halo of chill river-fog.

My beloved, I remain,

Ever and forever,
Your husband,
R. M. Renfield

Letter, R. M. Renfield to his wife
The banks of the River Sereth, below Fundu
1 November
My beloved,

We have journeyed through the day and through the night, and still I have no sight of Van Helsing and his company. I have, however, found signs of their horses, and the occasional marks of a camp. They seem to be taking a more inland route where possible, following narrower trails that climb the rolling shoulders of the hills through which the river winds its way down from the mountains, the better to see ahead along the river itself.

In the calèche it is not possible to do this, owing to the steepness and broken nature of the ground. Thus we can only press on night and day. Only once did robbers—Szgany gypsies—attempt to molest us. Fortunately the time was dusk, and I was able to slip from the coach as a mist, and fall upon them from behind in the form of a wolf. They fled almost before the confrontation had begun. I reassured Salaman, who had thought me asleep in the calèche the whole of the time, and took the opportunity to hunt in the woods in the form of a bat, and to take advantage of the presence of bona fide evildoers to refresh my strength.

Would that I could so refresh the strength of the horses, and of my servant. He is a small man of Sudanese extraction, a slave for many years first in Arabia and then in Constantinople. He did not mention the wolf and may not have seen me in that form, but he has become silent since then, and watches me from the corner of his eye. He has taken to wearing about his neck a *taviz,* the silver tube-shaped amulet in which a verse of the Holy Koran is sealed. I find the painful radience that emanates from it to be the same as that which imbues the crucifixes of the Christians. I long to know whether such an amulet would protect an Unbeliever, or a crucifix to guard a good Mohammedan or Hindoo, but know not who I could ask.

The Count himself, perhaps?

As we approach the mountains, the cold deepens, and at night the air smells of snow. Tonight when darkness falls, I shall ascend as high as possible in the form of a bat, and see if I can at least glimpse the red glimmer of the steam-launch's smoke-stack ahead of me on the river in the blackness.

If the saved can pray for the damned, pray for me, my beloved.

Forever, your husband,
R. M. Renfield

*Jonathan Harker's Journal**
1 November—evening
No news all day; we have found nothing of the kind we seek. We have now passed into the Bistritza . . . We have overhauled

every boat, big and little . . . Some of the Slovaks tell us that a big boat passed them, going at more than the usual speed as she had a double crew on board . . .

Dr. Seward's Diary*
2 November

Three days on the road. No news, and no time to write it if there had been . . .

Letter, R. M. Renfield to his wife
2 November

My beloved Catherine,
My adored Vixie,

This is good-by. In the form of a bat I have seen Lord Godalming's steam-launch upon the river, going much more slowly now owing to the narrowness of the Bistritza where it flows down out of the Carpathians, and the many rapids that result from the river's greater fall. Likewise as the mountains close in around the river and the valley sides steepen and draw near, it is no longer possible for Quincey Morris and his party to range over so much countryside. They must be on the river road some ten miles ahead of me. I will overtake both boat and riders tomorrow.

The night is very cold, the mountains that rise up on all sides of us thickly wreathed in snow-clouds. The road is in such ill repair, washed-out and undermined by repeated winter rains and floods, that a carriage cannot proceed farther in any case. I have paid Salaman off, and sent him away with the calèche and horses. He did not ask what I intend to do alone in this wilderness in the darkness before morning, but looked at me strangely when I said, "Go with Allah, my friend."

I am alone, as I have not been since I lay dead in Highgate Cemetery; since I knelt in such peace at your side.

Tomorrow night, in the form of a bat, I will overtake Lord Godalming's steam-launch, and will follow it until the hour when the tide turns, when it will be possible for me to go aboard. I know not how much crew they have, if any, nor exactly how long I will have before the tide's ebb in the distant ocean traps me aboard.

If the crew is small, it will be the work of moments to disable the pump that supplies water to the boilers and, if possible, to open the drains on the boilers themselves. I doubt, with Godalming's careful operation of the launch, that the boilers will remain untended so long as to explode, but they will certainly be damaged by being run dry for even a short length of time.

Then even the Count cannot punish Nomie, for deserting her task.

And that done, I shall be free. In what remains of the night I will seek out the shore-party of riders, show myself to them, and ask them what I asked Dr. Seward as we rode the Orient Express: for the quietus of death.

When the Count reaches his Castle, he will send out his call to me again, and if I still exist, I will have no choice but to go. To live as his servant always—to endure the company of the frightful Countess, the savage Sarike—surely even Hell cannot be more terrible.

And so my beloved ones, good-by. I shall, I hope, see you soon, if only briefly, but it will be a great comfort to me to know that you and I are at least on the same side of the great Veil that separates the living from the dead, and from the Un-Dead. I will miss my dear friend Nomie, and pray—if the damned can pray in Hell—for her eventual release.

Whatever happens tomorrow night, please know that through-out, my thoughts are only of you. When I die, it will be with your names on my lips.

With all my love, forever,
R. M. Renfield

Chapter Thirty

Renfield wondered, at various times during the following day, if the curious inability to enter any dwelling uninvited extended to boats, and if so, what he was to do about that. As he trotted along through the woods with the steady lope of a wolf—for it was in the form of a wolf that he ran—he glimpsed, down on the road, the tight band of a half-dozen horses, and what he thought were two men. But he could not see clearly in the brightness of the daylight, and dared not stop.

There would be time, he thought, to return to them, in the dark of the night.

When they'd skirted the town of Fundu, where the Bistritza River ran into the Sereth, it had looked to him sufficiently large and modern to support a coal-yard. Godalming would have stocked up there. Perhaps, Renfield reflected, he could have hired river-pirates there to attack the launch, but he doubted it. He didn't speak Slovak, for one thing, and for another, the rough back-country men who comprised the population of both boatmen and river-pirates seemed to have a wary instinct for the supernatural.

This was something, he thought, that he'd have to do alone.

For many nights now he'd timed the length of that sensation of power, of heightened strength, that came at the turning of the far-off tide, just as, during his days of enforced wakefulness on the way up to Veresti with Nomie in her earth-box, he'd timed the period of his ability to change his shape at noon. Part of Dracula's skill, Nomie had told him once, was simply his experience. He knew to the split instant when the tide would turn, and was ready for it; could feel the dawn coming with the exactness of a chronometer, and was poised to attack or retreat when the final sliver of sunlight vanished behind the shadow of the earth.

Still, for a novice vampire, Renfield didn't feel he did at all badly. He overtook the launch shortly after sunset, trotting through the underbrush of the bank as the darkness thickened on the water. Icy wind flowed down from the mountains, and the men on the few barges that he passed wore sheepskin coats and hats of wolf or rabbit fur. The road here was little more than a tow-path, and a badly eroded one at that. Here on the higher river the current was stronger, and the launch's engines labored, though Renfield could see she was running at full steam. Now and then a soot-black figure would emerge from the engine-room; in the ruddy glare from the door Renfield saw the young, clerkish face beneath hair growing rapidly as white as an old man's.

Jonathan Harker.

And if he is stoking, is it likely there will be a hired crew?

Wolf-Renfield watched, and for a long time saw no one else.

Then Godalming appeared, from the tiny cabin that was all the shelter on the launch's deck, roughly clothed in a bargee's heavy jersey with a knitted cap over his golden hair. He looked dirty and rumpled, and given the small size of the launch, Renfield's suspicion was confirmed. There were only the two of them.

Van Helsing must be ashore then, with Morris.

He felt it, the instant the tide began to turn. The launch had overtaken a small barge hauling iron, cloth, salt, and other goods up-river toward the settlements of the foothills; Godalming turned the bright electric searchlight on them, while Harker minded the tiller. The glare of the searchlight showed the big Romanian flag prominently displayed on the launch's jackstaff. Renfield wondered whom Godalming had paid for that, and how much.

Mist already lay on the river, so it was the easiest thing in the world to slip into it, and so across. Renfield didn't resume his human form until he was in the cramped dark of the engine-room. He'd been aboard a hundred such little steamers on the Hooghly and the Ganges, and found the pump without difficulty, at the far end of the battery of cylindrical black boilers. With a screwdriver from the neatly stowed repair kit, he ripped and shredded the leather drive-belt nearly through, then opened the cocks on half a dozen of the boilers, to let the water drain away.

In the dark of the engine-hold it might be hours before any problem was detected.

As mist, he flowed up onto the deck. The little Romanian barge was disappearing behind them in the freezing darkness. Godalming said, "We can't have taken the wrong way! If the Count continued up the Sereth instead of coming this way, he'll add fifty or sixty miles to the overland part of his journey. In country like this, and weather like this, that could be the better part of a week!"

"He can command the weather," replied Harker quietly. "And to some extent, he can command men. But Mina was right. Though he's paralyzed on running water, it's still the safest way for him to travel." His hand stroked the hilt of the huge knife at his belt.

Get closer to him! urged Renfield frantically. The two men stood six or eight feet apart, Godalming at the prow beside the electric searchlight, Harker amidships at the wheel. *Get closer and I can take you both!*

Neither moved; the moments of freedom and mobility were sliding away. *Stay in the hopes of being able to strike both and run the launch aground, or flee to avoid being trapped . . . ?*

His nerve broke. For an awful moment he thought he'd waited too long as it was, that he wouldn't be able to leave the boat: couldn't summon the will, the physical ability, to cross the water.

If they find me aboard, they'll know the engines have been tampered with.

Nomie will be the one to suffer for it, if I cannot kill them both almost at once.

If I throw myself into the river, I suppose I can wade out in twelve hours when the tide turns again . . .

He flung himself forward, with a sensation of icy tearing, of bitter cold somewhere in his chest. Then his flittering bat-wings bore him up, and he flopped, trembling, onto the river-bank.

With a great sloshing of her screws, the steam-launch churned on toward the next set of rapids. Renfield sat up in the wet weeds, chilled and exhausted from his daylong trot, wanting only rest and knowing there would be none for him, for he had left his earthen bed-roll far behind.

But he had succeeded, he thought. He had accomplished what the Count had ordered him and Nomie to accomplish—the first time the launch tried to climb rapids, she'd tear her engine to pieces. Now, in the few days at most that remained before the Count reached out to summon him to service once again, he was free, to seek what doom he could.

Drawing a deep breath, Renfield shifted that portion of his consciousness that controlled his shape, and felt himself melt again into the guise of a wolf. With luck, he thought, he'd be dead—truly dead—by morning.

* * *

Though it was after midnight, the shore party was still on the move, some ten miles behind the barge. Wolf-Renfield heard and smelled the horses before they came into sight in the broken and heavily wooded country of the banks; smelled Quincey Morris's chewing-tobacco and the more bitter stench of cigarettes. The scents of the night, the attenuated moonlight flickering on the water, were wildly exhilarating, and he found himself wondering if he could kill both men before he remembered that there was no longer any need for him to do so.

He was free. The night was his. His single dread was that the Count would feel himself safe enough to re-establish contact and control before Renfield could hail his deliverers.

He saw them now, from the shelter of the woods above the road. Six horses, two men, riding as swiftly as the dim moonlight would permit. The moon would set soon, and as bad as the road was, Renfield guessed they'd camp. Quincey Morris hadn't ridden the American cattle-trails for as long as he had without learning how easy it was to break a horse's leg in the darkness. A little to Renfield's surprise, he saw that the other rider was Dr. Seward, not Van Helsing as he had supposed.

Which can't be right, he thought, alarm-bells ringing in his mind. *Any of the men could have been left back in Galatz to guard Mrs. Harker. The logical guard is Seward: Harker knows the ground around Castle Dracula, Godalming can pilot the launch, Morris is the best rider and shot. They are the Rooks and the Knights . . . and they send a Pawn out, to do the work of the Queen-piece that the Persians call the Vizier?*

Where is Van Helsing? Were they really so foolish as to leave Mrs. Harker alone, or under the guard of hired help?

The horses would react to the smell of a wolf, the men, to the sight of a bat fluttering along in their wake. As mist, Renfield flowed down close to the river-bank, drifting and curling between water and road, listening for the voices of the men. Both were dog-tired, for they had been riding, Renfield guessed, almost steadily for three days, most of it without benefit of grooms to do the added work of looking after six horses. Once Morris's horse—a scrubby little Hungarian beast who looked ridiculously tiny beneath the Texan's six-feet-plus height—shied, and that soft Texas voice drawled, "Don't you go jigger on me, you slab-sided vinigaroon, I been scrapped with by *real* two-dollar Mexican plugs and you ain't even *in* it," and Seward made a ghost of a chuckle. But neither man spoke to the other until the crescent moon sank into the cloud-banks above the mountains.

"That's it." Morris drew rein. "Damn blast it to fucken hell. How they look?"

Seward dismounted, kindled a lantern that had been tied to the back of his saddle. "They seem all right." He moved among the other horses, feeling legs and withers. "I don't like this cold, though, nor the smell of the wind."

"Too damn much like Siberia. Or Montana." Morris kindled a lantern of his own, led his mount to a spot sheltered by rocks from the wind, and proceeded to cut and yank at the weeds and brush, to clear a spot for a fire. "Van Helsing and Mrs. Harker'll be higher up than we by this time, and God knows what the road's like up Borgo Pass, this time of year. All the guns in the world won't help, if they get caught in a deep cold and Mrs. Harker freezes to death. I wish a thousand times we'd left her in Galatz."

Seward said, "And I," but Renfield hardly heard him.

Borgo Pass? A qualm passed through him of sickness, of shock.

Van Helsing was going up the Borgo Pass.

That would mean . . .

"I understand that he has to do it," Seward went on. "You know it's useless to pursue a fox unless his earth has been stopped before him." He slipped bit and bridle from his horse's mouth, pulled free the saddle. The springing color of Morris's firelight made Seward's unshaven face look younger, thin and strange and very different from the neat, self-contained doctor Renfield had first encountered in the office of Rushbrook Asylum in the spring.

"Van Helsing knows what he's doing. I trust his judgement more than that of any man living, and I think Mrs. Harker will be safer in his company, even on the threshhold of our enemy, than she would be back in Galatz with one less experienced in the ways of the things that we fight. Harker told us, remember, that once at his Castle again he will have command of the gypsies who acknowledge him their lord. We'll be hard-pressed to fight all of them. And once we get close to the Castle, the Count won't be the only vampire with which we'll have to contend."

Nomie.

Renfield felt a chill pass over him, as he had at the moment of his own death.

He melted into the form of a bat, and flew away into the night.

Chapter Thirty-one

At the tide's turn he crossed the river and, taking on the form of a wolf, ran on into the growing day. The country here was truly rough and broken, thick forest alternating with stony meadows where sheep pastured in the summer. Ahead of him, the mountains were heavily curtained with snow-clouds, the wind bitterly cold. Though there was little direct sun, the daylight made Wolf-Renfield woozy and sick. At times he could barely recall who he was or what he was doing, save that he knew he had to reach the Castle. That he had to follow the twisting track up to the Pass.

Just before nightfall he passed a band of gypsy men, riding their shaggy ponies around a leiter-wagon, a sort of loosely built, skeletal farm-cart he had glimpsed negotiating the turns of the winding road as he'd followed the river northwest. The Count's mortal servants, he assumed, and wondered how Dracula communicated with them, and what bargain had been struck between the old boyar and the hetman of their tribe. There were about twenty of them, mustachioed and indescribably dirty, armed with knives but only a few decrepit flintlocks, very like the *badmashes* who robbed travelers in the passes of the Hindu Kush.

Like the Afghani robbers, Renfield thought, they almost certainly scorned the laws of the settled lands. Like the Afghani robbers, they would recognize and obey only strength.

His own resting-place far behind him, he loped on into the night.

He saw the Castle just after dawn on the second day. *In morning's splendor,* Wotan had sung—the real Wotan, the Wotan of *Das Rheingold*—*it lay masterless, and gloriously beckoned to me.*

The night had refreshed him, but he knew the weariness of daylight would be crueler still and harder to bear; it was difficult, even now, to set one aching paw down before the other. The Castle seemed unreachably distant, from the place where he came out of the woods, where the road climbed toward the Pass. It stood on a coign of rock where the eastward end of the Pass first narrowed, guarding the road that the Turks must traverse to invade the green lands beyond. Towers and battlements overhung the way, nearly five hundred feet above it. Indeed the morning's splendor dyed the grim walls pale gold, but all around it the snow-clouds made a pall of shadow. Even as Renfield watched, they closed upon it like a ghostly hand, hiding the walls from sight.

By the smell, it was snowing in the Pass before noon.

Through the day he trotted, stumbling with weariness and unable to rest. At the Castle he could rest, he thought—Nomie had told him that the earth of the Master would shelter the fledgeling, and vice versa. He wondered what the adventures of the Countess and Sarike had been on their way back home, and whether, when night came, they would watch from the walls for their Master's return.

By this time the steam-launch must have crippled itself trying to ascend the upper Bistritzia's rapids: Harker and Godalming would be forced to abandon it, and continue on whatever horses they could find.

Their delay would probably give Dracula time to reach the Castle in safety, but it would not affect Van Helsing's implacable mission. And the only thing that Renfield could think of more horrible than Dracula winning his race and summoning Renfield back to the Castle to be his slave, was the thought that he must serve him through Eternity alone.

When lying still in the shadows of the icy afternoon, he tried to sink his mind into half-sleep, to reach out to Nomie and warn her to flee, but he could not.

He could only stagger to his feet and trot on, praying he would reach the castle before Van Helsing did.

It snowed that night. *Guns will do them no good, if Mrs. Harker freezes to death,* Quincey Morris had said. Huddled in a cup-shaped bay in the rocks at the very foot of the Pass, trying to recruit enough strength to go on, Wolf-Renfield remembered Mina Harker's despairing scream, *Unclean, unclean!* and the touch of her mind as it sought for its Master. Recalled his dream, in the misty world between living and death, of the Count forcing the dark-haired woman to drink his blood, as Renfield had drunk the blood of Nomie and her sisters, to begin the transformation of human flesh into the deathless flesh of the vampire.

Once she had pressed her lips to the welling dark blood of the Count's gashed chest, it wouldn't matter whether Mina Harker died in the next moment or seventy years in the future.

The change to vampire had begun in her flesh. If Dracula remained in the living world, her mind and soul would be drawn to his, to be upheld, cradled, while her body died, then returned to the changed flesh within the grave. She would know the Count with the terrible, unbreakable intimacy with which Renfield knew the Countess, and Sarike, and Nomie. She would be his slave, under his domination as the three vampire women were, as Renfield was.

Forever.

Were I not here, running in wolf-form to thwart them, reflected Renfield sadly, *I would be one of Van Helsing's hunters, trying to save you, too.*

But that wasn't true, either.

If I were not here, vampire, I would be back in Dr. Seward's asylum, eating flies and trying to forget that I murdered my beautiful Catherine, my beautiful Vixie.

Though it was night and the strength of night was flowing into him, Renfield laid his head on his bruised and smarting forepaws and wondered if there was actually an answer to this conundrum somewhere, or if everything that had happened to him since the age of twelve—the age when those maniacal rages had first begun to twist at his mind—had simply been some gigantic celestial jest.

In his exhausted mind he saw her, one of the two people who had been unconditionally kind to him in his days at Rushbrook House. The only one who had talked to him as a man and an equal and not as a fractious, contemptible child. Far off, like the dim half-dream in which he'd seen the Count drink her blood, he was aware of her, her face pale in the wildly licking flare of a small campfire, her dark eyes following in fear as Van Helsing drew a circle around her and the fire, and with the meticulous care of an alchemist crumbled a Host, like a fine dust, into the snow of the circle. The air was filled with flying snowflakes, and Renfield was aware of the dark bulk of a small carriage, behind which sheltered four horses, horses who pulled at their tethers and thrashed their heads, their eyes catching the firelight in rolling terror.

Van Helsing, thickly bundled in a fur coat, was shivering with the cold. Mina, wrapped in rugs and sheepskins beside the fire, did not tremble, and her dark eyes seemed curiously bright. But when the old man came back to her, she clung to his arm, pressed her face to his shoulder.

Among the wildly whirling snowflakes, the firelight caught the red reflection of eyes. In his half-dream Renfield saw them, as Mina and Van Helsing saw them: the ghostly faces with their red-lipped smiles, the lift and swirl of the white dresses they wore. The gold of Nomie's hair, wind-caught like a mermaid's beneath the sea, and the storm-wrack of Sarike's and the Countess's.

As they'd hung in the air outside the Castle window in his earlier dream, calling to Jonathan Harker, they hung now in the mealy tumult of the blizzard, arms around one another's waists, reaching out.

Calling to Mina to come to them, to be their sister.

Nomie would be good to her, thought Renfield. But he'd seen how the Countess treated the youngest of her sister-wives, alternating caressing sweetness with almost unbelievable spite, as sisters sometimes do. Would the Count protect his newest bride from the others? Of course not.

He saw Mina shrink against Van Helsing's side, sickened terror in her eyes as she saw her fate.

She is freezing to death, thought Renfield despairingly. And as her body drifted toward death, so her soul was drawn toward the other three, whom the Count had chosen, seduced, and killed.

He saw the Countess smile, and point at Mina with glinting malice; saw her lean to speak with Sarike. But Nomie, floating behind them, only gazed across the barrier of the Holy circle at the dark-haired woman poised between living and dark Un-Death, and Renfield saw pity in her eyes.

*　　*　　*

Through the night he climbed the Pass, struggling against the slashing winds, trembling with hunger and exhaustion. Renfield felt the dawn coming, as he waded breast-deep in the new-fallen snow, and briefly debated transforming himself into a bat, for he knew he was still many miles from the Castle.

But the winds were still too strong for him to fly against, and by day, he knew he would be nearly blind. Then, too, he thought, he would not be able to shift his form again until the stroke of noon.

A bat could not take on a man.

So he fought his way through the drifts, and with the rising of the sun, the wind grew less. The world was transformed, ice-white and blinding, the rocks standing out against the marble of the snow like cinder-colored walls. Under his paws the snow squeaked a little, the only sound in the birdless woods. A little before noon he reached the road that turned aside up toward the Castle, and saw a man's churned tracks.

They were reasonably fresh, not more than two hours. The outer gate was barred, but the small wicket cut into the larger leaf of iron-strapped wood had been forced, the wood around its rusted hinges glaring yellow where a crowbar had ripped.

Wolf-Renfield slipped through, following the tracks across the deep drifts of the courtyard, to the stair that led up to the half-open door.

He'll search the chapel and the vaults, thought Renfield frantically. *The place must have a labyrinth of crypts and sub-cellars. I may still be in time. If I can hold him off, delay him until noon, when Nomie and the others can change their form, move about . . .*

If I can kill him . . .

Did they hear? he wondered. Were they aware of this man's footfalls, of the scent of the blood in his veins? Could they read his resolution in their uneasy dreams, as he searched through the vaults, pushed open the long-rusted hinges of those secret doors, descended the narrow, twisting stairs? With the preternatural senses of a wolf, Renfield listened, scented, seeking the faint creak of boot-leather, the reek of burning lamp-oil.

What he smelled, as he came to the top of a flight of descending steps, was blood.

A lot of blood.

Stumbling, trembling with weariness, Renfield slipped down the stairs.

He found the body of the poet Gelhorn at the bottom, curled together and with a look on his sheep-like face of shocked despair. He'd been dead for about two weeks. The Countess and Sarike must have killed him as soon as they safely reached the Castle. Throat, wrists, and chest—visible through his shirt, which had been half-torn from his body—were all marked with gaping punctures, and with smaller marks that had half-healed at the time of his death.

Wolf-Renfield sniffed briefly at the body, then passed it by.

Dr. Van Helsing's Memorandum*
5 November

I knew that there were at least three graves to find—graves that are inhabit; so I search, and search, and I find one of them. She lay in her Vampire sleep, so full of life and voluptuous beauty that I shudder as though I have come to do murder. Ah, I doubt not that in old time, when such things were, many a man who set forth to do such a task as mine, found at the last his heart fail him, and then his nerve. So he delay, and delay, and delay, till the mere beauty and the fascination of the wanton Un-Dead have hypnotise him; and he remain on and on, til sunset come, and the Vampire sleep be over. Then the beautiful eyes of the fair woman open and look love, and the voluptuous mouth present a kiss—and man is weak . . .

* * *

Sarike lay in the crypt beyond. Her head had been cut off, and a stake of fire-hardened wood protruded from beneath her left breast. Her thin white dress, and the velvet lining of her coffin, were both soaked with blood. Blood splattered her face and arms, and dotted the white garlic-flowers stuffed into her half-open mouth. It was their stench, rather than that of the blood, that turned Renfield's stomach, and he would have vomited, had there been anything within him to throw up.

Van Helsing had trodden in the blood, and his sticky track wove back and forth among the half-dozen tombs within that small crypt. The lids had been all wrenched off, and lay shattered on the floor. Renfield went straight to the last of them, the tomb where the Countess Elizabeth lay.

She was already beginning to crumble into dust. He knew it

was she by the dark coils of her raven hair, and by the gold ring on her hand. By the bloody footprint beside the coffin, Van Helsing had stood here for a long time, looking down at her as she slept.

Blood-tracks led out the door, into the deeper dark of the inner crypts.

Nomie, thought Renfield frantically, *Nomie, please be there . . .*

Please have hidden yourself, have concealed your sleeping-place, that he won't find you . . . That he won't come on you until I can be there to stop him, to kill him, to do whatever I have to . . .

That he won't come on you until noon, when you can wake, and sit up, and flee. When I can turn from wolf to man . . .

He listened, but though he smelled the fishy whiff of lamp-oil, he heard no sound, no creak of boot-leather.

A descending stair, in the wake of the blood-tracks and the smoke.

Then the far-off glimmer of lantern-light.

Staggering, Renfield limped down, to where a barred iron door closed the entrance to the deepest of the castle crypts. In the lantern-light beyond it Renfield saw the high tomb in its center, graven only with the name DRACULA, and all around it the torn-up flagstones where the gypsies had dug out fifty boxes' worth of graveyard earth for shipment to London. He pressed himself to the bars, invisible in the darkness, sick with horror and shock.

A smaller tomb lay perpendicular to the foot of the large one. Beside this Van Helsing stood in his shirtsleeves despite the brutal cold, the lantern at his feet, gazing down into the coffin, and on his face was a look that mingled pity and burning desire.

Blood splattered his face and splotched his clothing, dripped from his white sidewhiskers and hair. He held a hammer in one hand, a fresh, unbloodied stake in the other, and on the coffin's edge lay a foot-long scalpel. Renfield wanted to scream, *Nomie!* but could not.

He could feel the hour of noon, slipping to its slow zenith overhead. In the silence of the crypt Van Helsing's breathing was very loud. It was slow and thick, and his eyes had the look of a man hypnotized, caught by some terrible dream of self-loathing and lust.

Dr. Van Helsing's Memorandum*

Presently, I find in a high great tomb as if made to one much beloved that other fair sister which, like Jonathan I had seen to gather herself out of the atoms of the mist. She was so fair to look on, so radiantly beautiful, so exquisitely voluptuous, that the very instinct of man in me, which calls some of my sex to love and to protect one of hers, made my head whirl with new emotion . . .

* * *

Having spent years among the strange temptations of India, and months in the asylum at Rushbrook, Renfield knew that look very, very well.

We lure by our beauty, he remembered Nomie saying to him in London: *It is how we hunt. We disarm the mind through the senses and the dreams. How else would we survive? Men see us, and follow, despite all they know, drawn by their need.*

Van Helsing's mouth trembled, like that of a man beholding a vision; his hands shook, on hammer and stake.

The splattered blood, the violence with which the stakes had been been driven into Sarike's body, and that of the Countess, told their own tale. Furiously, desperately, Van Helsing had been killing, not only the vampires, but his own frantic desire for them. His own overwhelming shame.

His breath laboring, moving as if stake and hammer were both wrought of lead, Van Helsing brought them up. Braced the stake beneath Nomie's breast. Then stood again, hammer half-raised, looking down into the coffin with sweat pouring from his face and eyes stretched with madness.

Had he had human lips, a human voice, Renfield would have whispered, *Nomie, no . . .*

The crypt was silent, the lantern-flame unwavering on the vampire-hunter's motionless face and shaking hands.

Renfield felt the touch of noon in the crypt's darkness, through the snowy layers of cloud overhead. But even as he flowed into human shape in the darkness, laid hands upon the bars of the door, he saw Nomie sit up in her coffin. Gold hair tumbled over her shoulders, white sleeves fell back from white arms.

Stake and hammer slithered from Van Helsing's hands.

Blue eyes looked into blue. But while Nomie's gaze was calm, ready, filled with the peace of one who has passed decades beyond hope, Van Helsing's was wide with horror, shame, despair—and with the exquisite unbreathing anticipation of surrender.

Then Nomie leaned forward, took the old man's face between her hands, and very gently kissed his lips.

An instant later she dissolved into mist and shadows, and flowed away across the stone floor, to vanish into the darkness.

Dr. Van Helsing's Memorandum*

But God be thanked . . . before the spell could be wrought further upon me, I had nerved myself to my wild work . . .

Had it been but one, it had been easy, comparative. But
three! . . .

God be thanked, my nerve did stand . . .

Chapter Thirty-two

Letter, R. M. Renfield to his wife
(Undated)

My dearest heart,

It seems that there is after all yet more to write.

After arriving at Castle Dracula, and witnessing Nomie's escape from the vampire-hunter Van Helsing—through circumstances curious enough to constitute a miracle—I followed Nomie in the form of mist, down through the dark of the crypts and through the crevices of a vault that had been bricked up long ago. But time had had its way with the mortar between the stones, enough to admit the two of us before the short moments of noon had passed. There was no coffin in that crypt, only chest after chest of gold coins, and the skeleton of the wretched woman who had coveted them above all things. Yet the earth beneath the flagstones was the hallowed soil of the family tombs nevertheless, and in it, twined in Nomie's arms, I slept.

In my sleep I could feel the Count's approach, as once I had felt it while chained in the padded chambers of Rushbrook Asylum. He was coming, and even in his sleep, even with his mind closed against us, his wrath was like a pillar of cloud and darkness, approaching from the east and south.

"I heard the creak and gnashing of the wood, as the old man wrenched the doorways from their hinges," whispered Nomie into my dreams. In dreaming I could see again the coffin of the Countess Elizabeth, but the blood had dried upon her white gown and her black hair. Only dust remained, and a few fragments of bone, with the stake propped upright among them. The white garlic-flowers were still fresh, spilling from the mouth of the skull.

"Elizabeth had sensed Mina's coming from afar and said that she would be drawn to the Castle. We all thought Dr. Van Helsing was a servant she'd brought with her, or a man she'd ensorcelled to follow her, the way Elizabeth ensorcelled that poor little fool Gelhorn. When I asked why that 'servant' would have a *consecrated* Host with him—a thing not at all easy to obtain in these days—she only laughed, and said Mina would take care of that.

"'He thinks she will freeze to death in the night, and seeks to hold her within the circle so he can kill her,' Elizabeth said. 'Simple man. You saw his eyes, when he looked at her and saw the vampire beauty in her face. You saw how he watched her, and watched her, hungry and terrified of the hunger within him. He will not have the heart to drive in the stake. And if he does'— and she shrugged—'so much the worse. More kisses for the rest of us.' She never thought, you see, that he would have the tools in the carriage, to break through the Castle doors."

Van Helsing would be trudging back to his little camp in the Pass, where Mrs. Harker waited within the holy circle. I hoped they had armed her, and taught her to use weapons, for the wolves that would be drawn by the carcasses of the horses would have little concern for the Host, consecrated though it might be. I wondered what the Count would eat, when he returned to the Castle, for there was nothing there but bats. Even rats will not dwell where the inhabitants do not eat human food.

"To keep the Szgany loyal he never would permit us to touch them," Nomie remarked, a gentle voice within my dreams. "The villagers were wary and cautious, and travelers are few. For months, sometimes, we would live on bats. Can you wonder we were enraged at his plan to go away and leave us here to guard this place, until it might occur to him to return? And doubly so, to learn he'd started a second harem in your land to replace us? He'll choose another city now, another country to occupy. With you as his servant, it will probably be India."

"He could do worse," I said. "The governing classes all speak English, which he already knows."

The gold that filled the chests in our little crypt—filled them and overflowed onto the floor—would guarantee his welcome anywhere, and from Nomie's conversation while we traveled together, I knew that this was only a tithe of the treasure hidden in the castle.

"He, and you, will have access to books and to such culture as there is there," I went on. "Not like London, I admit, but better than re-reading Davila's histories of French insurgencies in the library here for the thousand and fifth time. And because of the European community there, neither he nor you will stand out. In fact, because the whites are perceived as superior in all ways to the natives, you will have a great deal more latitude than you would have even in London."

In our sleep I could feel her sadness, as if she laid her palm to my cheek. "And you, sweet friend?"

I thought of Van Helsing, gathering up provisions now—bedrolls, food, blankets against the freezing snowstorm that came sweeping down the Pass. "I will do what I must, sweet friend."

Writers—and certainly your appalling mother and your late unlamented sister, my love—speak casually and often of "a fate worse than Death," without understanding that such a thing can actually be. I, who have passed through death, or a half-death at least, have experienced that which is worse: eternal Un-Life, with my soul, my mind, my body at the command of an entity in love with both power and the pain of others.

He was coming. I felt his wrath from afar. Van Helsing, though he'd strewn the crumbled Host in the Count's actual tomb, had by no means "cleansed" even a quarter of the places where the Un-Dead could actually find repose, and of course the Host that he'd mortared around the broken-open Castle door would have no effect on a bat, or a trail of mist, floating in over its walls. The Castle would have had to be dynamited to render it unfit for the Count to hide in, and before that could be effected, even with Godalming's money, Dracula's gypsies would have dealt with the invaders.

It was indeed his Valhalla, offering both rest and the renewal of his strength.

"Why did you kiss him?" I asked her, and I felt her smile.

"Because he so much wanted it," she said. "And maybe a little, because he killed Elizabeth and Sarike, who have made me wretched for so many decades—made me wretched in the way that only those whom we live with, whom we rub along with night in and night out, year in and year out, can do. And perhaps to show him," she added softly, "that not all those who become Un-Dead are wholly monsters."

"Whyever you did it," I replied, "it was a fit revenge on the man. For you've given him something that doesn't fit in with his theories. Trying to make it do so will be a torment to him for the remainder of his days."

I asked her about her own journey, and whether the Countess and Sarike had attempted any assault on my agent Ross and his men. "Sarike tried," she said. "But Elizabeth and I drew her away. I told Elizabeth that it might be better, if instead of killing Ross, we kept his address and good will, in case we should need it later."

"And Gelhorn?"

"A truly obnoxious man," sighed Nomie. "He was forever boring on about the superiority of the Teutonic Race and its destiny to rule the world, and he seemed to think that because I am German I would agree with him. Heaven help the world— Heaven help Germany—if this 'Volk' idea gets taken up by politicians! Yet even so, I'm not sure he deserved his fate."

Knowing the Count would return in a mood of black fury, we discussed the preliminaries for the India scheme, which we knew would appease him. Which banks to use, and which of my false names would be safest for purposes of investment and transfer of another network of earth-boxes and safe-houses in Calcutta, Bombay, Madras, and Kathmandhu. I did everything I could to keep the names of my Indian friends and contacts out of it, knowing that these men and women would become the Count's likeliest early victims. With luck, I would find some way into true death before he could prise such information out of my mind.

The snowstorm now howled around the Castle's walls. Even in our dreams in the deep-buried crypt we could hear its cries.

"I have heard," I said to her, "rumor and legend of Masters who dwell in the mountains of Thibet, deathless creatures who were once mortal men. I wonder how the Count will get along, in proximity to them?"

"It would be interesting," said Nomie, "to seek them out."

"And more interesting still," I added, "to see if they would let you do so."

On that we truly slept, but in visions I could see the gypsy riders lashing their horses through the swirling flakes, see the rough-coated little ponies stumbling as they hauled the heavy leiter-wagon up the road that led to the Pass. I knew—for it seemed to me that the whole of the countryside around Castle Dracula breathed and whispered its secrets up to the Castle— that Van Helsing and Mrs. Harker had taken refuge in that little bay, high in the rocks, where I had lain exhausted that morning, and from its narrow entrance looked out over the plain below.

And as if I stood at Mrs. Harker's side—as if I rode on the wings of the snow-winds overhead—I saw the leiter-wagon's approach, within its ring of gypsy riders, thrusting on against the tempest. The earth-box in the wagon rocked and swayed, and I wondered if the Count were conscious, and if so, what he thought, helpless as a mortal man and drowsy with daylight. When the winds lessened and the clouds broke through, I could see the sun sinking toward the rack of storm above the mountains. With its disappearance, he would be free, and within striking-distance of his home.

From the south I could see riders coming, Harker's white hair like a blink of snow where his hat blew back, visible only to the far-seeing eyes of vampire dream. They must somehow have repaired the launch's engines, to make safe landfall hot on Dracula's trail.

Two men with six horses were galloping from the east, galloping hard: Morris and Seward, with their long hunting-rifles in their hands. In the sicklied yellow light of sinking sun and storm-wrack I saw them close on the leiter-wagon, saw the Szgany form themselves into a ring around it, knives and pistols flashing in the dying light. They were right below the rocks where Van Helsing and Mrs. Harker stood with rifle and pistol, blocking their path up to the Castle. Seward, Morris, Harker, and Godalming rode into the press of the gypsies and sprang— or were pulled—from their horses, striking and struggling where quarters were too close to shoot.

Harker and Morris sprang up onto the cart, Morris clutching his side where blood poured down. As the final rays of the sunset stabbed through the snowclouds, they wrenched the top from the earth-box, and in that instant I could hear Dracula's shriek, of rage and hatred and summons as the sun went down.

Then Harker's huge Ghurka knife flashed in that last second of golden sunlight, and Morris's bowie.

The image vanished from my mind.

Great stillness filled my heart.

Nomie and I lay awake, in one another's arms, in the gold-stuffed crypt of the Castle Dracula.

And we both knew we were free.

* * *

We climbed to the snow-padded southern battlement of the Castle, and stood in the swift-gathering dark, looking down at the Pass.

The Szgany were riding away in all directions, leaving the

leiter-wagon in the road. The wolves that the Count had sum-moned from all corners of the mountains trotted back to their interrupted repast on Van Helsing's four dead horses.

I supposed Nomie and I would be having bats for dinner.

If I had dinner at all.

I could see, against the clear violet of the twilight-veiled snow, five forms gathered around the leiter-wagon, bent over the sixth that lay on a spread-out blanket on the ground. Probably only a vampire could have smelled Morris's blood at that dis-tance. By the stillness of the others, the lack of even the smallest attempt at aid, I could tell the Texan was dead.

And I grieved with them, Catherine. A mere five weeks ago, with the recovery of my sanity, I realized that I had lost yourself and Vixie, my only and dearest friends.

Nomie's hand closed cold around my own. "Sweet friend," she said, and I looked down into her blue eyes. "You can go down to them now. I will be all right."

"What will you do?" I asked her, and she smiled.

"Exactly what you and I planned for the Count. I will con-tact Mr. Ross, and take over the false identities that you and your so-lovely Catherine established—and thank her for me, Ry-land, thank her, and you, so much!—and travel to India, where I will live like a Queen upon men who do evil. I will never forget you, Ryland."

I smiled, my whole soul feeling light and free, with the world and eternity opening like a night-blooming flower around me in the still iciness of the night. "Never is a long time, little Nornchen." With the Count's death, the winds, like the wolves, had been released from his grip. The clouds were dispersing over-head. The stars were like a thousand million lamps, each marking the start of an untrodden road to the future. In the stillness I felt that I could hear the earth breathe.

"I only wish . . ." she began, then stopped herself, and shook her head. She put her hand to my cheek, and whispered, "Good-by, Ryland. Kiss your Catherine for me when you see her, and your lovely daughter. One day I may meet them, by-and-by."

"When you do," I said, "they will welcome you with love. Until that time . . ."

Our eyes met in the starlight. "What is it," I asked, "that you wish?"

She shook her head. "It's better that you go."

"Tell me."

Her hands closed again around my own. Her voice was barely a murmur in the starry cold. "That you could come with me, sweet friend. That we could go to India together. That we could be friends, if not forever, at least for a very long time."

Gently—for even as a mortal man I had been strong—I took her in my arms, and our mouths met in a kiss.

We spent the rest of the night gathering all the gold we could from the four corners of the Castle, and before dawn I went down to Bistritz, to post a letter to Ross and another to my agents in Calcutta and Delhi.

My dearest Catherine, do you understand? I love you, and have always loved you—will always love you, in living or dying or the shadow-world of Un-Death. One day, when it pleases God, you, and I, and our lovely Vixie, and my beautiful Nomie will all meet, on the other side of the Veil, and after that, who knows? Who *can* know?

Until that time, we can only live as well as we can, and make our choices, as the ancient Persians said, for the Light rather than the Darkness. For even those of us in the Darkness do, it appears, remember the nature of Light.

I write this to you in the train-station at Varna, whence we are about to depart for Constantinople and points east. Already I seem to hear in my ears the music of sitars, and to taste upon my tongue the heady flavor of rice-beetles and the indescribable savor of white ants!

My beloved, I will write to you when we reach Calcutta.

Until that time, and always, know me to be,

Forever, your loving husband,
Renfield